SKY FALL

THE SHADOW GUARDIANS BOOK 3

CB SAMET

THE COMPLETE SERIES

Raven's Flight, prequel novella

Raine Down, Book 1

Rosalyn's Run, novella

Storm Surge, Book 2

Anka's Orb, novella

Sky Fall, Book 3

CB SAMET

THE
SHADOW GUARDIANS
TRILOGY

SKY FALL

3

CHAPTER

ONE

From his view across the street, Nico watched the redheaded woman turn off the lights inside her wellness shop. The scorching Texas sun had set, but the horizon still glowed light gray in the early evening hour behind the standalone building. An oppressive humidity hung in the air tonight, as it had every Southern summer night. His nostrils filled with the smell of hot pavement after sunset and a distant diesel engine running.

He'd been watching the attractive shopkeeper for two weeks and knew her pattern—what time she arrived at work, what time she took a lunch break, and what time she closed her store.

Sky Thoren had sky-blue eyes and long sunset hair. The name seemed appropriate, especially for a young woman who wore floral dresses every day and owned a wellness shop selling incense, tinctures, and herbal remedies.

How was this delicate creature related to the two deadliest women Nico knew? And why had they left her exposed and vulnerable for so long?

She'd been safe for years... until now.

His phone dinged with a text message from his brother.

Andrej. *You need to report back.*

Nico didn't respond and pocketed his phone. He had to focus on the task at hand. He sniffed the air, catching the scent of something deadly, like him.

Another foul predator?

Danger crested the horizon. Doomsday, some called it. Prophets of Vanir bloodlines around the world heralded its arrival. He glanced at the darkening skyline as instinct warned him something was wrong. The prophecy claimed three sisters were the only hope of preventing the apocalypse unleashed by Helen.

Helen. Hel. Goddess of the underworld.

Harbinger of a second Ragnarök.

But three Valkyrie sisters couldn't save the world if one of them was dead.

AFTER EXTINGUISHING THE INCENSE, Sky turned off the lights of her herbal remedy and wellness shop. She enjoyed closing time—eight o'clock on a Sunday night with no work on Monday. Mondays were for personal time, when she accomplished shopping, banking, and house maintenance. Once she completed those tasks, sometimes she went trail riding for enjoyment.

With her purse in hand and the front door bolted, she set the security system and exited through the rear shop door, locking it. The expansive Texas night sky glittered bright with stars against a darkening blanket of the deepest navy blue. Orion twinkled the most radiantly with its superstars shining bright—the red Betelgeuse and the blue-white Rigel. In Norse astrology, the belt of Orion was known as Frigg's distaff.

Is it keeping the chaos of the tangled threads of the world in order tonight? Sky wondered.

She hoped so. Somewhere out there, her sisters battled evil in the shadows. Sky had been left behind, but she told herself she wasn't bothered by that. She enjoyed her calm slice of Southern heaven. She would relish her quaint life until the day fate swept her into the oncoming war. For years, she'd heard whispers from the shadow world that one day, she and her sisters would step onto the battle-field and face the forces of darkness to prevent the end of the world.

The idea seemed too grandiose, too overwhelming to be true.

The humid air held a heavy silence as her sandals clicked against the pavement. She walked to her blue Prius while the strange sensation of being watched crawled along her spine. She'd experienced it multiple times this past week—enough to know she shouldn't dismiss the feeling. Perhaps the eerie sensations were related to her dreams of late.

But she wasn't unprepared. Both her shop and her home had protective wards to keep out dark creatures. She'd installed flood lights and a surveillance camera at the back exit when she'd first opened her shop. She carried pepper spray and a pocketknife in her oversized hobo purse. She'd done everything her overprotective sisters demanded—and then some.

Sky had never been a part of the danger in their lives, but she knew threats abounded, both human and supernatural. Meanwhile, a quiet battle was being waged in the shadows, one humans were unaware of.

She unlocked her car using her key fob and was moments away from being safe within her vehicle when shuffling noises approached from behind her. Thoughts of brutality and death crowded her mind. Someone else's thoughts.

Kill, kill, kill.

Her heart accelerated from zero to sixty with the roar of a jet engine. Her hand dove into her purse, searching for her bottle of pepper spray. Before she could turn to see who was ambushing her, something solid struck her head.

Pain jolted through her skull like a lightning bolt. Her world bloomed as hot and bright as that blue and white Rigel star before extinguishing altogether.

CHAPTER

TWO

Sky woke to throbbing temples as she lay in the back seat of a car—her car.

Wow, she needed to vacuum the backseat carpet. And there was the brooch she'd thought she'd lost last month. She blinked and struggled to clear her mind, recalling how she was in a predicament.

Kidnapped.

Her hands were secured behind her back with what felt like duct tape as her head pounded with a vicious migraine. Swallowing back the fear making her heart race, she clamped down on the urge to scream in terror.

From her position on the seat, she could see the thing driving her car. Mottled gray skin covered his bald head, grotesque with snaking veins over the surface. He seemed oblivious to the fact she'd woken.

She searched his mind, gleaning how he wasn't expecting her to regain consciousness—ever—after a blow to her head like that. He was already congratulating himself on killing her and wondering about the high praise he was likely to earn from his mistress, the dark queen, for his success—especially if the weak redhead was part of the sister trinity.

If Sky panicked, squirmed, or cried out, she would alert him to her wakefulness and lose the element of surprise. She didn't see headlights streaking on either side of the windows from other cars, which suggested they were somewhere remote. He drove fast enough to indicate they were on a highway.

Dump the body. Hide the car.

His thoughts were almost gleeful. The internal gloating leaking out of him at having succeeded in his mission to kill her heightened her sense of nausea. He even planned to take a picture of her corpse as proof of his victory.

She needed to call for help—send a telepathic SOS. She hadn't tried such a message before, but she'd sent thoughts of warmth, comfort, and friendship to her family previously, so why not a plea for help toward her sisters? Pushing the thought forward, she met a wall of pain.

As her head squeezed like a nutcracker threatening to burst her skull, she bit back a groan of agony. Some part of her telepathic ability must have been impaired by the blow to her head. A psychic call for help wasn't an option until she healed more, but she doubted she had time to wait. Fighting the urge to panic, she squeezed her eyes shut momentarily.

What would my sisters do?

Probably wait for the vehicle to stop and then take offensive action. Since the creature's speed and strength were likely superior to her average abilities, fighting him directly wouldn't end in victory. At least not hers.

Seizing the upper hand would require something entirely unsuspected, and she would only have one opportunity to make it count. She would have to be reckless and hope to Frigg she survived and the killer didn't. He wasn't wearing a seatbelt, which might work in her favor, but, then again, neither was she.

Sky slowly maneuvered her body into place, her shoulders

protesting against the torque on them from her arms being tied behind her. With all her might, she lashed out her leg and struck her captor in the side of his head. As he let out a grunt of pain and surprise, the car jerked under his grip.

She pushed herself forward, legs first, and hooked the toe of one sandal into the steering wheel. Yanking it right, she felt the vehicle dip and careen off the side of the road.

"What are you doing?!" he cried.

Tires screamed over the rumble strip before the Prius fishtailed off the shoulder. As the car spun out of control, her body tumbled through an explosion of shattering glass and agonizing pain before plummeting into a black abyss.

COLDNESS. *Darkness. Pain.*

Sky floated in a nebulous sea of agony. Every surface, muscle, tendon, and bone of her body hurt. Was she being tortured? Other sensations joined the pain—burning and itching like she'd been bitten by a thousand fire ants.

She dropped back out of consciousness.

Minutes or maybe hours later, voices echoed in the darkness. Was she hearing them or telepathically perceiving them? She didn't know.

"Is she okay?" Raine, her sister, asked.

"She's out of surgery. She'll heal. I'm sorry I failed you." This from a man's voice she didn't recognize, but the anguish in his tone was heartbreaking.

Sky drifted again, floating and anchorless in an ocean of obsidian water so thick it might have been oil. A voice, old and raspy like sandpaper, echoed around her.

Rain bleeds
Storm screams

Sky shatters

Hell's flames
   Hell's fury
   Hell's creations

On the night of day
   The battle of good versus evil
   Hell's wrath unleashed

Hell's army
   Beasts march to conquer
   Beasts march to kill

Three by three,
   Sisters, Valkyrie,
   Hell's wrath to free.

The end shall come
   Hell's will be done
   Blood flows until war's won.

Sky's imagination took her to a familiar dream—the dreaded battlefield. To the right of her stood towering snowcapped mountains, to the left, red-tipped, angry volcanoes. The stench of death filled the valley between peaks. Everyone had fallen—Helen's army along with Raine, Storm, Will, and Bryce.

Her family.

Somewhere, a distant voice cackled. A silver spear, pure and brilliant as moonlight, flew through the air on a trajectory to plunge into Sky's chest.

Her vision went blank as white-hot pain shot through her body. She heard a beeping sound, like alarming hospital monitors. The smell of death was replaced by the smell of antiseptic. She wanted to open her eyes but couldn't.

A large, warm hand slipped into hers. "Relax, *Raza de soare.* You're going to be okay." The absolute certainty and conviction of a man's gentle voice combined with the tenderness of his touch had her heart rate and breathing returning to normal.

She slipped back into a deep sleep.

Sky fluttered open a pair of dry, raw eyes. Several blinks passed before she could focus on her surroundings. Light from a single window shone on a sterile room of eggshell-colored walls. When she attempted the slightest movement, her entire body felt immobilized by an unyielding cast. She looked down at where she lay.

Oh. I am *immobilized by casts.*

Her arms hung suspended in the air, wrapped up to her shoulders in plaster. Both legs were in casts, one of which had various metal rods protruding from it like something from a science fiction movie.

The car accident flooded her memory. Not exactly an accident, per se, as she'd caused a crash to escape certain death. She hadn't died, but had her attacker lived?

She needed to get out of the hospital and reach out to Raine. Her sister would know what to do. As she attempted to move, agony coursed through every fiber of her body. She gasped.

"Whoa. Whoa. Easy." A calm, deep voice penetrated Sky's haze of panic. "If you jack up your heart rate, you'll garner all sorts of unwanted attention. You're in a hospital." The man's accent was difficult to place—well-enunciated, perhaps learned in the UK, but British English wasn't his native language. Eastern European, perhaps. Nowhere she'd ever been since she'd never traveled outside the US.

She focused on a man with disheveled dirty-blond hair standing over her. His square jaw and pale blue eyes looked concerned and compassionate. Whoever this fair-skinned stranger was, he wasn't the creature from her car.

"Get me out of these," she hissed. When she struggled against the casts, the pain bolting through her reminded her how she'd probably broken a third of her bones and dislocated every extremity when she'd tumbled inside her car.

"All in good time, *fluturaș*. You were badly injured, Sky. Do you remember?"

At the sound of her name, she stilled. How did he know her name?

"Who are you?" she asked, voice shaky with fear.

With his faded jeans and a navy t-shirt, he was obviously not on staff at the hospital. He had a face sculpted by the gods—high cheekbones, firm, defined jawline, and proportioned, narrow nose. Intense, glacier-blue eyes held a chilling sorrow.

"My name is Nico Wølfe. Your sisters, Raine and Storm, sent me to protect you. I'm helping the Shadow Guardians."

"Fine job you're doing. Did you arrive before or after my abduction?" At his pained expression, she immediately regretted her harshness. "Ugh. I'm sorry. That was uncalled for. I'm just... in pain."

She was also frustrated she couldn't get a read on this man. She could usually glean thoughts from people, but trying to read Nico was like scanning a book with no pages. How could she trust someone if she couldn't know his motives?

Shadow Guardians, he'd said.

Sky knew that term as something her sisters had discussed the Christmas before last. Shadow Guardians worked under a secret organization related to Norse bloodlines.

Nico's brow remained furrowed. "You're quite right to blame me. I shouldn't have let your situation escalate to this." His deep voice was a bottomless pit of sorrow as he gestured to her casts. "But I was following you with every intention of rescuing you when, to my dismay, your car kamikazed off the side of the road. I'm guessing you had a hand in that."

"More like a foot. Is he still alive?"

"No. The Dökkálfar who captured you is dead."

Dark Elf blood line? That explains the gray skin.

Her eyes roamed the room, noting for the first time the flowers, plants, and *Get Well* balloons along the windowsill.

"Please, can you pull off these casts?" she pleaded.

Nico gave her a wary look. "You were in surgery for twelve hours. Half a bloody day. The surgeons said it was like putting Humpty Dumpty back together—I had to search the internet for what that meant. You don't want to re-injure yourself."

"Please." She gave him her most imploring look. She couldn't stand to be imprisoned like this.

CHAPTER

THREE

Nico couldn't turn from Sky's imploring expression. She looked like a bird caught in a cage, longing to be free.

When he'd pulled her from the wreckage, she'd been so limp and broken he'd thought there would be no putting her back together again. Even the ambulance crew had seemed at a loss for how to begin stabilizing her tortuous limbs. But she'd miraculously still had a pulse and was breathing on her own.

He'd spent all night pacing the hospital waiting room, knowing he'd failed this woman and her sisters in his one responsibility to keep Sky safe. He had made Raine and Storm aware of the situation, and Raine and Will had dropped in briefly but then returned to their overseas mission. Hovering close by in anticipation of her recovery wouldn't make it happen any faster.

A few hours after surgery, when Sky had still been in the intensive care unit, Nico had felt a tightness in his chest ease when he'd noticed her face had already begun to heal.

The surgeon had said she would probably never walk again. Nico wondered now if she had any sensation in her legs, but she'd moved them as she squirmed, which he took as a good sign of recovery.

She may not be a warrior like her sisters, but to his relief, she shared their same healing abilities. Hell, she'd survived that crash—maybe she was a warrior—albeit a reckless one, risking her life like that. She'd taken a gamble she would survive and her abductor wouldn't.

Gingerly, Nico used his pocketknife to cut one edge and pried the cast off her right arm, anticipating she would scream in pain at any moment and the hospital staff would rush to her aid, tossing him out of her room. But her arm emerged, showing smooth, porcelain skin and no longer the eggplant bruising it had been when he carried her to the ambulance stretcher. The left arm was the same—healed.

She blinked at him. "You've got some super-strength."

"Remarkable," he said, running fingers along the healed arm and sending warmth zinging straight to his core. He pulled his hand back, reminding himself that carrying her broken body in his arms earlier didn't give him the right to touch her now.

"But I'm not touching the leg casts. There are metal poles embedded in your bones to stabilize them." He pointed at the apparatus. "The surgeon said they'd take you back to the operating room in a few days to remove those."

"It's okay," she said, a little breathless. "That's good for now. Oh, that's so much better. Thank you, Nico. Thank you." She struggled to move pillows and reposition herself. "How long has it been since the wreck?"

"Two days," he replied. "Forty hours, to be precise." He felt like he'd aged forty days in that time, worrying about her.

She grimaced as she tried to sit up straighter.

"Tell me what you need. I'll help," he said.

"Ah. A deep-tissue massage with yellow rose incense infusing the air followed by a warm bath. Kidding, not kidding. Can you just prop me up a little? Yes, please slide the pillow down a little. Uh. Perfect."

After two weeks of watching Sky from a distance, this was the closest he'd been to her—leaning over and adjusting her pillows while trying to keep his fingers from tangling in her adorably snarled hair. He also didn't want to disturb the IV in her neck where hydrating fluids infused her system. He supposed with four limbs shattered, the nurses had been forced to use a neck vein for intravenous access. Hovering close, he noticed a faint trail of freckles over her nose he hadn't seen before today.

His responsibility had been to keep her safe, and he'd failed. Because of him, she'd nearly died. When he'd found her—battered and covered in blood—he'd prayed for the first time in a very long time. Asking for her to live. Now, with her every movement, speech, or joke, he felt the tension he carried between his shoulders from worrying about her easing out of his body.

"Um. Sorry." The ring on his right hand had trapped strands of red. He leaned close, trying to free them one piece at a time and avoid pulling her hair. "There." Taking a step back, he shook his head to clear his senses of her sweet strawberry and honeysuckle scent.

She patted at her wild mane. "It's a mess, isn't it? I don't suppose you have a brush?"

Nico reached into a toiletry bag by the window. "I have a few things from your house—hairbrush, toothbrush, body and hair soap, lotion, deodorant, and a change of clothes." He handed her a brush.

"You went to my home?"

"Not inside. I met your mother there, and she and your roommate packed a few items," he said.

"You met my mother?" The incredulity in Sky's voice was growing, but she didn't sound mad.

Nico suspected it wasn't in her nature to be angry, judging by how quickly she'd apologized when she'd justly lashed out at him for not protecting her.

"She's a very pleasant woman. She and your roommate, Maddie, are worried about you, but I've kept them updated. Your parents will be by later this morning."

Sky reached back to brush her hair and grimaced. Besides broken forearms, her shoulders had been dislocated in the accident, and Nico suspected they were still healing on some level.

"Let me help you." He took the brush and moved close, detangling and smoothing her hair, careful not to tug too hard. He rubbed a hand over the strands after each brush—solely to smooth it down and not because he wanted to feel the silky texture on his hands. Having never brushed a woman's hair before, he'd not known how intimate the motions would feel.

She sat stiff as a board, letting him work the knots from her hair. Of course she would be uncomfortable. He knew everything about her, and she knew nothing about him.

Maybe he could remedy that. "Your sisters are Shadow Guardians, and I'm a sentry for the Council of Mjölnir. We eliminate threats—Frost Giants, Dark Elves, Fire Giants, and the like." He paused, giving Sky the opportunity to ask questions. He knew from her sister, Raine, that Sky at least understood the different bloodlines which had mixed long ago when the nine realms ended and survivors were trapped on Midgard—Earth. When she didn't speak, he continued, "Raine heard of a possible threat against you, so she sent me to guard you. As you correctly pointed out, I did a remarkably poor job of it. I can call her so she can confirm my role if you'd like."

Sky reached up and held his wrist, stopping his brushing motion. Nico looked into a pair of the deepest tropical-blue eyes. He had a disconcerting urge to kiss the freckles coloring her nose and cheeks. She was so breathtakingly beautiful, despite the fatigue under her eyes, that part of him wanted to kneel on one knee and swear allegiance to this Valkyrie before him.

What is this absurd pull I feel toward her?

She gave him a soft, closed-mouth smile. "I'm sorry I accused you of not doing enough. I'm sure I'd still be on the side of the road if not for you."

Her touch sent warmth through him, and he moved his arm so

that their palms touched. The light contact stole his breath. She was impossibly off limits, but he wanted more of this proximity to her.

"Aren't you two adorable!"

Nico's head jerked toward the doorway, his hand still touching Sky's.

A female nurse in blue scrubs entered, looking at Sky from head to toe. "I see you're out of your arm casts." She blinked several times, brown ponytail swishing. "That's odd. I thought the doctors would leave those on longer. What's going on here?"

"I'm getting better," Sky said with a voice of airy cheer which had the nurses furrowed brow easing into a glassy eyed daze.

Nico kicked the discarded casts under the bed to conceal the evidence that medical personnel hadn't been the ones to remove them.

"I'm grateful to everyone's efforts in taking care of me," Sky added.

The nurse's look of confusion faded, and she smiled at Sky. "My. You do look a sight better. Did your fiancé tell you he carried you in his arms out of a field as the ambulance was enroute? Such romantic heroism."

Sky released his hand and turned toward Nico. "My wh—"

When he shook his head and cast his gaze down, Sky snapped her jaw shut. That didn't stop her from glaring at him, which he found surprisingly adorable.

The nurse took a moment to listen to Sky's breathing with her stethoscope before whipping it back around her neck and withdrawing a syringe from her pocket.

"What's that for?" Sky asked.

"Blood thinner. Since you're immobilized, we don't want you developing clots." She moved aside the bedsheet and Sky's gown.

Nico looked away as the nurse gave an injection in Sky's lower abdomen. Neither one of them bothered to tell her how pointless it was to give a clot prevention medication to a woman with supernatural healing abilities.

"Can I get you anything?" the nurse asked, checking Sky's toes for circulation.

"Do I still need this thing in my neck?"

"The IV?" She thought for a moment. "I can take that one out and put a new one in your arm. You need one at all times while you're in the hospital." She gathered supplies, removed the IV, applied a bandage, and trashed the catheter once it was out.

"Thank you." Sky pulled the covers back over herself.

"You're welcome." The nurse turned and left with a promise to return soon to put in a new IV once she retrieved supplies.

Nico set the brush down and sat in the chair beside Sky, fidgeting with a spot of torn fabric on his jeans.

"Fi-an-cé?" She emphasized the syllables as she arched an eyebrow at him.

He shifted his weight and cleared his throat. "It was the only way they'd let me stay by your side. I can't protect you from the waiting room."

"You said the Dark Elf died."

"He did, but there are always more."

Silent tension impregnated the air.

"Where's my ring?" she asked, crossing her arms.

"Wh-What?" he stuttered.

"If you're my fiancé, how did you explain to them I don't have a ring?"

Nico crossed his arms. "I told them you lost it in the crash."

"And they believed you? No questions?" Her voice grew harsh as her eyes flashed with frustration.

"What questions?" he challenged, liking how her annoyance brought color back into her cheeks.

"Where I live, what I do. What my hobbies are. What's my favorite color? Standard questions to prove you're my fiancé."

Nico calmly recited her address and the description of her wellness shop straight from her website. "You like horseback riding."

"It's Texas. Half of the state likes horseback riding. We just don't all own horses."

"You're favorite color's blue."

She pursed her lips. "Statistically speaking, fifty percent of the population holds blue as their favorite color."

"Royal blue." The way he could endlessly stare into her eyes, he was beginning to think royal blue was *his* favorite color, rivaled only by the vibrant multicolored reds and oranges of her hair.

"How long have I been your assignment?"

"A fortnight."

"Favorite food?" she asked.

"You eat a lot of salad, but I'm guessing the side of strawberries is your favorite." He gave a teasing grin.

When she frowned, he knew he'd guessed correctly.

"And you're allergic to cats," he added.

She tilted her head to one side. "You are remarkably thorough." Her tone made the statement sound like a barb rather than a compliment.

He shrugged, but the truth was that he'd enjoyed learning about Sky. He certainly couldn't have claimed to know the favorite color of anyone else he'd ever covertly monitored.

But their time was drawing to an end, even if they'd only officially met minutes ago. Her sisters would arrive back in Texas in a day or two, and he would be ordered to move along to the next job. Storm had already given him an angry earful over the phone about his ineptitude.

His next assignment surely wouldn't involve anyone as lovely as Sky. Maybe it was better that way, because she'd damn near died on his watch. He clearly wasn't fit to protect a potato, much less a living, breathing human being—especially one who was part of the trio destined to save the world.

This was the first attempt one of Helen's pets had made on the youngest of the sisters. Nico suspected the escalation of violence was because of the nearing war, but the notion didn't ease his sense of failure.

Sky reached down and wrapped her knuckles against the cast on her leg. "I need to get these rods out of my bones so they can finish healing. Now, be a good fiancé and help me out, will you?"

Nico eyed the cast warily and swallowed.

FOUR

"Oh, my, sweet Sky!"

Sky looked to the doorway where her parents shoved inside her hospital room. Her mother wore a long dress of purple flowers, and her white hair flowed halfway down her back. Her father wore khaki shorts and a Hawaiian shirt. The pair looked more suited for a beach vacation than a hospital visit.

Sky smiled. She appreciated their eccentric appearances, which matched their personalities, and both were a welcome sight after what she'd just been through.

"So good to see you awake now. We heard what happened to you." Her mother bent over and kissed her on the cheek.

Sky could feel their relief like a warm blanket. "Hi, Mom."

Sky shot a look at Nico, letting him know he wasn't off the hook for getting her leg cast off. He eased back into one corner of the room.

"The doctors and Nico told us you flipped your car. Why were you driving so fast after work? You know there are deer and bobcat crossing the road at night. Oh, but you are looking better already. The first night we came, you weren't even conscious."

Deer and bobcat? Sky wondered what story Nico had told them about her accident. He must know her parents weren't aware of the supernatural world around them or the roles their daughters were playing in the shadows.

Her father leaned down and hugged her. "We brought your favorite... strawberry shortcake."

Strawberries.

Her spirit lifted before she glanced at Nico, who gave her a self-satisfied smirk at having guessed her favorite food.

"Oh my, Wyatt. We don't even know if she can eat yet. Can you eat, Dear? Do you have an appetite?" She looked down at Sky's legs. "Oh, heavens. Have they given you any prognosis?"

"I just woke up. I haven't seen the doctor yet."

"Ida, don't pester her about her condition. She's probably terrified."

Sky listened to the banter, which brought a sweet, homey feeling of comfort to her. She stole another glance at Nico, who also looked amused at the exchange.

"Well," Ida turned abruptly to Nico, "amidst this calamity, we met your fiancé."

"Ugh. No, Mom—"

Ida walked over to him and enveloped a stunned Nico in an embrace. "We're so grateful to you. Even if Sky didn't bother to tell us you existed."

"Ida—" Wyatt began.

"Well." She bristled. "We've met all of her boyfriends. There was John and Mac and Jeremy and the Frederick brothers—oh, not at the same time—" she added with a wave at Nico "—oh, and Wallace. I didn't even know you'd broken up with Wallace." As she talked, she moved Nico over to stand next to Sky at the hospital bed.

"Yes, we broke up," Sky said.

"Well, you've never been engaged before, so this must be serious. Honestly, Dear, we support whatever makes you happy."

Wyatt shook his head. "Ida, let Sky introduce her fiancé properly."

"Of course we want to meet him properly. I just didn't expect to be the last one to know. The hospital staff knew before her own mother knew."

"Mom—"

Ida took a step back. "But look at you two! What a lovely couple. Imagine, Wyatt, all three of our girls in love—and Sky engaged. Tissue, Wyatt, tissue." She flapped her hands at her husband, who dutifully produced a handkerchief from his back pocket.

Sky gave a quiet sigh. Her parents had probably suffered enough in the last forty hours. She could set the record straight later.

"Mom, this is Nico Wølfe. Nico, these are my parents, Ida and Wyatt."

Nico extended a hand. "Pleasure to formally meet you both."

Wyatt shook his hand.

"And what a dashing accent," Ida noted. "I meant to ask you yesterday what that is?"

"I was born in Romania. But I spent my primary school and uni years in London."

"My. And what brings you to Texas?"

"Your lovely daughter." He smiled.

Sky's cheeks flushed with heat. Was he serious? Nico sounded sincere, but he must be referring to the part where she was his assignment. The way he'd phrased it would only make future explanations to her parents about the snowballing lie of their engagement even more difficult.

Her mother placed a hand over her heart. "And he's charming!"

Nico winked at Sky, who barely suppressed the urge to roll her eyes at his performance. If her legs were free, she might have kicked him. She could throw her pillow, but that would probably hurt her aching shoulder.

"I only hope I can get her back on Thunder in no time," Nico added.

Sky narrowed her eyes at him.

He knows my favorite horse?

Ida cast a woeful stare at Sky's encased legs. "Yes, no time. Well, we'll let you rest, Dear. The charity bingo championship is tonight, and we have to set up for it. Unless you need us to stay. We can cancel to keep vigil at your bedside."

"No, Mom, I'll be fine. You should go."

Her parents were social butterflies—always on some committee or fundraiser. Their abundant activities kept their bodies and minds busy—too busy to pry into the strange lives their daughters led. Well, Raine and Storm had strange lives. Until today, Sky's had been fairly normal.

Now she was in casts and a pseudo-engagement to a handsome stranger who'd already endeared himself to her parents.

Ida and Wyatt shuffled out of the room after more hugs and goodbye waves.

Sky swiveled her head toward Nico. "Well, now you've met my parents. I guess the engagement is complete."

His smile faded. "Sky, I had no idea my fib would careen out of control and cause problems. I told only the hospital staff who then told your parents. I didn't lie to them directly. Admittedly, I didn't clear the lie either, for fear they'd have me evicted from your room."

Too easily, she said, "Don't fret." She should definitely make him fret. Everything about him—his smile, touch, effortless movements, and lean muscles—unnerved her. Yet she liked him smiling better than frowning and worrying, so she reassured him. "I'll straighten the issue out with them later. It was too much to tackle just now."

"You want your strawberry shortcake?"

"I would love a cup of coffee." She smiled sweetly and batted her lashes. "If you get these rods out of my leg, I can go get it myself."

Nico arched an eyebrow. "I'll be back with coffee. Don't wander off," he said in a teasing tone over his shoulder as he left.

"Jerk," she mumbled, but she couldn't help smiling.

"I heard that," he called from down the hall.

Super-strength and super-hearing?

She would have to watch out for Nico... strictly in a cautious, self-preservation manner and not because she fantasized about him brushing her hair—in a secluded, romantic wilderness... naked.

Ugh. Simmer down, Sky. That man is not your real fiancé.

After so many failed relationships of relatively short duration, she doubted she would ever marry anyone. Besides, there were larger issues to tackle—like the threat of Helen and the coming war.

Sky leaned forward and wriggled one of the steel rods that held her as an immobile hostage.

Oh, Helheim.

These things were going to hurt coming out. She appreciated the medical care. She had no idea how shattered, displaced bones might have healed. Thankfully, she wouldn't have to find out. She was, however, going to find out how painful removing rods from healed tissue and bone would be.

"Sky?"

When she looked up, the broad figure of her ex-boyfriend filled the doorway. He wore slacks and a polo shirt. His dark locks of wavy hair curved around his ears.

"Wallace? How'd you find me?" she asked.

"Mary Beth told me you were in an accident."

Mary Beth was a mutual friend. Because her mom was friends with Sky's mom, it made sense word had traveled through the grapevine.

He glanced up and down her stationary body. "Were you drinking?"

"What? Why would you jump to that conclusion?" She felt hot anger creeping up her neck and into her cheeks.

"I heard your car was totaled." Pacing the room, he ran a hand through his dark hair, agitation wafting off of him.

"I'm fine. Thanks for asking." Her voice was a hard block of ice. She didn't know the state of her car, but if her injuries were any indication, there would be no salvaging her Prius.

"Have they said when you'll walk again?"

"Why are you here?" Sky demanded, but she already had an inkling as his mind leaked his thoughts in angry, liquid tendrils.

He stopped pacing and put his hands on his hips. "Mary Beth said her mom said your mom said you had a mysterious fiancé."

Sky rubbed her temples. "You and I aren't dating, which means my current relationship status is none of your business." She also wanted to point out they'd only dated for a few months, but more than that, she wanted him to leave.

"Yes, but we only stopped dating a month ago. Dammit, Sky, I knew you were cheating on me." His tone turned seething as he resumed pacing.

Speechless, Sky gaped at him. What could she possibly say to him to diffuse the situation and his absurd claim? Every retort that came to mind would only irritate Wallace further.

If he'd perceived Sky distancing herself while they were dating, it was because she began noticing sparks of volatile temper flares. Nothing outright hostile—but enough quick tongue lashes, eyes flashing, and roughness with inanimate objects to convey to her that she needed to separate from the ticking time bomb beneath Wallace's easy smile and good looks. She figured those handsome, wholesome features had enabled him to get a visitor's pass with no hospital staff checking with her first.

He made a disgusted sound as he moved closer, towering over her while she remained vulnerable with half her body immobilized in the hospital bed.

Thoughts of hurting her pulsed through his mind, nauseating her as he debated how much damage he could do before he was caught.

Sky had no escape.

Sky maintained eye contact with Wallace as she eased a hand toward the remote with the nurse call button, but he observed the movement and slapped away the control. It flew off the bed then boomeranged back and dangled by the cord.

Sky glared at him, forcing anger to dominate the fear surging through her thudding heart. If Wallace moved to strike her, she would pull out one of the rods in her leg and smack him upside the head with it. Maybe. She didn't know the force needed to un-skewer her leg. She might not be strong enough to pull it out.

"*Ce puii mei!*" Nico appeared in the doorway and crossed the room in three quick strides.

Before Wallace could react, Nico shoved him into a wall. His forearm braced against the back of the bully's neck, and his other arm held Wallace's right arm behind his back. Wallace's face was smashed against the wall, and he let out a grunt.

How did Nico move so fast?

"Wallace, meet Nico. Nico, my ex-boyfriend was just leaving." She tried to sound coy, but her voice shook slightly from the combination of fear and anger at Wallace's intrusion.

Nico, who'd perhaps thought Wallace was a mixed or hybrid bloodline based on his forceful reaction, released him upon hearing he was her ex. Her protector took a step back, but his posture remained poised for a fight.

Wallace turned, face red with rage, and clenched his hands.

"You don't want to do that," Sky said, keeping her voice even.

Wallace blinked and faltered. He shook his head as if to shake straw out of his hair. Eyes unfocused, he looked back and forth between Nico and Sky.

"You're not worth it." Still fuming, Wallace stormed out of the hospital room.

"Did you just do something there?" Nico retrieved the coffee he'd set down on the armrest of the chair near the door.

Sky accepted the cup, holding it with two hands to mask their shaking and absorb the warmth after the cold fear from Wallace's confrontation. Looking away, she willed her trepidation to subside.

"Maybe." She blew on the steam dancing up from the surface of the drink. Black, the way she liked it. She hadn't specified what type of coffee she wanted. Had he guessed or had he known? Probably the latter.

"Thank you for the coffee. And the intervention."

"Did he hurt you?" Nico's voice sounded pained as much as worried, as if he thought this episode signified another lapse in his protection of her.

"No."

"I can protect myself," Nico said.

"Oh, I can see that." She looked down at the Styrofoam cup and frowned at what it would do to the environment. "I was protecting Wallace from getting hurt, not you. And I was looking out for me. If you get thrown out of the hospital for violent behavior, who is going to remove these torture devices from my legs?"

"He's your ex-boyfriend?" Nico asked, clearly avoiding the topic of the poles in her legs as she'd already established Wallace was her ex.

"Ugh. Yes. Wallace heard I had a fiancé and came to accuse me of cheating on him. Can't imagine whose fault that is. Hmm?" She sipped her coffee while looking pointedly at Nico.

Wallace's actions were on Wallace, but she wanted to steer the conversation back to the light banter they'd enjoyed earlier.

Nico shook his head with a grin as the worry the incident had caused melted away from his expression. "I leave you alone for five minutes—"

She cocked her head to one side. "Are you accusing me of being a troublemaker?"

"You clearly are." He chuckled, a deep rumbling that had her heart thudding in a completely different way than it had from her fear of Wallace earlier.

A woman in green scrubs entered the room. "Hello, Ms. Thoren. I'm Dr. Patel."

"It's your surgeon," Nico whispered to Sky. "Try to behave yourself."

Sky didn't have time to give him a snarky reply before the doctor gasped.

"Your... your arm casts?" she sputtered.

"You're a miracle worker," Sky said cheerfully, sipping her coffee again. The beverage wasn't her usual vitamin and turmeric laced home brew, but it would suffice.

"I am?" With a befuddled expression, Dr. Patel began examining Sky's arms—palpating the limbs and rotating the joints.

Nico took Sky's coffee to hold it out of the way for her.

"Impossible," said the physician.

"I'm a fast healer."

Dr. Patel moved down to inspect her legs.

Sky said, "Tell me about these rods. I see six."

Dr. Patel rubbed her chin. "Six stainless steel rods. Three in the proximal part of the bone and three in the distal part of the bone. They keep the fractured femur intact and aligned as it heals."

"Is there any additional hardware under the skin or in the bone?

Am I going to be setting off metal detectors for the rest of my life?" Sky didn't care about metal detectors, but she worried about having foreign objects embedded in a healed body. Would that cause chronic pain? Would pieces of metal work themselves to the surface like a splinter?

"No, we didn't need to implant any other internal hardware. Just these temporary stabilizers." Dr. Patel rocked back on the heels of her clogs. "Unbelievable."

Sky waved a hand. "I'm sure you went into medicine hoping to achieve the unbelievable. Besides, you probably have other patients to see and loads of other work. You don't have time to think about this right now."

"I have other patients to see."

"I'll be fine. You go ahead and see to those other patients."

"Okay. Thank you." The doctor nodded and left the room, looking slightly dazed.

Nico handed Sky's coffee back to her.

"You have impressive powers of suggestion," he noted in a tone indicating this was something he hadn't known about her prior to today and it perhaps made him nervous. Apparently, he didn't know everything about her from his observations and her sisters.

She nodded. "Mind manipulation is easiest when I'm suggesting something the person already wants or doesn't want. For instance, I suspected Wallace didn't truly want to fight you—a superior adversary. If I enforce my demands against someone's desires, it hurts both of us and it's a heck of a lot harder."

She took another sip of coffee. "For instance, if I tried to force you to agree to remove these torture devices in my legs against your will, I'd have to use a lot more effort and we'd both end up with migraines. Of course, sweet-talking hasn't worked, so maybe I should enforce my will." She let the unveiled threat linger, though she wouldn't force that on him, and he could probably tell as much from her playful tone.

She rarely used her power of suggestion with others because it felt too manipulative. Also, she didn't know if she could even use her powers on Nico. If she couldn't glean his thoughts, maybe his mind was unequivocally locked against her powers.

"Sweet talking?" He scoffed, light eyes glittering with humor. "You asked semi-nicely the first time and threatened me the second. You offered nothing to sweeten the deal."

Sky tapped her index finger on the sealed Tupperware container from the tray beside the bed. "I have strawberry shortcake," she purred.

Nico laughed—something wonderfully deep and melodic. "Okay, Valkyrie. I'll take them out."

HELEN WALKED DOWN THE HALLWAY, heels clicking on the pristine marble floor, and thought through her to do list: check on the status of her army in training, check on the shipment of armor she'd commissioned, and assign new tasks to the Fenrir fleet.

So much to do to prepare for battle.

As the French chemist said, *Le hasard ne favorise que les esprits prepares.*

Chance favors only the prepared mind. —Louis Pasteur.

And she would be prepared.

After swiping her badge, the laboratory door slid open, and she approached a man hunched over a microscope.

"Herman, how is the latest batch?"

He frowned, a pair of bushy eyebrows diving toward each other like porcupines about to duel as he scowled. "Not well. They're too fragile. Accelerating their growth has given you a larger army but a weaker one."

"*So ein Misthaufen!*" She stomped her foot as she swore in German. "I'm on a time crunch."

"I know, my Queen. Ever since we lost Apollo, the crop has been thinning."

"I know. *Ich bin wütend.*" She crossed her arms.

She'd had a healer in captivity until the Shadow Guardians had stolen him from her facility. After they'd infiltrated, she'd been forced to evacuate and abandon the multi-million-dollar lab. Without the healer, she had no one to fix her creatures.

Over the years, she'd nurtured Herman's creations with steroids and growth hormones, rushed to create a big enough army of more concentrated Norse bloodlines for the coming war. The stress on their bodies manifested with broken bones and poor wound healing.

Damn the Shadow Guardians. Always chipping away at my fleet, my soldiers.

Helen had launched her own offensive attacks. Her misfits had slain their share, though never a Valkyrie. Certainly never one of the chosen three. She knew better than to attempt to finagle a victorious ending outside of the prophecies, but the temptation to win before the heralded battle was too great.

She paced the lab. Despite her searching, the three had eluded her for years. She had no names, thanks to the infuriatingly vague prophecies. Nothing until eighteen months ago, when a Frost Giant assassin stumbled across two Valkyries. But the prophecy spoke of three sisters, so Helen couldn't be sure if they were her prize targets.

Still, two fewer Valkyrie in the world would suit Helen just fine. When they'd survived her explosion, she knew they must be the strong ones from the prophecy. She'd hit them with a bomb and only learned later it hadn't killed at least one of them, evident when the Jotun, Bolverkr, was reported missing and presumed dead. He had either died at the hand of a Valkyrie or gone into hiding to avoid Helen's wrath over his failure. Either way—her adversaries were out there.

Another possibility existed. The Hellfire—oh, she loved that name—missile had killed the two Valkyrie and the third sister killed the Frost Giant. Helen knew better than to make such an assumption. She would prepare her army with the expectation all Valkyries would march to their death on the battlefield.

Three by three.

Three Valkyrie sisters. But who were the other three? That information had eluded her all these years as well.

Fucking useless prophecies. Brothers by bond, whatever the hell that means.

Recently, one of Helen's many spies had found a woman he suspected of being a Valkyrie, perhaps one of the three, but she hadn't heard from the Dark Elf she'd sent to deal with her.

As Herman stuck his nose back into his microscope, Helen checked her watch. Turning on her heel, she walked back toward her office for her next meeting.

Victory and bloodshed were at the forefront of her mind as the fated battle neared.

CHAPTER

SIX

Nico arranged Sky's pillow and situated her covers, which had been draped awkwardly around the stabilizers. He steadily pulled back the cast on the leg without the stabilizers to reveal smooth, healed skin. Then he refilled the cup of water from the jug on her bedside table. The last thing he wanted to do was cause this charming woman more pain.

"Nico?"

He turned to look at her.

"Stalling won't make it hurt less." Her sweet voice was a melodious bubbling brook with Texan undertones. Because she hadn't been born in the state but had grown up there, he suspected she'd picked up the accent during her childhood.

He could listen to her talk for hours. Her clients at the wellness shop probably found solace and comfort in her lovely tone and caring mannerisms.

"I know," he grumbled. He handed her a small, clean towel from the bathroom. "Bite down on this."

She rolled it to make it long and cylindrical, placed it between her teeth, and nodded.

He positioned himself by her legs, a pair of smooth, lovely legs. "If I do ever get engaged, this is not how I envision spending the first few hours with my fiancé."

She chuckled through clenched teeth clamped on the towel.

Nico leaned over the bed and grasped the apparatus connecting the two sets of six pins and placed his right hand on her thigh to keep it still.

Then he pulled.

Sky bit down and covered her face with the pillow. Muted screams dissolved into sobbing. He tossed aside the bloodied apparatus and gripped Sky's hand. She squeezed it vice-like as she cried into her pillow. He felt like a total ass, even though he'd done exactly what she wanted.

He used a larger towel to lay over the holes in her leg and absorb the oozing blood.

After he pulled the sheet back over her, muffled sobs were still bubbling out from behind the pillow. His heart breaking, he crawled into the hospital bed beside her. The fit was tight because he took up two-thirds of the bed but worked with their bodies pressed together.

"Is this okay?"

The pillow bobbed up and down.

He tucked the covers more snuggly and stroked her hair. When she moved the pillow aside and rested her head on his shoulder, he slipped an arm behind her.

"Thank you." Even as she said the words, her pain-induced tears still fell.

Nico continued to run a hand over her head, at a loss for words. He thought about offering her a bite of the strawberry shortcake he'd "earned" but for which he now had zero appetite. He opted for silence.

After a few minutes, the soft crying stopped, and Sky's breathing became slow and regular. He looked down at her sleeping face and brushed aside a strand of hair.

Easing his phone out of his pocket, he texted Sky's sister, *She's resting. Healing fast like you said she would.*

Raine responded, *Any threats?*

Ex-boyfriend stopped by. Wallace wasn't much of a threat, but Nico was on assignment to report back all details.

Yeah, probably a few of those.

He blinked at the screen, unsure what to reply, if anything. Sky didn't seem promiscuous, so what was her sister implying?

Oh, he replied, recalling the many names of previous boyfriends Ida had mentioned.

Raine cleared up his confusion with her response. *Men flock to her sweet disposition, but when you have her power of perception, you see people's darker side before you get too attached.*

He read the message a second time. Men flock to her? Nico could see that about her—smart, beautiful, a sense of humor, and a little quirky. Sad, he thought, how her gifts stunted relationships, except if it was with men like Wallace, in which case her perception was powerful protection.

And what does she perceive about me? he wondered.

The thought that she might see into his darker side had his stomach souring. As far as he could tell, she wasn't frightened by him, and if she knew his secrets, she would be.

Nico texted, *I'll be on the lookout for any threats.*

Raine replied, *I'm sure few of her exes are real threats. The DE are the actual threats.*

DE. Dark Elves. And Raine was uncharacteristically rambling in a text message.

She's safe with me, he reassured Raine.

Thanks. We'll be back soon.

He rested his phone on his stomach and closed his eyes, thinking of the assignment when he'd met Raine, her husband Will, and Storm a year ago.

· · ·

Nico had been working for the Council of Mjölnir for over a year, relaying information about Helen's forces and feeling like he was contributing to the side of the good guys. He'd been instructed to go to the house at one of the council elders in Montana.

Usha had greeted him with cookies, lemonade, and the warmth of grandmotherly affection despite knowing who and what he was. She lived in a ranch style home decorated in mauve and taupe colors, and he'd sat stiffly on her worn couch, waiting to be given his next assignment.

Usha relaxed in a recliner that threatened to swallow her small, aging body whole. "You have an interesting bloodline."

He shifted his weight. "I didn't choose it."

"Of course you didn't. So why do you feel ashamed of it?"

"Because I serve a dark master."

Usha gave him an empathetic nod. "Despite that, you have shown your value to the Council of Mjölnir. We—myself and the rest of the Council—would like you to work with three very special women. Valkyrie."

His mouth fell open. "Three Valkyrie?" He'd heard the stories about the three sisters and their destiny to fight Helen.

"Yes."

His muscles tensed. The very mention of them could spurn Helen into tantrums of fury in an instant. "I'm honored, but I don't think that's a good idea. Especially given my curse."

A knock sounded at the door.

"Ah, they're here. See them in, will you?" Usha asked.

Nico swallowed but obediently answered the door. Two women and a man stood waiting. The blonde woman wore a navy suit, matching the tall, thin man's attire. The other woman had dark hair and deep amethyst eyes. She wore black fitted pants, a purple tank top, and a black leather jacket.

"Usha is in the living room," Nico said, noting their skeptical appraisal of him as he opened the door. "I'm Nico Wølfe, and I work for the Council of Mjölnir." He didn't see a vehicle and wondered how the trio had arrived.

"Will Decker." The man extended a hand. "This is my wife Raine and her sister, Storm."

As he shook the hand offered to him, Nico gave a slight bow of his head to both women. Storm scrutinized him with a scowl.

Where is the third sister? he wondered.

They entered the living room and took seats. Will helped himself to a glass of lemonade.

"Good to see everyone again," said Usha. "Storm, how are Bryce and Olivia?"

The violet-eyed Valkyrie's reserved, frosty exterior instantly vanished as she smiled, revealing a pair of dimples. "Doing well. Looking forward to the day they can come out of hiding."

Nico guessed Usha referred to Storm's significant other and his child. He marveled at how 'normal' these two Valkyrie seemed. He'd always imagined them larger than life, but they had families. Glancing down at the dark wood flooring, he felt the loss of something he could never have. He wouldn't allow himself a family, knowing what fate had in store for him.

Usha gestured toward him. "Nico has proven his loyalty to the Council. We are reassigning him to work with you. To help you in whatever capacity you need."

"Loyalty?" Storm glanced in his direction with unconcealed doubt, making him wonder if she had some ability to know what he was.

"Yes," Usha replied. "He works for the Council until the day his compulsion forces him to do otherwise. From now until that time, he will help you."

Storm turned and appraised him with those thunderous eyes and a look conveying that she'd ended the lives of creatures who opposed them and would have no problem ending his when he turned against them.

Perhaps when that day came, it would be a mercy.

CHAPTER
SEVEN

Helen strode past her assistant and through the foyer of her office building adjacent to the lab. Black and white abstract paintings adorned pristine white walls. After pointing a finger to the left, her assistant nodded confirmation that the creatures she was about to meet with waited behind the closed door. She'd once had chairs in her foyer but didn't like walking past the filth on the way to her office. Keeping them in a cramped room behind a closed door was a far better way to avoid them en masse and reinforce their inferiority.

"Send Andrej in," she said, crossing the threshold to her office.

An enormous black chandelier centered over the room illuminated her gargantuan marble desk. The iron tentacles adorned with spikes spanned out like stretching bare branches of a fiendish rose bush. The room had a white and black marble floor with blindingly pale walls and similar black and white paintings, resembling Rorschach inkblots. Helen liked to stare at them and imagine they were the bodies and blood splatter of her victims—past, present, and future.

Andrej Wølfe marched into her office wearing his usual black suit. As the lead alpha of the hellhounds, he was always polished and classy. Most of the rest of them slouched in torn jeans and smelled like the dogs they were. Andrej had handsome Nordic features with blond hair and blue eyes. Even his wolf form was an attractive, lean, and sinewy white, unlike many of the other dingy brown and gray dogs. He had a strong jawline and full lips on a mouth that obediently told her what she wanted to hear.

She'd been tempted to force him to bed, he was so damn sexy, but she wouldn't stoop to sleeping with flea bags no matter how devilishly handsome they were.

"Updates," she demanded.

He was newly in charge of overseeing the training of her entire army. The role was of a managerial nature, but it afforded her more time in proximity to him.

Because there were no chairs for subjects to sit, Andrej stood in front of her desk. Her creatures could stand or they could kneel, and occasionally they could die on her floor when they failed her.

"The new recruits are training well. However, due to some limitations in their strength, we anticipate an inability to achieve the full numbers of soldiers by the deadline you requested." His throat bobbed, his only sign of discomfort or nervousness.

Fortunately for him, this wasn't the first time she was hearing of delays. She might have lashed out at him, but she knew from the scientist, Herman, about the flaws in the genetic makeup. Attempts to rapidly grow her creatures had resulted in a higher than expected mortality rate.

She waved dismissively at him. "I am aware. Continue the training of the ones we have. I need a full headcount in one week's time. Jotun, Ildjotunen, Dökkálfar, garmr, and draugr."

"Yes, my Queen."

She liked her subjects referring to her as queen, especially as someday in the not too distant future, she would rule this planet. She considered herself a reincarnated version of the goddess of Helheim, but queen had such a nice ring to it.

Andrej was still standing before her.

"Something else?" she asked.

"My brother. He has not returned from his last assignment."

She stood and approached her subject. "What assignment, exactly?" She had far too many moving parts and pieces in her organization to keep track of every order she'd given.

"He was sent to spy on the US division of the CoM."

She walked slow circles around Andrej, trailing one finger along his shoulder and chest. Did he really care about some other dog from the same litter as him, or was he asking so he could linger longer in her presence? She'd bet he would love to bed her and claim bragging rights.

Pausing in front of him to look at a pair of succulent lips, she asked, "Which one is your brother again?"

What would his mouth taste like?

Her hand trailed lower as she wondered what he would feel like in the palm of her hand. Just one feel. One orgasm. No one would have to know. But secrets were hard to keep when her subjects gossiped.

Ugh. She missed Apollo. He was Vanir bloodline. No shame in that. She'd tied him down, stripped him, and had her way. Every way. Preferably screaming. And since Apollo could heal himself, she could ravage him time and time again. But those cursed Shadow Guardians had stolen him from her.

When she ruled Midgard, she would take who she pleased to bed. Perhaps Andrej could be so lucky.

Andrej's jaw ticked slightly. "Nico."

Her gaze shot to Andrej's eyes, and she bristled.

Yes, she remembered that dog. He had a way of annoying her, like speaking in half-truths about the missions she'd assigned. She had to be careful and precise when dealing with him. His loyalty was more forced than many of the other hellhounds she commanded, though he'd also been more competent than most.

He was too clever for his own good. Most recently, she'd sent him on a suicide mission to eliminate one of the Council of Mjölnir's leaders.

"He's probably dead." She waved a hand as she walked back to her desk. The gesture was intended to dismiss both the conversation and Andrej.

He didn't budge.

Yes, she liked this one's control. He didn't crumble at the loss of a sibling. Probably because she'd done far worse to Andrej during his initiation.

Broken, reassembled, and resilient while simultaneously obedient. Perfection.

"Very well." She held up a finger in the air and closed her eyes.

Since the shapeshifting wolves were descendants of Fenrir, controlled by Helen's great-great-whatever grandmother, she had a special connection with them. She could not only command them to do whatever atrocities she felt necessary but also telepathically connect with them. Of all the creatures to survive the loss of the Nine Realms, these were the only ones with whom she could remotely communicate.

Stretching her mind, she reached out for this one inferior, insignificant creature, and only because she didn't trust him. She had to make sure his absence wasn't insubordination.

Nico.

Nothing.

She shook her head. "I sense nothing. He is clearly dead. Only death can sever the connection between me and my dogs."

Andrej bowed slightly, turned on his heel, and left.

Helen picked up her phone and pressed the button to summon her assistant.

"Yes, Queen Helen?"

"Send in the dragon."

EIGHT

S ky woke the next morning in the dim room when the nurse aide took her vital signs at five am. Nico was gone. Better that he was—he'd seen her battered, unconscious, unclean in bed with atrocious bedhead, and red-faced, puffy-eyed, bawling like a baby. Even someone's real-life fiancé probably never saw such unsightly previews.

Ugh. Fiancé. Sky had a whole lot of unraveling to do on that front. Half of Texas probably knew by now.

Of her sisters, she was the only one not in a relationship. Raine was married to the charismatic FBI agent, Will Decker, and Storm was dating the physician and Texas gentleman, Bryce Chambers. Both of her sisters had found incredible men who knew about their gifts, supported their endeavors, and had gifts of their own. Will was a descendant of Heimdall and could travel anywhere in the world in a blink of an eye. Well, maybe ten blinks, but the supernatural ability was still impressive. Bryce had the gift of illusion and a powerful shield that had saved everyone's life eighteen months ago. His daughter, Olivia, had premonitions.

Sky had never progressed far enough into a relationship to

divulge her abilities. Proving her healing abilities would require she first injure herself to demonstrate their existence. Not appealing.

My fake fiancé knows.

Nico Wølfe knew too much about her for her liking. And yet he'd comforted her in her time of need—quietly emitting strength in an entirely nonjudgmental ambience. When had she ever been held by a man without sensing his discomfort or an ulterior motive?

'How long do I have to cuddle before I can get back to watching the game?'

'I have spreadsheets to review. I don't have time to just sit here and hold her.'

'How many times do we have to go to dinner and a movie before she'll sleep with me already?'

In fairness to the other men, since she couldn't read Nico's mind, any of those thoughts or worse could have been hidden from her, but she was grateful for the silence either way. The quiet stillness of his embrace was a welcome reprieve, which also worried her. She could become far too attached to the serenity of time spent with him.

When the nurse's aide left, Sky tossed off her covers. She stood slowly and tested her legs. They were a little wobbly and ached, but they would carry her where she needed to go. Right now, that was home. She had so much work to do. She pulled on the clothes Nico had brought for her—jeans and a pink floral blouse.

"Running off?"

Sky startled and spun around from where she'd been rooting in the bag for footwear. Nico stood in the doorway, two cups of coffee in hand.

"I'm going home." Fidgeting with the bag, she stared at the gorgeous man bearing the perfect early morning gift.

He extended a cup as he entered the room.

She accepted it, smelling the strong aroma. "Thank you."

"You don't want to leave AMA—Against Medical Advice."

"I don't?"

"Your insurance company isn't likely to pay for your stay if you leave without a proper discharge. I'm sure you've got a hefty surgery bill."

"Oh." She sat down on the edge of the bed. She had a small policy as an entrepreneur and couldn't remember how much of a hospital stay it would cover, but she certainly couldn't afford to pay for all of it out-of-pocket.

Nico sat in the chair and leaned back. "Stick it out a few more hours and use your disconcerting power of suggestion on your surgeon. See if she'll discharge you before you go AWOL."

"Okay." She sipped her coffee. She could wait. Mounds of medical bills were unappealing. She could also sit, drink coffee, and listen to this man's alluring accent all day long.

"But when it's time to leave the infirmary, you don't get to run out on me." He leveled his gaze at her, but instead of feeling intimidated, the expression sent heat through her body.

"Because we're engaged?" she teased.

"Because you're still under my protection."

"Right."

"My job is to keep you safe until your sisters return."

"Right." Job. *I'm the job. Keep little sister safe.*

She wasn't a child. She lived independently and owned her own shop. She was turning thirty this year, and she was only six years younger than Raine and four years younger than Storm.

Flashes of leaving her business at closing time the other night were followed by images of the blow to her head and the car crash. Fine, so she did need protection, but she didn't have to like it... or the fact that she did actually like it. Like him.

"Are you okay?" Nico interrupted her thoughts, studying her face.

"How long am I going to need protection? You can't be my guardian angel forever."

Nico choked as he was taking a sip of his coffee. He sat up, wiping his mouth. "I'm far from an angel, Sky."

She grinned, liking his reaction and the use of her name. "Are you hiding demons under your halo?"

His pale blue eyes flashed silver at the word *demon* before his expression eased back into neutral.

Oh, you are *hiding demons.*

Enticingly intrigued, she wanted to know what secrets Nico Wølfe bore, but they weren't established friends where she felt she could simply ask. A fake engagement gave her no right to pry.

"I'm your protection until Raine reassigns me."

"You think that will be when she gets back?"

"Quite right."

"Well, I have a lot to do in the next few days. I need to check on the shop. I have a wellness session at the senior citizens' center tomorrow night. And I need to research these dreams I've been having." She clamped her mouth shut before revealing anything else.

"Lee Ann is taking care of the shop. Maddie is doing the senior citizens' session." He held up a hand when Sky opened her mouth. "She will take the brochures and the basket of remedies."

"Okay, they get half price."

"Senior citizen discount. She's aware."

"How did you know all of this?" But Sky knew the answer—Nico had been spying on her as much as protecting her. Then he'd charmed his way into the confidence of the people closest to her while she'd been unconscious. Oddly, his actions felt thoughtful instead of controlling because they'd been done on her behalf with no apparent benefit to himself.

Instead of an answer, he said, "Tell me about the dreams."

Damn rambling.

She eyed him over her coffee cup as she sipped. He'd saved her life and knew more about her than any man she'd been intimate with, but she wasn't ready to discuss her dreams. Not with him. Not yet.

NICO WAS ABOUT to press Sky a little for those dream details when Dr. Patel arrived for her morning rounds. She looked perky, as though she'd already consumed several cups of coffee. Her clogs squeaked on the shiny floor.

"Good morning, Ms. Thoren. You're looking remarkable. And…" She faltered. "And dressed?" She bent over and felt along Sky's legs. After a gasp, she said, "Your stabilizers? You're mobile."

"I'm all stable on my own. No need for stabilizers. They came out last night."

Dr. Patel straightened, anger and confusion in her furrowed brow. "They don't just come out."

That they don't, thought Nico. A man with lesser strength wouldn't have been able to remove them, and he'd damned near cried when Sky had out of anguish over the suffering he'd caused her.

"Life is hard," Sky said softly. "We take miracles when we can get them."

Nico watched Sky work her power of suggestion. Her voice acquired an even pleasantness.

"Miracle?" Dr. Patel frowned.

"Anyway, you're probably under pressure to discharge patients as rapidly as possible to cut costs. You don't want to keep someone here who's ready to go home."

"You might be ready to go home."

Sky smiled again. "That's the spirit."

"I'll work on your discharge paperwork, but it may take some time." Dr. Patel left, looking dazed.

When she was gone and out of earshot, Nico gave a wistful sigh. "Must be marvelous to always get what you want."

Sky rubbed her temples as if the effort of suggestion had cost her. "I don't." She narrowed her eyes at him and he chuckled.

"You don't use those skills unless you have to. Yes, so you said. Now, about those dreams," he pressed.

"I'm not comfortable talking about them."

"Okay. Then let me tell you about mine." He set his coffee down on the tray beside the still untouched strawberry shortcake. "In a land of fire and ice, an army of undead arises—Hel's army, except she goes by the name Helen. The descendant of the daughter of Loki will command them—the undead and an army of mixed breeds, including Jotun, Ildjotunen, Dökkálfar, and garmr."

"An army of Frost Giants, Fire Giants, Dark Elves, wolves, and draugr—undead." Sky's face drained of color. "And they are met on the battlefield by Valkyrie," she finished.

Nico nodded. He'd suspected her dreams would be the same as hybrids of the Norse realms across the globe were reporting. By the rising frequency of these dreams, some suspected the war was drawing near.

"Not just any Valkyrie are leading the battle," he added.

Sky cast her eyes down at her twisting fingers. "Three Valkyrie."

"Three sisters. Three Shadow Guardians."

"Yes." Her voice sounded slightly breathless.

"These are not just dreams, Sky."

"Prophecies." She swallowed but obviously wasn't surprised to hear his words.

"Helen is amassing this army. You and your sisters—by the power of three—are the key to stopping her."

She blinked. "Three by three. Not just three sisters, but their mates. An army against six. The next Ragnarök."

"The end of Midgard."

"But I'm not a warrior. I don't have my sisters' abilities."

"They had to develop their skills. You will, too. I saw a woman who risked her life to kill a Dark Elf the other night. I saw you on that battlefield with Hel's army. You had a bow and arrow." The vivid memory of the dream with Sky looking like a warrior sent gooseflesh along his skin. He remembered the first time he'd seen her in real life from a distance and had been overcome with an overwhelming sensation to drop to one knee and worship that woman because of what he'd seen in his dream.

She gave a strained smile. "I know my way around a bow and arrow. I used to shoot while horseback riding when I was younger."

"The way Raine tells it, you out-rode your sisters."

She grinned. "Maybe I did."

Sky would become an amazing Valkyrie, he was sure of it. Too bad he had to distance himself and wouldn't be around to see her reach her potential.

CHAPTER

NINE

Nico helped Sky into his rented Silverado. Already, the summer Texas sun was beating down, although it was barely noon. If the humidity wasn't so oppressive, he could have better tolerated the heat. The truck's air conditioning blasted at full power to cool off the interior.

Sky had been discharged from the hospital, and he'd secured her Get Well flowers in a bin in the bed of the rental truck. Then, he'd texted her parents and sisters to let them know he was driving her to her house.

Sky buckled in as he closed the passenger door. After walking around, he slid into the driver's seat.

She smoothed her hands over her jeans. "I need a new phone."

"I can help with that." His mind immediately went to the burner phones he routinely purchased. He would need to get her a standard one and see if she had her data backed up somewhere.

"Really? Thanks."

He started the engine and left the parking lot. "Anywhere you need to stop before home?"

She chuckled. "Looking like this? No, definitely not."

To his eyes, after having seen her on death's door, she was a picture of beauty and health. She'd showered in her room while they'd awaited the formal discharge. Now, her red hair was down in loose waves with her red highlights illuminated by the sun, and her skin had a rosy hue. Her eyes shone bright and vibrant. The smell of strawberries and honeysuckle replaced the hospital's antiseptic odor.

Her gaze slid to him and back to face the front of the truck. "I guess you already know the way to my house."

"Quite right."

She fidgeted with a hole in her jeans.

"Does going home make you nervous?" He hoped it wasn't him making her uncomfortable.

She lifted her eyes to him. "I know what's next. I mean, I know the next part of the story... the battle. I know I need to prepare for it. I guess I thought I had more time."

Because the urge was too strong to resist, he stretched a hand over and took hers. Soft, warm. He wondered what holding that hand would feel like on a daily basis. But he didn't have the right. She was a Valkyrie. A chosen one.

And one day, he would betray her trust.

"There's still time," he said, unsure if he was trying to reassure her or himself.

"We're going to my parents' for dinner tonight."

"We are?" he asked.

She nodded. "The invite is coming soon. Raine and Storm will be there, and they're going to tell us they've discovered the exact day of the showdown."

"They are?"

Eyes glistening and doleful, she said, "We have until August twenty-third to prepare."

"Do you see a lot of the future?"

"No. I can't see the future, aside from my dreams, which are never clear. This is me picking up on my sisters' thoughts and feelings. This is knowledge they've recently gained and will share, not a premonition."

He relaxed at the reassurance she couldn't openly see the future, but only slightly. How much of his thoughts and feelings could she sense? Did she know he was attracted to her? Did she know the fear gripping him at his inevitable betrayal of her?

He doubted it, since she wasn't afraid of him.

He squeezed her hand before letting it go. "And what am I thinking?" He managed to ask the question playfully, even as his gut clenched in trepidation at what she might say.

"You want to know what's for dinner." She winked.

"I am hungry."

"Actually," she narrowed her eyes at him, "I can't read you. It's both maddening and wonderful at the same time."

He chuckled nervously. "Why is that?"

"Maddening because I don't know why you're the first person whose thoughts I can't read. It can't be related to different nationalities. I've met a mixture of people from different countries. But," she held up a finger, "it could be related to your powers. You're fast and strong. Are you Asgardian?"

The truck jerked slightly under his hands when they shook, and he gripped the wheel tighter. "No. What's the wonderful part?"

She rested her hands in her lap. "When I'm with you, the world is silent. No whispers trickling into my head. I only knew what my sisters were up to because I intentionally stretched my psyche for that information. When I'm in close proximity to people, their thoughts waft toward me, and I have to make an effort to close my mind to them. With you, I have quiet peace... you know, when you're not harassing me." She rolled her eyes.

He grinned, not revealing the mix of emotions swirling through him—relief that she couldn't read his mind and see his attraction for her and the evil lurking deeper, delight that his presence gave her respite from her powers, and regret that she would be safer if she knew the truth and banished him.

Not to worry, he assured himself. They were having dinner tonight with her sisters, at which time he would be properly reassigned to a different task not involving Sky because of his failure to protect her. He would no longer be a danger to her and her family.

"Hey," Sky slid her hand back into his, "don't worry. Mom and Dad are making bar-b-que. Dinner will be delicious."

Nodding, he gripped her hand a little tighter. No, she definitely couldn't read his mind.

He cleared his throat. "You should know I'm a spy." There, now she would know not to trust him.

"A spy?" Her eyes widened in shock.

"I work for Helen, and I spy for the Council of Mjölnir. I've provided intelligence on Helen's inner workings over the years."

"Sounds dangerous."

"I'm sure if Helen ever discovered my misbehavior, I wouldn't live to regret it. Not that I would regret it. I'd die happily knowing I was her undoing." He said the last statement with the same acidity he felt about the subject.

"Don't say that. No death for you. Don't go back to her. I forbid it." Her tone was spoken in mock authority mixed with a surprising tinge of worry.

He glanced at her, concerned by the angst in her voice and debating how to shift the topic or lighten the mood. "Is that so?" he asked with a playful arch of his eyebrow. "What makes you think you have a say in the matter?"

"Chosen Valkyrie, remember?"

"That title earns you the right to storm Hel's battlefield, not to command me," he teased.

She huffed. "You can't simultaneously protect me and return to the goddess of the underworld. So, do your job and stay as my protector."

"Your sisters may have a different assignment in mind when we see them."

"Why did they assign you to me? Seems like spy and bodyguard are two very different roles."

"I've done both over the years. The US leader of the Council of Mjölnir assigned me to you. Considering your condition when we met, it was probably not one of her better decisions."

"Pfft. Stop beating yourself up about that. If Raine and Storm wanted appropriate protection, they would have told me about you and introduced us. Then you would have been by my side instead of ten paces behind me."

She had a point.

Except... Nico frowned. "I asked them about a direct introduction, and their response was that you wouldn't accept it. Apparently, they'd tried an assigned bodyguard thrice before, and you dismissed them as intrusive."

"Oh, yeah, so I did." She chuckled, apparently recalling the details of the incidents.

"Besides, I don't think Storm wanted us acquainted. She neither likes nor trusts me. She only accepted my role as protector for you because Usha, the leader, declared it so."

Sky snorted. "Storm neither likes nor trusts anyone. Don't take it personally."

Ah, but Storm knows what I am, Nico thought.

She had good reason to distrust him.

When they arrived at Sky's house, Maddie, her roommate and Bryce Chamber's mother, was there to greet them. She wore her dyed blonde hair so large and airy, Nico suspected it could be used as a flotation device. But he'd discovered her heart was as big as her hair when he'd told her about Sky's injuries and she'd immediately offered to help.

In his early protection of Sky, Nico had learned about her roommate. After Bryce had been attacked at his own home, Maddie had moved in with Sky for safety in numbers. In addition, Sky had fixed her home with protective wards years ago against the dark bloodlines. Maddie lived with her now, except when she left for a week every month to spend time with Bryce and Olivia, who mostly lived on Storm's yacht to avoid Helen's detection.

Sky's house was a quaint three-bedroom craftsman bungalow with a low-pitched roof and wide eaves with exposed rafters. Tapered square columns framed the small porch.

Nico kept pace beside Sky as a protective gesture against another attack and because he could see she was still unsteady on her feet after the accident, despite her assertions to the contrary.

"Oh, it's so good you're back home," Maddie cooed. She wore jeans and a mint green blouse.

"Hi, Maddie," Sky hugged her when she reached the porch. "I guess you already met Nico."

"Very charming." Maddie beamed and winked at both of them.

"Good to see you again, Mrs. Chambers." When he and Sky reached her doorway, Nico hesitated and stiffened. "You have wards," he recalled feeling them like an invisible tingling barrier the first night of his assignment when he roamed outside this house. This would be the end, he thought. Sky would discover he was evil when he couldn't cross her threshold.

"Yes." She looped an arm through his. "But they guard against creatures intending harm. My protection spells don't apply to my savior."

With that, they stepped through the veil of magic, and she led him through the front door.

"Savior?" He wasn't sure about that. He neither deserved nor wanted such an accolade. And would those wards snap back in place to protect her should he one day have harmful intentions?

"Savior and tormentor," she amended, playfully and patronizingly patting his arm.

SKY FELT REVITALIZED after a bubble bath. As she rummaged through her closet, deciding what summer dress to wear, she bobbed her head to music from her laptop playlist. Without her phone, she settled for the slightly tinny sound of her computer speakers, playing an upbeat Lady Gaga song in keeping with her current buoyant spirits.

She probably should dread the core family reunion because it signified the danger to come, but she was too happy at the prospect of having all her family and their significant others under one roof to let minor details like an impending apocalypse dampen her mood. Such a gathering hadn't happened since Christmas a year and a half ago.

She took her time selecting her dress and drying her long hair to look perfect for the occasion.

"Sky?" came a tentative male British voice.

She'd been so wrapped up in her own excitement she'd almost forgotten the gorgeous man inside her house.

She wondered what magic he possessed to enable him to detect her wards. He'd never answered her question about whether or not he was Asgardian, but her sisters were, and they couldn't detect her wards. She knew that because she could sense their thoughts.

Nico must be something else entirely.

"Yes?" She set down her brush.

"You may already know this, but dinner is at six. Raine is bringing Will, and Storm is bringing Bryce and Olivia."

"Almost ready. I'll bring you and Maddie."

She topped off her look with a pair of dangling gold earrings, exited her bedroom, and walked into the kitchen where Nico was pouring a small glass of orange juice. He wore jeans and a black t-shirt stretched over his broad, muscular chest. A very fine chest she'd laid her head on only yesterday and wouldn't mind doing again right now.

Maddie lunged on the couch reading a Nora Roberts novel.

"I took the liberty of ordering you a phone we'll need to get..." Nico's voice trailed. He spilled the orange juice as he stared at her for a moment. "Sorry." He rushed to close the jug and shove it back into the refrigerator. "What were you saying?" He snatched up a rag and started wiping at his mess.

Maddie watched the awkward exchange with an amused twinkle in her eye.

Sky grinned. "I wasn't saying anything, but perhaps I should say thank you for ordering me a new phone. Are you okay?"

He gulped down the orange juice before turning back to her. "Sorry. You're an exquisite woman, and my reaction was unprofessional."

She widened her smile, not knowing what to say at the delightfully honest words. One day when she had an actual fiancé, she hoped he would stutter, become flustered, and spill juice at the sight of her.

"Oh, uh, I almost forgot." He fished a hand in his blue jean pocket. "I've been meaning to give this back to you. They took it off you in the emergency room." He held out a necklace with a twisting Celtic design.

Gasping in delight, she rushed to grab it. "Thank you! I thought I'd lost it in the crash. Thank you so much." She took the necklace, put it around her neck, and tried to re-clasp it. She really needed a mirror to see what she was doing.

Nico walked around behind her. "I'll help," he offered, taking the necklace from her hand.

She held up her hair as he fastened the clasp. With his presence so close and fingers brushing her neck, the gesture felt intimate. Though with his mind closed to her and his expression hidden behind her, she didn't know his feelings about the act.

Suddenly struck by her own vulnerable emotions, she swallowed. "Are we ready to head out?" Her voice sounded dry. As soon as she felt him release the secured piece of jewelry, she stepped forward, needing a little space.

"You do look gorgeous," Maddie chimed in. "I made pie."

She headed toward the refrigerator. "So, how do you want me to play tonight? Nico here just explained to me how his little lie to stay close to you blew up like a bonfire turned wildfire, and half the town now thinks you're engaged." She pulled out a peanut butter pie and balanced it in her palm.

Sky smoothed the front of her skirt. "Yeah. Mom was so delighted I couldn't bring myself to tell her at the hospital after what she'd been through with my accident. I'm going to do my best to clear the air tonight."

"I don't know," Maddie began, eyeing Nico as she spoke. "He's a looker and saved your life. I say hang onto him."

"I can't *hang on* to my fake fiancé just because I think he's a great catch. Relationships don't start in the engaged status."

Nico looked back and forth between the women. Clearly deciding not to join the conversation about this topic, he changed the subject. "Shall we go to dinner?"

"We shall." Sky said, enjoying the burning shade of crimson in Nico's cheeks.

CHAPTER

TEN

While Nico helped Maddie out of his rental truck and held the pie, Sky bounded up her parents' porch steps and let herself inside the house.

Nico's gaze darted around the darkness, all senses on high alert for another attack, but he perceived no threats nearby. Sweet molasses permeated the air and mixed with freshly mowed summer grass.

"It smells incredible," Sky was saying when Nico and Maddie reached the foyer.

"Wyatt made bar-b-que pulled pork to die for!" Ida gushed. "Melts in your mouth. Honey, you're a picture of health." She turned toward Nico, who stood to Sky's right. "Oh, Nico!" She gave him a hug—full Southern style, as if they were reuniting after weeks of absence rather than having just seen each other yesterday.

Sky shifted her weight on her feet. "Yeah, Mom, about Nico."

"Granny!" Olivia skipped into the room and into Maddie's arms as she knelt to receive the hug.

"My sweet baby girl," the woman declared, wrapping her arms around her granddaughter.

The reunion warmed Nico's heart. He knew Bryce and Olivia lived on a boat and wasn't sure how often Olivia was able to see her grandmother.

Behind Olivia, Bryce entered the room wearing jeans, boots, and a button-down shirt. "Hey, Mom."

"Never trust an atom," Olivia told Maddie. "They make up everything."

Maddie laughed. "I like that one."

After a quick hug to his mother, Bryce approached Sky. "And hey, Sunshine." He wrapped his arms around her. "Olivia is going through a joke phase."

"Why was the math teacher suspicious of prime numbers?" Olivia asked Sky.

"Why?"

"Because they were all odd."

Sky giggled. "Cute."

Bryce glanced at his daughter with an adoring gaze before turning back to Sky. The girl was all buoyant youth, reminding Nico a bit of Sky.

Bryce kissed Sky's cheek. "Glad to see you've bounced back from your accident. I wanted to visit, but Olivia and I have been in the Gulf. Are you feeling okay?"

"Recovering. Thanks."

When Bryce stepped back from Sky, he extended a hand to Nico. "Bryce Chambers."

"Nico Wølfe." He shook hands firmly with the Texan, a little amazed this friendly cowboy was Storm's significant other.

"Good to meet you. Storm mentioned you."

Nico wondered in what context the Valkyrie had spoken about him to Bryce, but the man didn't seem to cast any doubt or negative vibes in Nico's direction.

"You knew about the engagement?" Ida asked Bryce.

The man's brow furrowed as he looked back and forth between

Nico and Sky. Her cheeks flushed in what appeared to be a mix of frustration and exasperation.

When Sky threw a look of daggers at Nico, he realized he'd been grinning at her. He schooled his expression.

"Mom," Sky said on a sigh, "I'm trying to tell you that—"

"Engagement?" Storm said, voice striking the room like a thunderclap.

All eyes turned to the front door where Will, Raine, and Storm stood. Will and Raine wore the same outfit Nico had always seen them in—matching navy-blue suits, though Will had a blazer and she wore a vest. He was long and lean with a narrow nose and sharp eyes that took in everything around him like one might expect from an FBI agent. Raine had blonde hair, usually in a ponytail, but tonight she wore it straight and long down her back.

"What engagement?" Storm asked, her violet irises boring into Nico.

He didn't know if her hostility toward him was because of what he was, his failure to protect Sky from the Dark Elf, or the word engagement being used in the context of her younger sister. Probably some combination of all three.

Nico began, "I—"

A shrill alarm filled the air.

Ida flapped her arms. "Oh, Wyatt! You and your baked potatoes. He's always setting the smoke detector off." She flittered out of the room with Maddie after her. "Open the windows. Open the windows!"

Olivia giggled, and Storm scooped her up into her arms.

"No engagement," Sky said to Storm. "Just a misunderstanding."

Will stepped forward and shook hands with Nico. "Good to see you again."

"Likewise."

"Wait," Raine interjected. "Mom thinks you and Nico are engaged?"

"You know how she is... drawing conclusions when she sees a handsome man in proximity to me."

Raine nodded, and Will's mouth quirked in bemusement.

Nico's eyebrows raised, surprised at the way Sky seemed to be protecting him and the lie he'd allowed to perpetuate.

"Engagement?" Storm asked again.

"Look," Sky snapped, "I'm trying to clear the misunderstanding."

She seemed more frustrated by Storm's tone suggesting the engagement was preposterous than by misunderstanding the situation, making Nico wonder what Sky gleaned from Storm's emotions.

Raine snorted. "Good luck with that."

"You could start by not standing so close to each other," Storm said.

Nico glanced down at Sky who had slid closer to him when the smoke detector had been set off. Or had he moved closer to her?

With a petulant jutting of her chin, Sky looped an arm through Nico's. "You know what? You can take your disapproval and shove it up your boat. Mom is happy, so I'm going to let her be happy. I can manage the fallout after we deal with what everyone is gathered to talk about."

Nico gave a squeeze of support to Sky's arm as he avoided direct eye contact with Storm and her arched eyebrow of incredulity. He suspected only one of the sisters of the deadliest Valkyrie he knew could get away with mouthing off to Storm without losing a limb.

"We do need to talk," Will said.

"Yes," Raine agreed. "But after dinner and not within earshot of Mom and Dad."

Plates filled with bar-b-que pulled pork, baked potatoes, and coleslaw. The smells of sweet sauce, tangy vinegar, and buttery spuds permeated the dining room where everyone sat to enjoy the meal.

Sky sat next to Nico. She savored the meal as light conversation flowed. Discussions ranged from Olivia on Storm's yacht to Storm's travel blog to Will and Raine's next trip on behalf of their work for the FBI, which Sky knew was actually work for the Council of Mjölnir.

When a lull in conversation struck, Ida asked, "How about we all address the elephant in the room?"

The three sisters glanced nervously at each other. Bryce and Will looked at their women while Nico curiously observed the entire group. Olivia looked around as though expecting to see an actual elephant.

"Mom, what are you referring to?" Raine inquired, voice slow and steady with caution.

Ida heaved out a breath. "I know you're not FBI, dear. And Storm hasn't been living a carefree life traipsing around the world just to create her travel blog for ordinary humans to enjoy. And I don't believe for one minute Sky lost control of her car, without her seat-belt on, and nearly died—only to be walking a few days after multiple broken bones. I think it's time we all stop pretending your parents don't know who and what you are."

All three women's jaws dropped open.

"You know about us?" Raine asked, glancing at Sky as if clearly wondering how she, of all people, hadn't known.

At the same time, Storm said, "We've been trying to protect you."

"I never sensed anything," Sky sputtered. She could glimpse her parents' thoughts, but they were always tame—the next bingo night, the next garden harvest, or the next wine-down Wednesday. She wrung her napkin in her lap.

Ida looked at them with the sort of compassion and pity only a mother can achieve. "Of course, I knew. Sky, when we figured out your gift, we had an enchantment placed on us to protect us, Wyatt and I, from your abilities. We—"

"All this time?" Storm demanded, an edge to her voice as if they'd had a right to know their parents had known.

"All this time," Ida confirmed. "I've known all of you were

special, known you're destined for great things. That you've already been achieving great things, even if I don't know the specifics."

"You should have told us. We could've been more prepared." Storm shook her head vigorously even as Bryce put a hand on her shoulder. "We were so unprepared."

Anger and frustration pulsed out of her. Nico glanced at Sky as if noting how Storm's rage was impacting her like a throbbing heat-wave striking her psyche.

"You're wrong," Ida said gently. She continued despite Storm's rising, pursed-lip frustration. "What has happened as you've gained more knowledge? What has happened as each of you have slowly united with purpose?"

Sky considered the escalation of events as she knew them. For years, Raine and Storm had worked in isolation from each other, chipping away at evil. When Storm joined Raine's ranks in the Shadow Guardians, the goddess of the underworld had thrown a smart bomb at them. Now, after a period of relative safety, Sky had been attacked.

Sky cleared her throat. "The stronger we become and the more we unite under the supernatural shadow world, the more Helen homes in on us."

Ida nodded. "I kept information from you for so many reasons. I didn't want your childhood and adolescence burdened by the rumors of toxic battles and a destiny of bloodshed. And I trusted my dreams. They warned me that the longer your power and strength weren't fully realized, the longer Helen would be unable to find you. The necklaces I gave each of you can only protect you so much from Helen's attempts to find you. In fact, I had one made for Olivia." She glanced at Bryce. "Don't let me forget to give that to her before you leave tonight."

Sky's hand went to the charm on the necklace she wore. She felt a chill of realization as images running through everyone's minds crashed against her like waves on a cliff. All this time, Helen had searched for the sisters unsuccessfully. She knew the prophecies, had even tried to kill all prophets to silence the inevitable truth. Despite the seemingly limitless resources at the woman's disposal, she was late finding the sisters. Not until a few days ago had she found Sky and sent the Dark Elf, but even he hadn't been sure she was one of the three sisters.

Storm blinked, as if processing their mother's claim while her anger at the situation visibly deflated.

"Mom's right," Raine began. "In all this time, Helen hasn't come after us directly. She only attacked us during our dream walks, a time when we were gaining more power. If she'd wanted to thwart the prophecies, she could've come after us when we were defenseless and unskilled."

Nico shifted his weight. Although Sky couldn't glean his thoughts, he clearly knew something about Helen and her efforts to find her and her sisters. He'd admitted to being a spy, after all.

Will held Raine's hand. "Agreed. A woman like that would've had the resources to track the three of you down a long time ago. Maybe she just couldn't find you, protected with the necklaces and the separation, as Ida suggested, until now."

Until now, the words echoed in Sky's mind.

"Protected?" Storm asked, throwing her napkin on the table. "Helen almost killed all of us with a bomb."

Nico quietly said, "She wasn't the one to find you, though. Bolverkr, the Frost Giant, did by happenstance. Not Helen. She didn't find Sky until now, and it wasn't for lack of searching for all of you over the years. I'm not sure she even knew Sky was one of the sisters when she sent the Dark Elf. Sometimes she gets wind of someone—a light elf, a Vanir, a Valkyrie—and eliminates a potential threat before it can manifest against her."

Silence settled among the group for a long moment.

"I guess it's time for my dream walk." Sky swallowed. "I'm the weakest link."

Nico shook his head slightly in obvious disagreement at her last words but stayed silent.

"Oh, I doubt that," Ida said with a chuckle and an adoring grin.

Raine looked sad, but Sky felt her oldest sister had already accepted the truth. Sky formally needed to join them as they neared the fulfillment of the prophecy. Storm's pale and stricken face reflected her feelings that she'd failed Sky somehow. Storm had spent all these years as an assassin, hoping her work would protect her family, only to learn her mother already knew. In addition, now Storm was forced to accept she couldn't alter their destiny.

Sky had to join them.

Sky told Storm, "Oh, please don't be so upset. We all know it needs to unfold this way."

Under the table, Nico slipped a hand into Sky's, and she squeezed it, grateful for his gesture of emotional support. Storm glanced irritably at the pair of them, the look reflecting the overall sour mood pouring out of her like mist from dry ice. Sky wouldn't dive any deeper into her sister's psyche, as she didn't want to open her senses and receive what she knew would be a potent dose of Storm's anger. Instead, she focused on Nico's comfort and her mother's calm ambience.

"You've kept me safe for so long, both of you." Sky looked back and forth between her sisters. "But we have to face what's coming. I need to be prepared, and I need all of you to help me do that." She looked around the table at each of them. Even Bryce, Will, and Nico. Maybe the prophecies heralded three sisters, but these men were also an integral part of their team.

Three by three.

Her sisters were stronger with the love and help of Will and Bryce supporting them. Even on the battlefield in her dreams, these men were fighting alongside them. Glancing down at Nico's hand in hers, she tried not to read too much into his gesture, but in the short time she'd known him, he'd more than earned her trust.

"Daddy, what are they talking about?" Olivia asked in hushed tones.

Bryce leaned over and kissed his daughter on the top of her head. "I'll fill you in later, sweetie."

"Well," Maddie interjected cheerfully, "it seems we can continue this discussion at another time. Who wants pie?"

Nico stared at the flames of the outdoor fire pit in the backyard of the Thoren estate. Initially, he'd thought having an outdoor fire in June was absurd, but he found the ambience relaxing and conducive to discussion. They sat in six chairs in a circle around the dancing light with Raine and Will's seats and Bryce and Storm's pushed closer together. Nico wouldn't have minded closer proximity to Sky, but he didn't want to indulge his feelings for her or fuel the fire of Storm's obvious dislike of him.

Inside the house, Ida and Wyatt cleaned the kitchen, having insisted on their children discussing matters on their own while Maddie and Olivia played chess in the lounge room.

"We need to distance ourselves from Mom and Dad," Storm began. "Physically, not emotionally. I don't want Helen launching an attack at us while we're here and putting them at risk."

Raine nodded. "I agree. I know Sky put wards on the house, but I'd feel better if we weren't bringing danger to their doorstep."

"My home isn't big enough for six," Sky said.

Six, Nico noted. Surely, she couldn't possibly think he would join the next part of their journey.

"Usha's ranch?" Will asked.

"Yes, my thought exactly," Raine said. "She has space to train, and Sky can do her dream walk in relative safety there. We have a solidified date now, so the rest is just preparation."

"We have until August twenty-third. Freyfaxi, according to Olivia's premonitions," Bryce said.

Storm added, "Freyfaxi marks harvest day, dedicated to the god of harvests. I think there's some sick parallel with Helen wanting to harvest the world for her apocalypse."

Nico observed the group dynamic. Seeing everyone together for the first time was illuminating. Raine was the practical older sister, a little less impulsive and without the mood swings of Storm. Despite Storm's angst, she seemed to have the best interests at heart for the people she loved. Sky, meanwhile, absorbed everything from everyone with strong, understated compassion, as though she would spare them any emotional pain if doing so was within her power.

None of them could stop their destiny, and he knew what a bitter pill it was to have no control as The Fates—Nornir, in Norse Mythology—dictated your life as if you were a mere puppet on a string.

"So we're all moving to Usha's ranch to train there," Bryce clarified.

"Life off the boat for a little while," Storm said with a reassuring pat on Bryce's leg.

"Olivia and I will like that," Bryce said.

"What about Nico?" Storm asked. "We're all together now. Sky will be safe with our group. He could be reassigned by the Council."

He felt the words like a stab to his gut. Nothing Storm said was untrue, and her tone hadn't been harsh, simply matter-of-fact. He deserved harsh. He deserved to be kicked out of the club for having failed to protect Sky, who could have died in the car accident. At the same time, he hated the thought of being reassigned. He wanted to stay and be a part of them, even if his dismissal was safer for everyone.

As he waited for the group to cast their votes, a war raged inside him. He simultaneously wanted to stay and go. Rather than making eye contact with anyone, he stared at the fire so as not to betray his feelings—although they were so muddled within him that he didn't know what he could possibly betray.

"He stays." Sky didn't look at him even as he did a double take at her words.

"I don't know if that's a good idea," Storm said.

"The Shadow Guardians assigned him to me, and I feel safer with him. If he doesn't have some more important work he needs to be doing, he stays."

"Safety in numbers," Will offered, looking at Raine. "And Usha speaks highly of him."

"At this point," Bryce added, "there probably isn't a more important job than keeping Sky safe."

Raine took a deep breath. "If Sky feels safe, I think that's the biggest indicator he should stay."

Nico hazarded a glance at Storm, who stared at Bryce with her mouth agape. She turned a pair of narrowed eyes back to scrutinize Nico. Now was his chance to recuse himself. Sky would be safe in the care of her family. Nothing could be gained by his further involvement. His presence could only be to the sisters' detriment.

Walk away, Nico.

Instead, with a sinking realization of what a selfish bastard he was, he stayed seated and remained silent.

ELEVEN

S ky woke to the smell of coffee. She started to walk out of her bedroom but hesitated when she remembered Nico was staying on her sofa. Last night, when everyone had parted ways, Storm, Bryce, Maddie, and Olivia had stayed at Sky's parents' house. Will and Raine had teleported back to their place in Virginia, and Sky and Nico had gone to her house.

Now he was in her home, making coffee and... did she smell eggs?

She should make herself presentable. Ha. He'd already seen her at her worst. What was another morning of bedhead? Besides, if they were all going to be living under one roof in Montana to train, they would have to acclimate to seeing one another first thing in the morning. Rather than brush her hair, she swirled it up in a messy bun and slapped on a clip to hold it out of her face. She left on her sleeping attire—yoga pants and t-shirt—but pulled a house sweater over her.

When she walked into the kitchen, Nico was standing over the stove, adding cheese to an omelet. He wore jeans and a fitted white t-shirt. She'd never seen anything so delicious first thing in the morning.

"Good morning, *Raza de soare*." He greeted her with a smile.

"Is that Romanian?" She made a beeline for the pot of coffee, doing her best to ignore the way her body wanted to melt around his muscles at the sight and sound of him in her kitchen.

His smile faltered. "Yes. Sorry. It means sunshine. That's Storm's name for you. I shouldn't presume to use it."

She poured herself a cup and sniffed the fragrant aroma. "Any man who brews coffee for me, ready upon awakening, can call me Sunshine."

"Any man?" His lips quirked.

"Any fake fiancé who stood by my side during surgery and—" she leaned over his shoulder, crowding his space "—who cooks me breakfast."

"Ah, well, that narrows it down, then."

She forced herself to move away and around to the other side of the counter, where she sat, sipping her hot coffee when what she needed was a cool fan.

"Are you seeing anyone?" she asked before she could stop herself.

He was mid flip with the omelet, faltered, and nearly tossed the entire thing out of the pan. "What?"

"Are you seeing anyone? So far, I haven't managed to undo the spreading fallacy of our engagement, so I need to know if I should be prepared for a jealous lover who might plot a smear campaign against me on social media." She secretly congratulated herself on covering her impulsive question with a plausible reason for having asked it.

"No. Dating has not been feasible in my line of work." He slipped the now finished omelet onto a plate and slid it over to her. "I am unencumbered to continue to be your fake fiancé. Although, there won't be a need for the farce in Montana. Everyone who will be there knows we aren't a couple."

Pity, Sky thought. The more time she spent with Nico, the more time she wanted to spend with him. Yet she couldn't tell if the feeling was mutual. He seemed to like her close and even holding hands, but they'd driven home last night with no contact. He'd been lost in thought, so she'd given him the silence he seemed to have needed.

He'd stayed the night in her house, all the while keeping his distance despite having called her an "exquisite woman." He seemed preoccupied ever since she'd invited him to stay longer with the group.

She took a bite of the omelet. "Mmm. So good."

He leaned toward her with a smile. "Easy to make it taste good when you keep so many fresh ingredients."

She shoveled in another mouthful. "No." Pointing with her fork to the masterpiece, she added, "This takes skill." She eyed him, wondering what other skills he possessed.

Straightening, he turned his back to her as he washed the frying pan. Could he read her thoughts? He seemed to become antsy when her imagination wandered to steamy places with him. No, he could probably see the desire in her expression. She'd always been told she would make a terrible poker player.

"Will promised to pick us up to take us to Usha's ranch this afternoon," Nico said.

"And so it begins."

Training.

The final countdown.

SKY WANDERED HER BEDROOM, trying to focus. She'd dressed in a spaghetti strap sun dress with sunflowers and yellow sandals.

She needed to pack... for Montana. She'd never had an extended stay so far from home. Her mom and Maddie had agreed to look after the shop.

Pausing, she realized she also needed to bring supplies from her shop with her. She would have to put some thought into what remedies might be needed for the six of them training on a ranch. Fortunately, they would also have a doctor in the house. That thought conjured images of when Bryce picked shards of glass out of Storm's wounds after Helen's attack. Sky shuddered, not wanting to ponder what nightmare the she-demon would put Sky through during her dream walk.

From one shelf, she picked up a photo of her and her sisters trail riding in their youth.

Montana. She'd bet trail riding there would offer some amazing views. She'd never lived outside of Texas. Sure, she'd traveled on vacations around the states, but this sure as Frigg would not be a vacation.

In Montana, she needed to survive a dream walk and training. Somewhere in that time, she would have to see a dwarf about a weapon. Hopefully, he would tell her a bow and arrow were hers to wield. Besides being familiar with a bow, she didn't want to get close enough to any of the creatures to use something as barbaric as a sword or spear—no offense to Raine and Will. She couldn't lasso like Bryce, and guns were so loud. And complicated. They had chambers and safeties and magazines and clips. People accidentally shot themselves all the time.

No one accidentally shoots themselves with a bow and arrow.

She was deep in thought, tossing clothes into a suitcase, when she heard the warning bark of her neighbor's dog. Looking out her window, she saw Wallace standing in her yard. He wore jeans and a green collared shirt with his dark hair neatly slicked to one side.

Not even needing her ability to sense his rage, she could see anger in the glint of his eye and the flush of his cheeks.

"Nico," she said on a breathless exhale, dropping her clothes and dashing toward her living room.

He was probably still in the kitchen, unaware of Wallace's presence.

The boom of a shotgun accompanied the shattering of glass. She skidded to a halt at her sliding back porch door as it splintered into a thousand tiny pieces. Fortunately, she'd stopped before she was in the path of the flying shards.

The gunman's eyes held a crazy glee. He noted Sky, but his gaze searched for Nico. Wallace's malicious intentions wafted off him like foul body odor. He wanted to shoot Nico in order to make Sky suffer her betrayal in loneliness.

As her ex approached, Sky glanced around her home's interior, not seeing Nico. Her heart pounded wildly beneath a tightened torso. Too bad she didn't already have a bow and arrow, because she wanted to shoot Wallace right between the legs.

He spun to his left, like perhaps he'd spotted Nico, and raised the shotgun. She couldn't see what he aimed at, but she wasn't taking any chances.

Summoning her psychic powers, she forced Wallace to point the barrel at the ground as he fired. He shrieked in agony when the shotgun spray ravaged his foot. Pain lanced through her temple before she walled up her mind to him.

As he fell back, a wolf, large and gleaming white, leaped onto his chest. The animal snarled and snapped as Wallace whimpered, pleading for his life.

Just as fast as the animal had appeared, it bounded off. Sky stepped over the glass and outside, where she took the shotgun from Wallace. "I'll call you an ambulance."

When she took a step back, two brawny arms gripped her biceps.

Nico had appeared. "Are you okay?"

She nodded. "Yeah, just a headache. He was coming for you."

Nico kept one hand on her arm as he pulled out his phone and called 9-1-1, requesting police and ambulance.

She set the shotgun down inside the house, well out of reach of her stalker, before grabbing a kitchen towel and hurrying back outside to Wallace.

Nico stood close, still on the phone.

She looked down at Wallace. "I can help slow the bleeding, but I won't come near you if you're going to continue to be a threat."

"Help me. Please, help me."

. . .

After Wallace was carted off in an ambulance and the police conducted their interview of her, Sky wanted to give in to exhaustion and sink into her sofa. She'd told the officers everything, excluding her mental interference that resulted in Wallace shooting himself in the foot and the wolf she'd seen. She wasn't sure that part had been real anyway.

While she'd given her statement, Nico had texted her sisters about the situation and boarded up the sliding glass door. Sky swept up the last of the shattered glass while Nico finished his statement.

"How are you feeling?" he asked as they stood in her kitchen.

"Like I shot somebody." If she was this shaken after one encounter with a single human, how would she manage the terror of the battlefield?

"I suspect authorities will rule his gunshot as a self-inflicted wound. Accidental. Meanwhile, he's likely to be charged with aggravated assault with a deadly weapon." He turned, fixed her a glass of water, and handed it to her.

She took a sip of the cool, refreshing liquid. "I may have left the fake fiancé lie in place when talking to the police. It seemed easier than trying to explain its origins."

He gently squeezed her forearm. "It's alright. When they addressed me as your fiancé, I figured you'd said that, so I didn't dispute it."

She nodded and took a long drink.

"Are you packed for Montana?" Nico asked.

"Almost. I need to go to the shop for supplies. And can we stop off at a friend's house? I'd like to say goodbye to Thunder."

"Certainly. You know you don't need to ask permission as if I control your schedule. I'm here as your protector, not your guardian."

"In the South, sometimes we ask to sound polite when we aren't really asking." She batted her eyes at him. "I was trying to be polite."

"How would one know if a question wasn't a question?"

"Let's say you replied, 'No, we can't go see the horse, it isn't safe.'

I would have asked, 'Excuse me?' Not because I didn't hear you, but because I'm giving you time to reconsider your stance on the matter with the slightly veiled threat that there are consequences should you not change your mind."

He chuckled. "I see."

CHAPTER

TWELVE

Wheatgrass crunched beneath Sky's sandals as she walked toward the fence. On the other side of the dark wood beams, a white horse lifted his head to look at his visitors.

"This is Thunder? Is he yours?" Nico asked.

"No," Sky lamented. "I don't have the land or money for a horse. The Umbers are family friends. They bought horses because they enjoyed looking at them, but they're not so keen on riding. They let me ride to keep him in shape and accustomed to human interaction." As she talked, the horse walked over to them.

"Nico, meet Thunder. Thunder, this is Nico." She rubbed fingertips on the short hair between the horse's eyes.

When Nico extended a hand, the horse sniffed suspiciously. His ears whisked back as he snorted and backed away.

Sky frowned. "Sorry, he's usually friendlier than that." Although she couldn't read animals' minds exactly like humans, she could sense their feelings. To Thunder, Nico smelled like a predator.

"Quite all right. I've never ridden a horse. I'm sure he senses my uneasiness."

A man of mid-fifties in worn jeans, a t-shirt, and leather boots approached, waving a hand and squinting under the sun. "Afternoon, y'all."

"Mr. Umber." Sky smiled. "Good to see you. I was introducing Thunder to my friend, Nico."

"Little hot for a ride." Mr. Umber offered a hand to Nico who shook it.

"Pleasure to meet you. Beautiful animal you have."

"Do you ride?" Mr. Umber asked.

"Alas, I do not. Never have."

"Well, that's a shame. Say, what's that accent you're sporting?"

"UK over Eastern European."

Mr. Umber's lips curved. "Expanding your horizons?" he said to Sky. "Good for you." He smiled at Nico. "She don't normally ride with boyfriends."

"Oh, I'm—"

Sky interrupted Nico as she slipped an arm through his. "Was there something you came to discuss, Mr. Umber?"

Mrs. Umber was known to be a town gossip. As nice as the couple was, these were not the people to mark the starting point of unraveling the lie. Sky needed to tell her parents the truth first.

"Oh, yeah." He rubbed the back of his neck. "The missus's folks are in poor health."

"I'm sorry to hear that," Sky said.

"Thing is, we need to live closer to them to help out for a spell. In Florida. Gotta shut down the ranch here for a while."

"Oh." Shoot. She was about to move to Montana. How could she horse-sit if she was nearly two thousand miles away?

"Other thing is, we're thinking of selling Thunder."

"I'll buy him," she blurted.

What was she thinking? She didn't have money or land for a horse. Maybe she could borrow money from Storm. But where to board him? Her parents had a few acres, but it wasn't fenced for livestock. Maybe she could impose on Bryce and his land.

"I was hoping you'd say that," Mr. Umber said. "Your money ain't no good here. Payment's knowing he'll have a loving home. You've been buddies going on ten years now. Don't know how many more he's got left, but he'd want to spend time with you."

She beamed. "Thank you. Can you give me a few days to work out where to stable him?"

"Of course. You can keep him here as long as you need to."

"Usha's?" Nico suggested.

"You don't think she'd mind?"

"No."

Mr. Umber extended a hand. "Sold. I'll send you an email with papers transferring ownership rights."

Sky shook his hand robustly. "Thank you so much!"

He chuckled, dipped his head, and walked back toward the house.

She hoisted herself onto the fence and then climbed onto Thunder's back. Leaning over, she basked in the warmth of his soft fur and musky horse scent. Her dress was now covered in horsehair and dirt, but she didn't care.

Oh, to forget my worries and ride off into the sunset on a horse.

Thunder held his head high, ears twitching as if ready for her command to move.

"This is the horse," Nico said. "The horse from our dreams."

Our dreams, as if they shared them together in the months before they'd even met.

She thought back to the dream which seemed to fade so quickly during the daylight hours. "I do remember a white horse."

"Do you want to ride? You could take a turn about the pasture." He looked up at her from the other side of the fence as if dazzled by the sight of her.

Unsure what to make of Nico's intent stare, she slid off the horse. "No. Will is waiting to hear from us, and I still want to stop by my shop for supplies."

NICO CARRIED A CARDBOARD BOX, following Sky around her shop as she filled it with jars and bottles. He asked about them, and she explained what each was for—rosemary, yarrow, ginseng, bilberry, chamomile, turmeric, elderberry, and more. She had soothing lotions, tinctures for healing, and teas for different ailments.

He thought back to her sitting on Thunder, bareback and wearing a dress with the blue Texas sky behind her. Now, he admired the brain beneath the beauty—a wealth of homeopathic knowledge. Magnificent.

The worry that had shadowed her expression after Wallace's attack had faded into serene peacefulness. Nico was touched she'd taken it upon herself to protect him from her ex, even though a human would never get the drop on Nico. He'd smelled the hot-tempered Texan and had been planning to lure him away from her home when she'd intervened. Nico had been impressed she'd kept her wits about her to overpower an angry man with a shotgun.

Nico couldn't fathom why Raine and Storm let him stay on as Sky's protector. First, he hadn't done a stellar job, and second, they knew what he was. Obviously, Sky didn't, or she would distance herself, but her sisters should've protested any further involvement on his behalf. Did they know something he didn't?

In any case, he could protect Sky until the day Helen ordered him back to her side. Sky hadn't seemed bothered knowing he was a spy. She hadn't batted an eyelash or asked him how she would know he wouldn't double-cross the Shadow Guardians.

I don't deserve her trust.

Nico would fall on his sword before he would hurt Sky. But his actions weren't always his choice. He could look at himself in the mirror and swear he wouldn't harm one hair on the heads of any of the Valkyrie, but he honestly didn't know whether he could keep that promise once Helen issued a command.

No.

He would make sure he never set foot or paw on that battlefield to fight against any of them. And yet, in his dreams, he was there. He stood, watching the fighting unfold. From his view, he couldn't discern which side was winning, but he was definitely there, a detached observer.

He would have to ensure he never joined them and, therefore, couldn't be forced to fight against the Shadow Guardians.

He set the box on the counter. "Listen, Sky—about joining everyone at the ranch. I don't think it's a good idea. I appreciate your nomination, but I should decline."

She stopped packing her supplies into small boxes filled with protective confetti made of recycled paper. "Is this about the spy thing again?" Her light voice was teasing.

"Yes. I'm not to be trusted." He kept his tone grave.

"We've been over this," she said, amused rather than irritated. "I do trust you. Besides, we need you there for more than eye candy."

"Eye candy?" His lips quirked.

"Don't get me wrong, you are all sorts of eye candy—and you cook, so bonus points—but you were Helen's spy. You know stuff, right? You have insight—maybe even into her weaknesses, depending on how close you were to her."

Too close.

Nico shuddered. "Are," he corrected.

"What?"

"Present tense, 'you are Helen's spy.'"

"Same difference."

He placed his hands on Sky's shoulders and turned her toward him. He would have to spell it out to make her understand.

Stomach tied in knots, he said, "I am Fenrir bloodline. We serve Helen—not by choice. She will make me betray you. All of you. You cannot trust me, Sky."

Big blue eyes brewing with compassion stared back at him. She blinked before her mouth opened in surprised understanding. "Hellhounds serve the goddess of the underworld."

He dropped his arms and stepped back. Now she would give him the rejection he deserved. He diverted his eyes to the floor as he waited for her dismissal, but warm hands cupped his face. "You were the wolf standing on Wallace."

Nico swallowed and nodded. Where was her anger? Her disgust? Her outrage?

Was he not explaining the situation fully enough?

He looked earnestly into her eyes. "Helen sent me to infiltrate the Shadow Guardians. My orders were to get close, learn weaknesses, and report back. I was upfront with the Council of Mjölnir, and they took me in despite what I am so I could play the role of dual spy. Double agent."

Sky took a step closer to him. "Helen gave you orders to spy but not orders to not disobey or tell us about her organization?"

"No. I'm free to plot against her... until the day she discovers my betrayal." He stepped back, trying to free himself of her sweet scent and ill-placed compassion.

His heart was pounding so hard he thought she might hear it. Why was extricating himself from this assignment so difficult?

"What have you told her? Helen. What have you told Helen about all of us?"

He paused a moment. "Nothing."

"Nothing?"

"I didn't tell Helen about this assignment—about guarding you. She doesn't know I'm in contact with any of the Valkyrie sisters. She hasn't contacted me yet—not with force, anyway." He thought of Andrej's text he'd ignored. "At some point, she'll summon me. If she learns I'm with the chosen Valkyrie, I could be your undoing."

"She can summon you anytime?"

He nodded. "The compulsion to obey is undeniable. She rules the wolf shapeshifting descendants of Fenrir."

"Oh, Nico." Sky wrapped her arms around his torso and pressed her head to his chest.

He tried to back away, confused by her kindheartedness, but the counter stopped his retreat. Placing his hands on her upper arms, he fully intended to push her off of him, but his grip tightened. He lowered his head, resting it on top of hers and feeling those silky red locks. He didn't deserve her empathy, but he indulged in it for a moment.

"You understand why I have to leave?" he asked.

"No."

He pulled back. She gave him a little space even as she kept her arms around him.

"No?" He frowned.

"I understand why you think you should leave. But the bottom line is we need you—we need your intel on Helen. You're meant to be with us, Nico."

He took a shaky breath. She was saying 'we need you' but her eyes were saying 'I need you.' This was a terrible idea, but he couldn't say no to this woman, even if not doing so could be the death of them both.

Lowering his voice, he surrendered. "I'll stay as long as I can."

She smiled, bright and wide, lighting her face like sunshine.

She was so close, it would take no effort at all to pull her up to him, lean in, and press his lips to hers. He would bet those lips tasted as good as she smelled. They held the pose as if each waiting for the other to make a move. She stretched toward him.

The door chime dinged, breaking the spell between them. Sky stepped back, cheeks pink, and smoothed the bottom of her dress. She turned and greeted a customer, explaining how she would be out of town for a bit.

Nico used the counter for support until his legs felt more balanced. Staying, he realized, meant all sorts of emotional entanglements that could be as harmful as his curse.

THIRTEEN

Iridescent multicolored light faded around them as a glassy blue Montana sky filled the space above them. Hills and tall grass flourished in every direction. Sky took in what would be her home for the next twelve weeks. The house, twice the size of hers and probably five thousand square feet, boasted a long wooden porch and two stories. It wasn't dirty so much as weather-beaten. The home fared better than the barn, though, which appeared to be in neglect and disrepair. Sky didn't see any livestock, so perhaps the structure was entirely unnecessary. She hoped they could make this place a temporary home for Thunder.

Nico stood beside her with his pack slung over one shoulder and her luggage in his hands. Although not an actual fiancé, he'd dutifully taken her luggage and waved her off when she'd said his gesture was unnecessary. Truthfully, she couldn't manage the two gargantuan suitcases by herself. In her defense, she'd had to pack for a long leave of absence from her home and bring an assortment of herbal remedies for who knew what they would encounter on a ranch in Montana. And of course, all work and no play would make for a dull time here, so she'd brought a few dresses, should the occasion call for it.

Sky and Nico followed Will to the door, which creaked open as they made their way up the steps.

A small woman with dark skin and black and wiry white hair slicked back in a bun greeted them with a warm smile. "And then there were six. Three by three, Hel's wrath to free."

Will jolted. "Huh. I remember that from the Noble prophecies. Three by three. I'd forgotten that. All this time, I was thinking of only the three sisters."

"They are not complete without the love you give them," Usha said.

Sky forced a smile, though she worried Raine and Storm may have perpetuated the fiancé lie if Usha thought she and Nico were a couple. She could sort that out later. She didn't want to start introductions with the leader of the US district of the Council of Mjölnir by correcting her.

"It's great to meet you," Sky said.

Nico bowed his head slightly. "Mrs. Bashki."

Usha smiled with familiarity at him, and Sky felt their connection for a moment. They knew each other, she gleaned. Usha had been the one to recruit him, and even the one to assign him to her as a protector. Sky had imagined her sisters had orchestrated his involvement, but it had actually been Usha.

Not wanting to intrude further on knowledge others hadn't shared with her yet, Sky walled up her sensing abilities.

"Please come in," Usha said. "We have much planning to do. Your sisters have gone to town for supplies."

Usha stepped to the side, and the three of them crossed the threshold into her home. The furniture in the entryway and living room was dark cherry red. Matching sets of curtains, rugs, and upholstery boasted varying prints in mauve.

The journey up the stairs was a slow one. Usha's small, bony body climbed at a painstaking pace, like the tin man in desperate need of oiling his joints. The snail-paced ascension made Sky appreciate the ease with which she climbed stairs, uninhibited by the discomforts of old age. She wondered how much of an imposition the six of them descending on Usha's home would be. They would need to make a chore list and ensure their presence wasn't creating work for the woman.

When they reached the top, Usha explained, "The room to the right at the end of the hall belongs to Storm and Bryce. The one here in the middle is for Raine and Will." She walked them down to the other end of the hall. "And this is for you two."

Sky glanced at Nico, whose face morphed into a look of shock and mortification. This might have been the first time a single man had looked horrified at the idea of sleeping with her. She didn't have to be a mind reader to know his thoughts. She would have enjoyed navigating the intricacies of a forced sleeping arrangement, but Nico was clearly uncomfortable with the idea.

She shook off the sting of rejection and told Usha, "We're not a couple."

No more fake fiancé. No more perpetuation of the lie. Those thoughts inexplicably made her a little sad. Perhaps if their almost-kiss in her shop hadn't been interrupted, Nico would feel differently. Perhaps she would have to recreate a moment of proximity and find out. Navigating the emotional world without access to Nico's mind was proving to be a challenge.

Usha smiled. "My mistake. Nico can sleep in the office downstairs. There's a fold out that you can make into a bed."

THAT EVENING, the six of them sat down to eat, with Usha at the head of the table. Nico breathed deeply the scent of steak, roasted carrots, and creamed spinach. They passed food around and filled their plates. Will had picked up takeout from a restaurant Bryce had sworn had the best steaks in all of Texas. The FBI agent certainly used his transporting talents to their fullest. Nico wouldn't want that ability. Such magic would have made him all the more able to follow Helen's orders expediently.

"Oh, this is so good," Sky said, appearing to savor a piece of steak.

The others agreed.

"No Olivia tonight?" she asked Bryce.

He smiled. "She wanted a few more days with Maddie. She'll love the opportunity to ride here if we can bring Dolly and Faith."

"We were hoping to bring Thunder as well," Nico said, noting Sky's smile at his words and his body's instant warmth in reaction. If this was his body's response to her smile, he'd definitely dodged a tricky situation by having separate sleeping quarters, though her look of hurt had been a surprise to him. Perhaps he'd misinterpreted. She couldn't possibly want to share a bed with him. They barely knew each other. Of course, that hadn't stopped her from trapping him at the store, where he'd nearly kissed her.

"After dinner, I'll put wards up on the house to keep us safe," Sky said, mercifully unable to read his mind.

"Olivia will be joining us off and on," Bryce said. "I'll feel better when the wards are up."

Sky continued, "I was also thinking we'll need something like a rotating chore list—things like cooking, cleaning, laundry."

"I agree," Raine said. "I can work on that."

Storm took a sip of the Cabernet Usha had served with dinner. "We also have ranch work to divvy up."

"Ranch work?" Sky asked.

"Mending the fence, fixing the barn, and house repairs," Storm explained.

"I'll make assignments," Bryce said. At Sky's worried expression, he added, "I'll pair the experienced with the inexperienced."

"I thought we were here to train." Sky shifted her weight, as if keenly aware she was the most inexperienced fighter and needed every waking moment for battle training.

"You'll get plenty of training," Storm said. "Indoor and outdoor projects between training will help keep your muscles moving and build them stronger."

"So, train, chores, train, chores, train?"

"Basically."

Nico observed the exchange as he ate his steak, the back-and-forth volley like watching a tennis match between sisters.

"When do we work on spiritual well-being?" Sky countered before chomping on a piece of carrot.

"When the sun goes down," Storm said flatly.

Lips quirking, Sky waggled her fork at Storm. "Are you and I talking about the same spiritual well-being? Because what I do when the sun sets and what you do," she gestured at Bryce, "are probably not the same thing."

Bryce chuckled as Storm gaped at her. "You can meditate or whatever soul remedies you need to do at night. During the day, we train. Part of that training is getting this place back into shape."

"Sir, yes, sir," Sky said in a mocking and insubordinate drawl. She grinned as if suddenly reminded of how much fun it was to push her sister's buttons.

Nico enjoyed the moment as well but kept his expression schooled. He didn't need to give Storm another reason to despise him.

Will smirked, clearly enjoying Sky riling Storm as much as she did. Nico liked the way her brother-in-law and Bryce seemed to feel a protective edge toward her while simultaneously enjoying her antics.

Usha clasped her hands together. "Because you all need to work as a team, there will be team-building exercises as well."

"Ooh. Fun!" Sky said, her enthusiastic tone suggesting team-building appealed far more than training to fight and pumping new life into this run-down ranch.

Storm's expression turned concerned, as if she thought the

activity would involve trust circles and falling into each other's arms. "Team building?"

"It'll be fun," Raine shared Sky's sentiment.

"I've some experience with team-building exercises. I can help design them," Nico said. As long as he was here, he wanted to contribute on every level—training, ranch restoration, and team building.

"Excellent," Usha said. "Raine and Sky will make a house chore list, Bryce and Will are to list needed repairs, Nico and Storm will devise a training list. Work starts tomorrow after Sky's dream walk."

CHAPTER

FOURTEEN

"You can't wear that," Storm said, gesturing to Sky's outfit.

"What's in your hand?" Raine asked.

Sky looked from the joint in her hand to her white spaghetti-strap sundress and thick soled sandals. "I applied sunscreen," she told Storm. Even if she blistered, she would heal.

Storm crossed her arms, giving Sky a more pronounced scrutiny with her gaze. "You'll be walking for twenty-four to thirty-six hours. This," she gestured to all of her, "isn't practical."

"Comfortable is the epitome of practical," Sky retorted with haughty playfulness.

"What's in your hand?" Raine repeated.

Sky held up the slender object. "This is a joint. Mary Jane, pot, weed, hash. I borrowed it from Mom. Technically, since I'm going to smoke it and not give it back, borrow isn't the right word."

Now Raine crossed her arms. "You intend to smoke weed on your dream walk?"

"That doesn't sound safe," Storm added.

"I will not smoke it on my dream walk. I will smoke it *to enter* my dream walk."

"What?" Storm blinked.

"Will that work?" Raine's brow knit.

Storm looked at Raine as if surprised she hadn't rejected the idea outright. "Is that cheating? That sounds like cheating."

Sky scoffed. "This isn't an algebra test. This is neuropharmacology."

Raine and Storm glanced skeptically at each other.

"Look," Sky began, "the whole point of dehydrating and starving oneself is to trigger the brain into a state of hallucination. Marijuana triggers the sensory portions of the cerebral cortex to induce hallucinations and an altered sense of space and time. This way, I'm not risking death to achieve the same effect. Cultures across the world have been using pot for this purpose for millennia."

Storm turned her back to Sky and spoke to Raine in an aside, even though Sky could still hear every word, and even if she couldn't, they were both broadcasting their thoughts loud and clear. "Did our Sunshine just outsmart your entire cult?"

Raine rolled her eyes. "The Council of Mjölnir is not a cult. And, yes, what Sky is proposing is actually a good idea."

"Why didn't the Shadow Guardians know about this?" Storm persisted.

Pursing her lips, Raine replied, "I don't know. Maybe drug-inducing hallucinogens are frowned upon. Maybe they don't want to encourage inhaling dangerous substances."

Storm snorted. "They do understand we kill people, right?"

Raine threw up her hands in exasperation and looked at Sky. "Do you see what I've had to put up with for the last year and a half?"

Sky gave them a lopsided grin of pure delight at the three of them being united and all the old pestering resurfacing because of it.

"I guess we can try your way," Storm told Sky with a shrug and a wink.

"Yay!" Sky clapped her hands. "Besides, this way, you can stay close in case Helen crashes my dream walk. No offense, but I really don't want her to drown me in a river or shred me with glass." She shuddered at the memory of how terrible Storm had looked.

"That's actually a very smart plan," Raine said.

Sky wagged a finger at her. "Maybe you could say that with a little less shock and awe in your voice? For the record, of the three of us, I'm the only entrepreneur who owns a house. Clearly, I'm the brains of the operation."

"Um," Raine scrunched up her face, "Storm owns a multi-million-dollar yacht."

"And a private jet," Storm added.

Sky squared her shoulders, affronted. "Well, herbal remedies are obviously not as lucrative as assassinations. It's not my fault if the world's priorities are askew from improperly assigned values."

Storm grinned. "Sunshine, you are by far the smartest and most well-adjusted of the three of us."

"Thank you."

"No matter what Raine says," Storm added.

Sky rolled her eyes.

"So," Storm said, looking back and forth between her sisters, "is this the part where we circle Sky and sing *Kumbaya* as she smokes dope?"

Raine sighed. "Apparently, but let's skip the singing."

"Fine by me," Storm said.

Sky stuck out her bottom lip. "What's wrong with singing? I love singing."

NICO WALKED circles around the group in the barn where Sky sat in the middle on a mat with her eyes closed. A puff of smoke rose above her head. He wrung his hands, feeling more nervous than he'd felt on previous hazardous assignments. He'd heard from Raine how dream walking could be dangerous. Helen had attacked the other sisters, who wouldn't have survived without Will's and Bryce's interventions.

At least Sky wasn't physically leaving the ranch, unlike the long walks the others had done. Still, Nico knew first-hand how deadly Helen could be. He'd seen the she-demon bathed in the blood of the creatures she'd killed, whether for battle, betrayal, or just because she was having a bad day. He'd also seen her perform rituals to steal power from dying mixed breeds.

Although he could see Sky smoking her peace pipe, his worry didn't ebb. What if she was attacked in her dream state and no one knew she was fighting for her life because her body rested while her mind or—Odin forbid—her soul was tortured somewhere else? There were too many unknowns.

Leap of faith, Usha had said.

All well and good unless it killed you. The thought was accompanied by his low growl.

"Stop pacing, Nico. It's annoying," Storm scolded as she played with one of her knives, a habit Nico found equally annoying.

"I keep waiting for him to cluck 'duck-duck-goose' and tap one of us on the head," Bryce said lightly, running his golden lasso through his fingers.

The thing crackled with power, like the low hum of an electrical transformer. Nico instinctively disliked it, knowing what it had been capable of in Norse mythology.

"Do kids still play duck-duck-goose?" Raine asked.

Bryce frowned. "Olivia and I are a little rusty with what kids do since we've been home schooling on a boat for a year and a half."

"When this is over, we can all play," Raine said in a tone suggesting she wanted the conversation folded into silence.

Nico made a mental note to search the internet for information on this duck-goose fowl game so he could understand the reference. He tried to recall if his childhood had games.

Nothing fun surfaced in his memories. Almost nothing.

He'd been inseparable for a time from his brother. They used to play in the woods near his parents' home, enacting fantasies of two young princes battling an evil king invading their land. The memory caused an ache in Nico's chest for the brother he'd lost to Helen when she'd turned him.

Nico's head grew fuzzy from inhaling the second-hand smoke wafting from the joint. No one else seemed to be affected, but no one else had his canine sensitive sense of smell. He blinked his eyes several times.

Storm sucked in a breath. "Where'd she go?"

Nico froze. The center circle was bare where Sky had been seated on the floor a moment ago.

"Helen," he snarled, an icy fist of worry squeezing his heart.

Raine held up a hand. "We don't know that. Sky just entered her dream walk. Both Storm and I went to a different dimension. I visited Yggdrasil and Storm Valhalla. Neither one of us ended up where we started. Will?"

The FBI agent sat with his eyes closed. "Working on it."

"He'll keep his focus on Sky and know the moment she's back in the tangible world," Raine explained.

"You mean she won't return right back here?" Nico asked, voice raised in concern. He ignored the way Storm scrutinized his behavior, his angst over her younger sister.

"Raine and I teleported somewhere else," Storm reiterated.

Nico ground his teeth. Leave it to the queen of the macabre to make him feel worse. His vision blurred as his stomach churned. He needed to get out of this smokey barn and clear his head.

"I'm going to go look for her." Nico stalked away from the group.

"Wait, Nico," Raine began, but he didn't slow.

He was the best tracker of anyone he knew. He and his brother had hunted in wolf form growing up. Little had they known it served as a sort of training for the day Helen summoned them to hunt for her benefit. Hunt the innocent.

Except this time, he needed to track Sky and save her from

Helen's wrath. Maybe he couldn't travel to another dimension, but he couldn't remain idle while Sky was in danger.

When he left the barn, he stepped into an unfamiliar wilderness of tall trees and moist, cool air—not summer in Montana. Had he inhaled enough marijuana to overload his senses and take him, body and mind, to another dimension? And was he in the same one as Sky? He raised his head to the air and breathed deeply.

Sweet honeysuckle and strawberries.

Sky.

To the east.

He took off at a sprint.

FIFTEEN

Sky sat in Usha's barn, out of the warm sun, but the heat in the barn grew stifling despite the open doors at each end to let a nonexistent breeze flow through. Closing her eyes, she settled cross-legged on the mat.

"Stop pacing, Nico. It's annoying," Storm said.

Tuning out her protectors surrounding her—all five of them—she breathed deeply of the marijuana. It filled her lungs as it filled her mind. Unaccustomed to smoking, she coughed several times.

Bah. How does anyone use this stuff regularly?

A sensation of drifting filled her, like floating among clouds, weightless. The murmur of voices in the barn faded.

When she opened her eyes, everything around her grew sharper with a distinct outline. No longer in the barn, she sat at the edge of a cliff. In the distance, a city with towering buildings glinted gold and copper.

Asgard.

Noises seemed enhanced, from the predatory cry of a hawk, to the scampering of a lizard across the rocks, to the low rumbling of a wolf.

Wolf?

Sky peered in every direction until she saw a white wolf as large as a man standing with his tail to her, alert and watchful. Was he protecting her?

Beyond him, she didn't see any danger.

Am I in my dream walk?

"Nico? Aren't you gorgeous?" she told the wolf.

Was it him? She'd only had a fleeting glimpse of him when he'd been at her house.

His ears shifted, but otherwise, he remained still as a statue. His fur was white as fresh snow.

She scooted toward him and extended a hand. "Are you really here?" She could read horses and dogs but couldn't get a read on this creature's emotions.

Must be Nico. Unless it was a hallucination brought on by drug use. Ugh. She would fantasize about the one man reluctant to be with her.

He turned his head to stare at her.

She sucked in a breath at the magnificence of his pale blue eyes. His intense but non-threatening gaze suggested he didn't intend her harm.

After a long moment with Sky unmoving and hand extended, the wolf stepped forward. He placed his head beneath her hand.

Sky restrained her urge to squeal in delight as she sank her fingertips into his soft fur. Something electric and wondrous filled her at touching him. She buried both hands in his coat, needing to relish in the connection they shared.

"Do you feel that?" she asked him.

When the wolf closed his eyes as she stroked him, Sky knew he felt the connection, too. He opened his eyes, staring into hers, and she swallowed at the intense emotion as it lifted her essence to euphoria. Was this the pot? No. Some exhilarating bond was forming between them.

"I belong to you, Nico." Sky said, feeling the truth of the words. It was a commitment, not a sacrifice.

The wolf dropped his head into her lap as if making his own pledge to her.

Does he belong to me?

She rubbed his head, wishing for one fleeting moment that she could hear his thoughts, feel him. Instead, she listened to his steady breathing, resigned to know she would simply have to ask him later about this encounter.

The wolf, who'd been perfectly still, quickly pulled his head back. He spun and dashed away into the thick foliage.

She pushed to her feet. "Wait. Where are you going?"

But he was gone.

Sky sighed. What if the THC had made her imagine the interaction?

She looked back to the sky, which had turned a tumultuous gray. The surrounding landscape shifted to a white, flat land with a background of snow-capped mountains. Smoke billowed from one of the mountain tops. To her right, a lake boiled, steam rising into the air.

Volcanoes and snow.

Fire and ice.

"Sky Thoren."

She turned to her left to see a tall, slender man with a long, thin nose and dark hair in waves to his shoulders. He wore blue and white pants and a tunic.

"Loki."

Why would the trickster of the gods be the one to guide her? Raine had spoken to Thor, and Storm had met with Odin and Frigg.

Loki gave her a broad smile, handsome but mischievous.

"Was that your wolf?" she asked.

"I assure you that creature belongs only to you."

Did he? She liked the sound of that. Regardless, she was here with a purpose.

"I'm here for advice," she told Loki.

"You're here for enlightenment."

"I suppose. Apparently, a war is coming. I don't really understand my role."

"Let us walk together, young Valkyrie."

She took a position beside him, snow crunching beneath her sandals and breath condensing in the air but not feeling the cold.

Loki linked his hands behind his back. "Three sisters must fight Helen to prevent the downfall of Midgard."

"Yes. Three sisters and three men. And Helen is a descendant of Hel—your daughter." She couldn't conceal the accusatory tone in her voice, which seemed not to faze him. "I've been told about the war, but my sisters are fighters. I'm a healer—the fluffy flower child of the bunch."

"Just because you haven't exploited your fighting talents doesn't mean they don't exist. You will master the bow and arrow before the battle."

Bow and arrow. *Whew.*

His words matched the dream she'd had—the one she shared with Nico. Sky recalled the long summer days of youth spent horseback riding and shooting arrows at hay-stuffed targets. Of course, slaying scarecrows and fenceposts differed from targeting vicious, moving creatures with murderous intent.

The Dark Elf in her car had been the first truly evil being she'd encountered, but somehow she was supposed to help fight an army of them.

"You know I can't offer advice if you don't ask questions," Loki said.

She narrowed her eyes at him. "Is your advice trustworthy?"

He smiled—big and wide, reaching his gleaming eyes. "For you, it is."

"You say that to all the ladies?"

Loki pressed a hand to his heart in feigned shock and mortification. "Dearest Sky, you are family."

"I've read what you've done to family. You cut off Sif's hair."

"I made the dwarves create six great items for the gods, including Mjölnir," he countered, tone all boasting self-satisfaction.

"You killed Hreiðmarr's son."

"Who was disguised as an otter. Honestly, that was his own poor planning."

"You lured Idun out of Asgard, and she was captured."

"I rescued her. No harm, no foul." Loki waved a dismissive hand.

Sky grunted her skepticism but decided to divulge her concern anyway. "I don't want to be the weakest link in the battle. The wobbly leg of a tripod. The flat on a tricycle. What if my lack of skill or experience results in injury, or worse, to one of my sisters? What if my failure results in the next apocalypse?"

Loki stopped beside one of the boiling lakes and looked at her. "You are all of equal capacity but varying approach. I can't fight the way my brother can, and yet, I have my uses in battle. You'll find your role as you train. Find your strengths and play to them. Fight with your mind as much as your body. And there can be no power of three without all of you. Fear is natural under the circumstances, but don't let fear restrain you. Accept it, but don't allow it to control you. Don't let it prevent you from fully embracing your destiny."

"Destiny, huh? Does Destiny know I've never physically fought anyone? I own a natural remedy store fighting arthritis with turmeric."

"Destiny knows what's here." Loki pointed a long, slender finger at her heart. "And here." He moved his hand to her forehead and in one quick motion tipped her head back with the thrust of a fingertip.

Sky fell backward, grasping and clutching at the air. The pit of boiling water rose to meet her. She screamed, but the moisture that engulfed her was warm, not hot.

She sank to the bottom, falling out into a column of rock filled with air as her body turned vertical. Her feet hit an obsidian rock floor.

Taking in her surroundings, she noted the chamber in which she'd landed was made of black stone, somehow jagged but still reflective, like polished lava rock. Sconces burning with blue flame lined the walls. Offset against one wall stood granite steps leading to a throne made of oily black skulls. A blonde-haired woman in a black dress sat confidently with crossed legs. She had chiseled cheekbones and irises as dark as midnight.

"Aren't you a pretty little fragile thing?" purred a voice laced with disdain.

"Helen." Sky spoke the name on the exhale of a shaky breath.

The woman gave a cruel smile, as if gloating at the obvious fear she caused Sky.

"Do you think you're a match for my power, Valkyrie?" Her voice had a raspy German accent.

Sky probably looked more like a drowned rat than an exemplary warrior for good. Of course she wasn't a match for Helen, but Sky wasn't alone—or wouldn't be on the battlefield. Technically, at this very moment, she was utterly alone and completely vulnerable.

The woman stood from her throne and sauntered toward Sky. "I will strike down your sisters and any bloodlines supporting the Guardians. I will wipe every last drop of your blood from the earth and watch it boil. When I'm done, humans are next." She had pale skin with large eyes and might have been beautiful if not for the soulless black of her irises.

"Why are you filled with hate?" Sky asked. Her heart pounded as she glanced around, hoping to form an exit strategy.

"Don't you see the injustice of it all? Ragnarök ravished the realms, destroying each of them. And which one is left standing when the dust settles?" Helen let out a cold, humorless, cackling chuckle. "The weakest one. Midgard." She spat. "And what is our species subjected to? Millennia of diluting our blood with filthy humans, making us as weak as them. But I have the strength and the resolve to do something about it. I am making the bloodlines powerful again."

"You wouldn't have barged into my dream walk if you didn't feel threatened by me."

In a blur, Helen was in Sky's face, snarling. Long, boney fingers lashed out and curled around her neck.

Jolting in surprise, she grabbed Helen's wrist with both hands, trying to tear away the grip crushing her larynx. She couldn't breathe, and lights danced before her eyes. The arm was immovable. Absolute terror flooded her body.

Helen flashed her teeth in a snarl. "I will end you. I will end all of you."

CHAPTER

SIXTEEN

I will end you.

Helen's words cut through Sky's mind as she flailed in the she-demon's unyielding grasp. If she allowed another sixty seconds of suffocation, Sky was fairly certain Helen would be right. Blackness crept in at the periphery of her vision.

Fight with your mind as much as your body, Loki had said.

In a desperate move, Sky unleashed a psychic punch, shoving all of her pain and fear at Helen.

The woman shrieked in surprise, her hand falling away as she took a step back in wide-eyed shock.

Free of Helen's grasp, Sky stumbled backward, gasping for air and tripped on a ledge of rock, losing her balance. Instead of falling onto the hard stone floor, the obsidian surface was a lukewarm liquid pool that swallowed her whole.

Sky thrashed, uncertain because she couldn't identify the surface. Panic gripped her with a wave of jolting fear. When she opened her eyes, she saw a light and swam toward it. Kicking her way furiously to the surface, she finally broke through, panting for air.

"*Raza de soare*, I've got you." Nico's powerful arms grabbed her and pulled her out of... she looked around in shock... a river tributary. The landscape was once again Montana.

Her throat was still too swollen to talk. Shaking her head, she breathed heavily as Nico pulled her into his arms. They sat on the riverbank while she caught her breath, wet clothes soaking him. She was shivering even though the mid-summer sun beat down on them.

"Sorry. Got... you... wet," she said when she could finally talk again.

"I'm not worried about that. I'm worried about you." He rubbed a hand up and down her bare arm.

"I'm okay."

He pulled back slightly and looked into her eyes as if needing visual confirmation of her claim. His gaze scrutinized her face, dropped to her lips, and then settled on her neck. Scowling, he asked, "What happened to your neck?"

"Helen. I finished my dream walk with Loki and dropped into Helen's lair." Sky didn't know if what she'd seen had been reality or still part dream, though. "She tried to strangle me, but I got away."

"Loki? And you saw Helen?"

"Damn trickster. Raine gets Thor, Storm gets Odin, and I get Loki," Sky complained. "Why do I get the conniving one?"

"Did he trick you? Did he send you to Helen?"

"I don't know."

Had Loki sent her to Helen to challenge Sky's feelings of weakness? Had he intended to put her in harm's way, or had her encounter with the goddess been inadvertent?

"Maybe Loki chose you because you're clever. You'd see through any deception he might attempt." Nico kissed the top of her head.

"I didn't expect him to shove me into a boiling lake."

"Boiling lake?" Nico resumed rubbing soothing hands up and down her arms.

"Well, it looked boiling, but turns out it was nothing more than a small ravine."

Will, Raine, Bryce, and Storm appeared in shimmering rainbow colors.

"Interesting choice of baptism." Storm said with a smirk, though she shot Nico a look of warning as if he wasn't allowed to hold and pamper her younger sister.

To Sky's relief, he didn't budge under the look.

"You just vanished right before our eyes," Raine said. "How did Nico find you?"

"Helen attacked her," Nico said.

Storm's eyes widened as she straightened. "What happened?" she demanded.

Although reluctant to leave Nico's arms, Sky stood and wrung out her dress's skirt. "I appeared in a land of fire and ice—Iceland, I think. Loki bestowed his words of wisdom and sent me on my way. But I ended up in Helen's lair where she said she would kill us all, followed by ridding Midgard of all humans. Then, she tried to strangle me."

Nico stood and shook the water off as he listened, attentive to her every word. Had Nico not already seen her bloodied, broken, and incapacitated in the hospital, she might have been self-conscious about her current state of dishevelment. But he'd seen her at her worst and hadn't shrunk away yet, so what was a little water?

"How'd you get away?" Storm asked.

Bryce took a step closer, lifting Sky's chin to inspect her neck.

"When I threw a telepathic bolt of lightning, she backed off." Sky remembered the way Helen had shrieked in surprise, a reaction that gave Sky some measure of satisfaction since the she-demon had every intention of killing her.

"I didn't know you could do that," Raine said with enough awe to counteract Storm's disbelieving stare.

Seemingly satisfied Sky wasn't in need of doctoring, Bryce dropped his arms and stepped back from her.

"Neither did I," Sky said. "I guess you find new strengths when it's the fourth down and the offense is on the ten-yard line."

Storm blinked at her, but Raine and Will nodded in understanding at her football reference.

Bending over, Sky wrung her wet hair.

"Did he tell you your weapon?" Storm asked. Of course she'd want to know the weapon.

"Bow and arrow."

Storm relaxed slightly, leaned against a tree, and fiddled with one of her knives. "Ah, well, that makes sense."

"I haven't played with my bow in five years." Sky smoothed her damp dress. "Stop grinning, you dirty-minded fool," she said to Storm. "That wasn't a euphemism for anything."

Nico's cheeks reddened at the sisters' exchange.

"You were always the best shot with a bow," Raine said.

"Unmoving, inanimate objects," Sky countered.

Storm shrugged. "We'll get you some practice. You know... before it's life or death."

"Swell."

"Brok, the dwarf weapon maker, will help," Will added.

"Right."

"What else did Loki tell you?" Raine asked.

"Gave me a nice pep talk. Oh, but there was a wolf."

"A wolf?" Storm's eyes narrowed as she glanced briefly at Nico and Raine.

Nico shifted his weight as he stood.

Ah, so Storm knows Nico's secrets.

Sky felt the tension between Storm and Nico. Her sister wanted to protect her, and she gleaned Storm knew about Nico's curse to obey Helen. Meanwhile, the fearless wolf turned sheepish and wilted under Storm's glare.

Because he agrees with her that he shouldn't be here.

Sky didn't need superpowers to figure that much out. Well, she wasn't letting him go, even if the pair of them disagreed with her.

She felt a connection with Nico she'd never had with any other man, despite his mind being closed to her. She'd be damned if she would let his doubts and self-deprivation interfere with what they might have together.

"The most gorgeous white wolf with blue eyes. He let me pet him." Sky lifted her chin in defiance.

Storm twisted one of her knives in her hand with dizzying dexterity. "Didn't we teach you better than to pet wild animals?"

"Come on," said Raine, "let's get you in some dry clothes and we'll have lunch. We'll start training tomorrow."

HELEN WOKE, screaming into a dark room as her head pounded in agony.

Wretched Valkyrie bitch.

She tossed the covers off and made her way to the bathroom, where she splashed cold water on her face to dispel the night sweats.

So, the third Valkyrie had made her dream walk. These dream walks of theirs turned out to be nothing but a tease, showing Helen her adversaries but stealing them away before she could prematurely kill them.

The prophecy of war would come true.

But an army against three women? They couldn't possibly defeat her product of years of preparation. She'd seen nothing spectacular in any of them. The first, Helen had only glimpsed flailing in a river. The second had a warrior's body and an insolent mouth but had cowered before Helen's power. The third was all soft edges—except for her mind. But her little display of psychic force had cost her. Helen doubted the redhead could maintain such magic in the face of a raging battle.

Still, something of which to be mindful.

The Nornir had given her these glimpses for a reason—small insights into the Valkyries. Were the fates showing her how triumph would undoubtedly be hers, or was there another lesson here?

She would have to reflect more, but not now. Now, her temples throbbed from that Asgardian witch.

She hadn't suffered headaches this dreadful since childhood—since those days she'd spent locked in her parents' basement with no food and little water. She looked in the mirror, and for a moment, saw that small girl from long ago.

Her mother and father had locked her away after the small trifle of killing their pet dog. She'd only been curious. What eight-year-old didn't ponder the magnitude of life and death? They had gone to her grandmother's funeral, where everyone mourned the loss of a life, but Helen had felt nothing. She'd only known the woman as a grumpy, shriveled thing whom she'd been forced to visit a few times a year. She'd wanted to understand this mystery called death which people feared and shed tears over. Perhaps by killing something, she would understand.

When she'd watched the life drain out of the animal's eyes, she understood death. Understood the power of it. When her parents came across her soaked in the pet's blood holding a knife, she under-stood the fear of it. Their expression of absolute terror gave her power.

They'd locked her in the basement as they argued, trying to decide what was to be done with her. There was something wrong with her, they'd said. And she needed help. They talked of sending her away. Institutionalizing her. They clearly cared more about their dog than their daughter. She was loath to think she was related to those powerless things. So, before they could institutionalize her, she took her understanding of death one step further.

SEVENTEEN

Sky's lungs burned. "How much more?"

"That's one mile," Nico said as he kept pace jogging beside her. "I think your sisters are planning on five miles, but you can stop at three."

"Three? Shit." She glanced over at him. "You're not even... breaking... a damn sweat. You're not even... winded."

Sky was slender, but she hadn't kept her figure through cardiovascular exercise. She ate healthy and was a model for anyone coming into her shop looking to lose weight through dietary modifications. She sold naturopathic appetite suppressants, but she advocated that the best way was eating the right foods.

"I run a lot," Nico said. "Don't worry. You'll build your endurance."

"You guys are going to kill me before I even make it to the battlefield."

They'd started the morning with this run but had already laid out plans to see Brok after lunch. Tomorrow would be a day of sparring, followed by archery in the afternoon.

At the two-mile mark, Sky couldn't push herself any farther. Her heart was beating like a jackhammer. She stopped, bent over, and took deep, gasping breaths.

"Well done, but don't stop. Stretch your torso up like this and walk the next mile to cool down."

Looking up at him, she admired the way his t-shirt clung to his muscular chest when he stretched it.

She straightened and started walking. "You can finish your run without me."

Ahead of them spread the empty path. Raine, Storm, Will, and Bryce had disappeared back at the quarter mile mark.

"Until your training is done, I'm still your assigned protector." He kicked out a twig on the side of the dirt trail into the grass as they walked. "Besides, I enjoy walking with you." Softly, he added, "I like spending time with you."

Her stomach did small, giddy flips at his words. "Pff. That's probably something all fake fiancés say." She tried to break the tension from his last statement but, but the truth was, "I like spending time with you, too."

She wanted to ask him about the dream walk, but her courage escaped her. What if he hadn't been there? What if he didn't want to talk about it because he seemed to think his wolf shapeshifting abilities were something of which to be ashamed?

She'd never considered herself lacking in the gumption department, but apparently her determination was partially attributable to her being able to read thoughts. With that power blocked toward Nico, so was her temerity. At least, for now.

COLORS GLOWED AROUND SKY, Raine, Nico, and Will as Usha's ranch faded from view. The landscape transformed into lush green grass in front of a pile of wood and rubbish.

Sky had changed from jogging clothes into a dress and sandals. Nico wore jeans and t-shirt. Will and Raine wore their navy suits.

"Still very cool, Will," Sky said, watching the colors fade. "I love the rainbow colors. Can you transport on the move?"

"Yes," he drew out the word distractedly as he scanned their surroundings. Reaching over his shoulder with his right hand, he unsheathed his sword by pulling it out of thin air. Technically, he was withdrawing it from its storage in the Bifröst, but it looked like thin air except for the faint, rippling rainbow glow. "But you have to consider how you'll still be moving wherever you arrive if you travel in motion."

"Ah. So if you fall off a cliff, don't transport to a parking deck," she said.

He nodded. "Preferably a body of water if gravity is going to slam you into something, even then it can't be a great height. Anything over ninety feet is still deadly. Water or not."

"What happened here?" Raine had pulled her baton and looked braced for a fight.

Nico was on alert, nostrils flaring and eyes wide.

Raine, Nico, and Will positioned themselves to create a protective circle around Sky. As she had no physical weapon, she didn't mind. She scanned the area, trying to find the threat the others were prepared to fight. Opening her mind, she sensed no danger.

A run-down house, clearly not up to code, squatted among tall grass and was partially obscured by vines. Rusted appliances in varying shades of orange and brown decay littered the yard. Off to one side was a haphazard pile of wood, perhaps once a structure. Among all of this, she saw and sensed no monsters.

"I don't see anything," Sky whispered, "except that this dwarf clearly needs lawn maintenance."

"His workshop is in shambles," Raine said, gesturing to the pile of wood.

"That was a workshop?" Sky frowned.

Will moved in a slow circle, still apprising the area. "When Storm and Bryce last came, Brok told them he was being intermittently attacked."

"Is he still alive, and if so, how do we find him?" Nico asked.

"We can ask Usha if she's heard where he moved. I don't have a contact phone or email for him." Raine kicked the toe of her boot at a toilet lid in the grass.

Recalling what Loki told her about using all of her skills, Sky extended her senses further. Music, rhythmic pounding, heat, and a cavern.

"Follow me." She stepped over a lumpy tire and around a rusted anvil as she made her way toward the collapsed shack.

Raine, Will, and Nico followed her, keeping their protective stances at her flank.

"Under there." She pointed to corrugated sheet metal laying on the ground atop scattered lumber.

Nico bent and lifted the tin, revealing steps down into darkness.

Sky held up a hand to the others.

Brok? She sent him a mental push. Although she could sense him down there, not sneaking up on a man who made weapons for a living seemed like the prudent thing to do.

"Come on down!" a gruff voice called. "You and whatever man is helping you."

Raine nodded. "That's his voice. Why don't you and Nico go while Will and I stand guard out here?"

"You have errands," Sky protested. "I don't sense any danger."

"I don't smell any danger," Nico added. "Metal, sweat, filth, and teriyaki flavored beef jerky. No danger."

Raine glanced around again, unconvinced. "When you're safely inside, let me know."

"Okay." Sky started to step down, but Nico put an arm out to stop her.

"I'll go first. Bodyguard, remember?"

Yup, bodyguard. Not fiancé.

And she was definitely not checking out his ass as he descended the stairs.

She followed, soon struck by the heat wafting toward them from the bottom of the steps. A room spread out, filled with wall-to-wall weapons and smelling like coal and copper. On a counter sat a bottle of Coke and a bag of opened, unfinished beef jerky. In the center of the room, an enormous telescope sat on a central counter. It looked to be crushed in the middle, like a massive fist or Mjölnir itself had struck it.

Brok stood at just over four feet tall and wore a brown, long sleeve jumpsuit that Sky suspected was fire resistant. He had meaty, grease-stained hands, matching the dark smears of grime on his face. A long wiry beard of dark brown hair complemented an unruly pair of eyebrows so haphazard Sky wanted to trim them into submission.

"Sky Thoren, the youngest and fairest of them all. Welcome to my humble lair."

"It's an honor to meet you," she said. "Were you attacked again?"

"Yeah. Poor Sunna is out of commission. Fixable though." Brok patted the misshapen telescope. "Seemed pointless to rebuild the workshop, so I'm just working from the basement level." He turned toward Nico. "You're with her?"

"I'm her protector." Nico extended a hand and shook Brok's.

All good, Sky told Raine. *I'll call you when we're ready for pickup.*

She sensed Will and Raine leaving the immediate vicinity.

The dwarf turned and picked up two pieces of copper colored leather from his workspace counter. "I've got these beauties for you." He placed one piece of leather in her hand.

The material was soft and supple, as if oiled and worked with care and diligence day after day. Runes had been carved into the leather and infused with gold-colored ink.

"They're beautiful. What are they?" Sky asked.

"Defense and offense," Brok said proudly as he took one in his hand and slipped it over her wrist, a small elastic portion of it stretching to fit. It extended halfway up to her elbow. "These babies are infused with uru nanoparticles. Impenetrable." As he talked, he pulled the second one onto her other arm.

"I can feel the power in them."

Brok took a step back. "Now, extend your left arm like you're holding a bow. Very good. With your right arm, reach back behind you as if pulling an arrow out of a quiver, keeping your left arm extended."

She did as he instructed, feeling the singing hum of magic down to her bone marrow.

"Bring the imaginary arrow around as if you're nocking it."

As she did so, a bow of semi-translucent sparkling gold and an arrow of the same champagne color materialized before her eyes. Mouth gaping open, she pulled back on the arrow, and the glowing bowstring obliged. When she let loose, the arrow flew across the room, embedding in the wooden wall beside an ax. Speechless, she took a step back and dropped her arms to her side. The magical bow vanished, as did the arrow in the wall.

"Wow," she said, feeling a little breathless.

Nico walked to the wall and inspected the hole left by the vanished weapon.

Sky repeated the motions, faster this time. Left arm raised, her right arm pulled the arrow out, drew it back, and fired. As before, the bow and arrow appeared with the motions of her hands. She let it fly a foot to the left of where Nico stood. The arrow sunk into the wall.

When she dropped her hands, all magic vanished but the puncture in the wall remained. "That's amazing."

Brok's eyes twinkled in delight at her appreciation. "I needed to come up with a way for you to have an unlimited supply of arrows. This works."

"I love it."

The dwarf pulled out an index card with a name and number on it. "I guess you know the next steps. See the tailor about your outfit." He turned toward Nico. "Let's see about getting you a weapon, shall we?"

Nico shook his head. "I am just helping the Valkyries. I'm not joining them on the battlefield."

"But, Nico—"

"I don't need a weapon or magic clothing."

She didn't like the utter defeat and finality in his tone. She opted not to argue with him in front of their host, though the prophecy said three by three. Who else, if not Nico?

Brok looked back and forth between Sky and Nico's unspoken exchange. He grunted. "Sure, kid, whatever you say. Come back and see me when you figure out your destiny."

EIGHTEEN

Back at the ranch, Nico stood by as Sky extended her left arm to demonstrate her new magical weapon to the entire team. With her right, she pulled a magical arrow from an invisible quiver, took aim, and fired. She looked magnificent, with poise and focus. The arrowhead embedded in a wooden fence post three hundred feet away.

Sky grinned at her audience. A sadness struck Nico to think about how the pride and self-satisfaction she felt now would be replaced by a warrior's bleak determination when she stepped onto that battlefield.

Would she lose that bubbly, light innocence floating around her after a fight to the death? Perhaps she would keep both her spunk and her grit. She seemed to balance the difficult and the fun. She had faced down Wallace and his shotgun, only to be sweet and flirtatious in her shop later.

The memory of her proximity stirred all sorts of uneasiness in Nico. He'd wanted to kiss her, at least as much as she had wanted to kiss him. She didn't seem to understand how a real relationship might destroy them both if he was ever forced to hurt her family. The best he could do was keep his distance and keep his hands to himself.

'*I belong to you, Nico,*' she'd said as she'd stroked his fur.

He felt the same but didn't know if her words had been spoken in truth or because of the hallucinogen she'd been breathing. If she hadn't meant what she said, he didn't want the pain of hearing that truth. If she'd spoken from the heart, he didn't want the responsibility of breaking her when he was once again summoned to serve Helen.

Sky fired three arrows in a row, each landing within an inch of where the last mark had hit.

"That's amazing," Bryce said.

Will nodded with pride and appreciation. "Woman, you are going to be deadly on that field."

Storm stepped closer, inspecting Sky's leather vambraces. "Incredible craftsmanship. These markings, the style. I wonder if Brok had Anka tattoo the leather."

Anka, Nico recalled hearing from Usha, was a tattoo artist who had created Bryce's and Jake's shields.

"I need to practice while riding Thunder. Practice in motion and maybe even with moving objects."

"I can help with that," Bryce said. "I'll create moving illusions for you to shoot."

"As soon as we have a section of fence repaired to keep Thunder in, we can bring your horse here," Storm said.

Family, Nico thought as they all worked to help and support each other. *And love.*

The team had this advantage over Helen's army. Her subjects did her bidding out of fear, ingrained training, a mutual desire to see the world rid of humans, or some combination of all three. Nowhere in the mix was love or compassion. He could see how these things brought strength to this group. Their love gave him hope they would be enough to bring the goddess of death to her knees.

And send her back to hell.

THE NEXT DAY, Nico set to work on his chore list. Step one, clean out the barn. He started with organizing piles of usable items—old saddles, rusted bits, buckets, hammers—and unusable items—moth eaten blankets, broken rakes, and rotten wood. After that, he would clean what was salvageable.

A shadow in the corner caught his eye. He spun, hackles raised, but his attacker was too fast.

Storm backed him into the wall, pinning him there with her arms.

How had she moved in on him with such stealth?

He growled slightly before reining in his temper.

"I don't know what you're playing at, Nico."

"What?" he snarled.

"This thing between you and my sister."

"I told you. I made up the engagement in order to stay close to Sky at the hospital. The lie was the only way to protect her."

Still glaring at him, Storm let go. "As amusing as that was, it doesn't explain why the two of you are casting longing gazes at each other."

"I—"

Shit.

He let his anger deflate. He didn't have a good explanation, and Storm would see through any lie he attempted.

She took a step back and crossed her arms expectantly.

Nico reached up and rubbed the back of his neck. Under the weight of the purple flames in Storm's eyes, he finally said, "I like your sister."

"I see that. Does she know?"

He grit his teeth. She was asking if Sky knew his curse, but he opted to stall. "That I like her? Probably."

Storm shook her head and frowned. "Does she know that you're Helen's pup? Does Sky know she can't have you?"

He met her stare. After a few beats, he looked away. "Yes."

Storm's gaze softened, which did nothing to eliminate the lump in his throat. "Good. Then she'll come to the right conclusion."

He'd thought the same when he'd told Sky, but she hadn't distanced herself yet.

Storm's brow furrowed as if she saw the turmoil of his feelings and had a rare moment of compassion for him. The expression was almost as unnerving as when she played with her knives.

"I'm sorry for your curse. You seem like a decent guy otherwise," Storm said.

He stared down at his boots as he felt the weight of his own self-loathing. "Knowing what I am, Sky still asked me to stay and help. We have... chemistry."

Storm frowned, but her voice stayed soft. "Stay and help us train and prepare. But don't emotionally destroy her by letting her think there's a future between you two when there isn't."

She was right, of course. The best-case scenario was if Helen was destroyed and that freed him of his ownership, but she could command him to commit many unforgivable acts before that occurred.

"I can count on you?" Now it was his turn to look hard at her, teeth clenched and jaw firm.

She cocked her head to one side.

"If I become a threat to anyone, you'll end it? End me?"

If he was going to stay here and endanger everyone, he needed to know Storm wouldn't hesitate to do the right thing.

She cast her gaze aside and swallowed. "You can count on me," the assassin said, resignation and truth in her voice.

When the Shadow Guardian walked away, leaving him alone in the barn, he thought about the first time he'd met Helen.

At the age of eight, his parents had driven him and his brother Andrej outside Zalău with no forewarning. The car ride had been quietly oppressive, as Nico could sense his parents' fear.

When they arrived and parked, a half-dozen frightened boys and girls he didn't know piled out of various cars under the watchful eye of two stoic men in suits. In retrospect, Nico suspected those men had been Frost Giants. He and Andrej had huddled close together.

Everyone's parents stayed in the cars as the children were marched into the forest. Snow crunched beneath Nico's feet and his breath condensed on the frigid winter air. He knew enough from the bizarre situation and secrecy of it all to feel a sense of dread and foreboding.

His pants, coat, and hat did little to combat the bone-chilling cold. The Frost Giants in overcoats herded the children a distance through snow and barren trees until stopping near a stream. Nico couldn't pinpoint what had compelled him to stop, although all the children simultaneously halted. Wide eyed with fear, he looked at his brother, who appeared just as terrified.

A woman emerged from the white bleakness. Her skin was as pale as the frost with light golden hair flowing down and peeking out of a blood-red cloak over a black velvet dress.

"My children," she purred. "My pups." She gestured to them all, small and shivering. "Bow before me," she commanded in a deep, forceful voice. She spoke in German, but one of the Frost Giants translated into Romanian. Oddly, Nico had begun to bow even before the translation was complete. The compulsion couldn't be denied. Unable to resist, Nico dropped to his knees with Andrej beside him.

"You are Fenrir's descendants," she continued with a gleam in her dark eyes. "You belong to me. I will summon you to my side when I need you. Until then, remember your place."

The cold ground instantly numbed his legs. Around him, the other children all fell to their knees, some sobbing and others glaring at the woman.

She raised her hands. "For now, let the wolves run wild."

At that, every one of them doubled over in agony, screaming. Nico's body was being torn apart—bone from ligament and tendon from muscle. Pain and heat escalated beyond anything he'd ever experienced.

When the blinding agony relented, the long, high-pitch cries of children were replaced by howls.

Nico opened his watering eyes. Surrounding him were a dozen wolves of varying colors—black, gray, red, white, and brown. He was terrified at first, but as he watched them nervously glance around at each other, he realized he could smell their fear.

Some of them put flaring nostrils to the snow-covered ground, a few sniffed each other, and others nipped or growled at other wolves. He looked down to see two white paws in the snow. Eyes darting for Andrej, he saw a pair of familiar blue eyes staring back at him around pure alabaster fur.

In a panic, Nico took off at a sprint. Beneath his torso, four limbs moved in smooth coordination with powerful muscles flexing and extending. He wasn't sure how long he ran—between trees, around shrubs, and over hills, kicking up snowy puffs of white powder.

At last, he stopped when he came to a stream. Water pooled in one section. He dipped his head and lapped up the icy water, glimpsing his rippling reflection. He was all white, but his eyes were the same glacier blue as in his human form. His snout was long and narrow, and he had control of his ears to flick them in one direction or another. Crisp sounds assaulted his hearing—the babbling stream, a bird landing lightly on a branch, the fall of snow from over-burdened branches.

The noise of another animal running heralded Andrej's arrival. He caught up to Nico and halted in front of the water. Looking at his new form, Andrej growled at his own reflection.

The brothers took off running again, and Nico wondered if he could spend his entire life running free and never facing that dreadful woman and her ability to completely control him.

"I will summon you to my side when I need you," her words echoed in his mind.

Skidding to a stop on a hill, he lifted his head to the sky and unleashed a long howl of protest.

NINETEEN

"Afternoon, class, I'm Will Decker. I'll be your shooting range instructor for the day."

"Very funny," Sky said, crossing her arms as she stood in front of a table of guns. She was Will's only pupil, because she was the only one of the group who didn't know how to use a weapon. A gun, she corrected herself.

With a huff, she added, "I'm going to use a bow and arrow. I don't see why I need to know how to use a gun."

Her sisters had insisted on the training, but Sky hated the loud weapons with their obnoxious smell.

Will nodded. "Your bow is amazing, don't get me wrong. And maybe that's all you'll end up needing. But hear me out about guns, because at some point in the battle, you may want to pick one up and use it." Before she could protest, he added, "Let's say you're knocked on your butt, crawling in the dirt, with a Dark Elf bearing down on you, and you don't have enough space to do the whole bow and arrow maneuver? What if your left arm is broken? So while you're shuffling in the dirt with your left arm broken, you notice the corpse of a Frost Giant beside you has a gun you can take. Good thing for you, your dashing brother-in-law taught you how to shoot."

She narrowed her eyes at him but didn't argue.

He gave her a broad smile and rubbed his hands together. "Let's get started, class. Raine and I like Glocks. This is a 19 and this a 17. The 19 is slightly smaller with about a half inch shorter barrel. Standard magazine capacity for the 17 is 17 and 15 for the 19."

"The bigger number is a smaller gun?"

"Yes. In fact, there's a Glock 26, which is even smaller."

She put her hands on her hips. "But with bullet caliber, bigger is actually bigger."

Will shrugged. "I didn't design them. I just use them. These are semi-automatic, meaning it self-loads a bullet into the chamber—ready for the next time you pull the trigger."

Sky looked at the guns and then at the target. Will had placed it only fifty feet away.

He continued, "We'll try out the Glocks as well as Storm's P320 Compact. It's lightweight and holds twenty-one 9mm rounds."

She slipped on the earmuffs and picked up a gun, disliking the hard, cold feel of it. "Okay. Let's do this."

LATER THAT DAY, with ears still ringing from firing weapons, Sky rode on the four-wheeler behind Bryce. Barbed wire and tools were crammed into the back compartment. The hot summer sun beat down on them so ferociously that she could feel the heat through her baseball cap. Dressed in jeans and a t-shirt, she'd also preemptively put on leather gloves for the work ahead.

The landscape was a beautiful mix of rolling hills and mountains. She thought she could live in such a tranquil place until she envisioned it covered in three feet of snow. Equally breathtaking in view, but way too cold.

When Bryce pulled the vehicle to a stop near a stretch of dilapidated fence, Sky hopped off. He wore a determined expression with a hint of anticipation, like he wanted nothing more than to spend the day immersed in manual labor.

He squinted up at the wispy clouds as he pulled on his gloves. "Why don't you grab that spool of barbed wire, and I'll bring the tools over."

She hauled her load over toward the fence. "Here ya go, Mr. Chipper."

"I don't think anyone's ever referred to me as chipper before, but I am in a good mood. I've always enjoyed working with my hands. That's why I became a surgeon."

"Do you miss it?"

"I do miss it. Can't practice medicine on a boat, and keeping Olivia safe is a priority." Using sheers, he clipped the shorter strands of wire with Sky following his lead and winding up the snippets. "I miss that feeling of changing lives. But then I remind myself that's exactly what we're doing now. Beat Helen and change some lives. Maybe all lives."

"You've certainly changed Storm's. For the better," she quickly added. "It's like you ground her. Like she was floating—a ship lost at sea, and you're her anchor, her moor. It's a beautiful thing."

Sky sensed Raine and Will's role in grounding Storm had to do with seeing the pair of them married and then working together. This had sparked the possibility in Storm's mind of how she could have love, too, despite the future they faced. Seeing them happy had planted the seed that had grown into possibilities once she'd met Bryce.

He grinned. "Funny thing is, I feel the same way about Storm. She helped me discover who I am and who I'm meant to be in the supernatural world."

"It's great you're going to propose. I'm looking forward to another brother-in-law." As soon as the words were out of her mouth, she clamped her hand over it.

Bryce cocked his head to one side.

"I'm so sorry," she rushed to say. "I didn't mean to glean that information. That was private." She scrunched up her nose.

He chuckled. "You must be hell to buy a birthday present for."

"Sorry. Your psyche is kind of screaming it, though."

"It's okay. I've been thinking about it for quite a while. I just... the thing is, she's been engaged before, and I don't know what her reaction will be. I don't want to bring her pain."

"Bryce Chambers, physician and illusionist, you will bring my sister nothing but happiness. She loves you, and she's healed from the heartache of the past. A proposal from you will cause pure joy."

"Thank you. I believe that was just the pep talk I needed."

Sky couldn't see the future, but she had felt Storm's devotional love to this man and his daughter. Storm wanted to marry him, she just didn't know it yet.

They set to work repairing the fence, trimming rusted wire that had broken loose or slackened under the strain of Mother Nature's weather extremes. Lastly, they re-fastened new strands to replace the old.

"What about you and Nico?" Bryce asked, wiping sweat from his brow as they stopped for a water break.

Her mouth twitched. "There is no me and Nico. He's here to protect me and train me."

"You have four other people who would risk their lives defending you here. And you really believe you need a bodyguard at an isolated ranch in Montana?" Bryce asked teasingly.

"Okay, Mr. I-can-throw-a-shield-up-faster-than-Dirty-Harry-can-draw-his-gun. I don't have swords and spears and magic lassos. I'm just an herbal shop owner extraordinaire."

"Who also has power so immense she can punch Helen in the frontal cortex and stun her."

"Yeah," she giggled, "I did that."

"And the bow and arrow out of thin air? Nobody I know can do that, and if I tried to replicate it, my illusion would just sail right through the target."

"I admit, I feel safer with Nico around." She huffed. "Fine, I am mildly attracted to him." From the look in Bryce's eyes, he saw through Sky's use of the word *mildly*.

"That's good to hear, because I'm pretty sure his attraction to you is a little stronger than mild. Maybe not full-blown caliente scorch-your-tongue, but it's there."

"You're being ridiculous. He likes to annoy me. I saw the look on his face when Usha incorrectly thought we were a couple. He was mortified. He continues to remind me how he's only here for my protection."

Bryce gave her an amused arched eyebrow but didn't argue with her. "Okay." She sensed what he'd really wanted to say was, *'are you sure you're interpreting his behavior correctly?'*

After the dream walk, she wasn't certain of anything except that Nico seemed more guarded around her. She would get to the bottom of their feelings for each other—at some point between the endless training and exhausting chores.

Nico sat beside Sky, his standard spot because all the couples were paired beside each other at the long, rectangular table for dinner. Usha sat at the head.

Platters filled with seasoned meatloaf, garlic mashed potatoes, and cheesy broccoli covered the tabletop. Everyone passed the food and helped themselves, creating a clinking, almost melodic sound of serving spoons and forks clicking against ceramics.

Each night, Nico found the routine relaxingly domestic. During the day, he worked with Raine or Will on repairs to the barn while Sky was whisked away to other chores or training. The rotation was good for building rapport. Because they would take the battlefield together, building trust was imperative among the five of them.

Meanwhile, no one can trust me.

No one should trust him.

He had to plan his exit strategy. Helen hadn't contacted him to force his return. Enough time had passed that he was beginning to think she couldn't. Why? Was there some invisible barrier because of his proximity to the chosen trinity? Since this battle was to take place in Iceland, perhaps parting ways with the group was as simple as not being transported with the team. Then, he couldn't be forced to fight against them.

If the barrier to Helen's commands was related to his proximity to Sky or this group and Helen's power over him resumed when they were separated, he would still have no way of reaching Iceland in time for the battle.

And yet, deep down, he knew he'd be there. His dreams told him so. However, other Norse mixed breeds were having similar dreams, and the prophecies said only six would battle against Helen.

Long before he'd heard the location was Iceland, he'd seen it. Before he'd met the Shadow Guardians, he'd known what each of them looked like. Raine and Will with their sleek navy-blue suits, Raine's blonde hair pulled back as she wielded a spear. Will brandished both sword and gun in a blaze of bright color.

In Nico's visions, Storm spun through the swarm of her enemies, knives fast as lightning and deadly. By the time Hel's creatures realized they'd been cut, they were already seconds away from death. Bryce wielded his glowing lasso in one hand and a gun in the other. The golden rope functioned like an extension of himself, knocking his enemies to the ground, where a bullet finished them. The wolves gave the cowboy a wide berth, knowing the history behind the design of that rope—the ribbon which had once held Fenrir himself.

Lastly, was Sky. Her hair flowed in ribbons of red, gold, and brown as she sat on top of a white horse—Thunder, Nico now knew —firing arrows. Magical arrows. He'd been in awe the first time he'd seen her in his dreams. The love came later. The love came when he'd seen her everyday life at the shop—the way she cared for others, was generous with her advice and her time, and how she interacted with him. Devoid of judgment.

Had Helen known of his dreams, she could have forced him to divulge information about the Valkyrie—their weapons and their fighting tactics. He'd watched the battle from the sidelines of his dreams often enough to know them all. He could be forced to betray them in the worst way.

Yet Nico suspected Helen would never ask. It would simply never occur to her that her dogs possessed intelligence or insight. She dismissed them as ignorant and only as useful killing tools. And she wouldn't hesitate to order him to kill any or all of them at this table.

"Penny for your thoughts?" Sky's sweet, whispering voice drew him out of his deep thinking.

Looking up, plates across the table were now filled, some partially eaten except his own. All eyes were on him.

He picked up his fork. "I was thinking about battle strategy. We should spend a half day discussing it. You need tactics that play to each of your strengths." He took a bite of meatloaf and chewed.

"That's a good idea," Will said.

"You make your suggestion as though you'll be the one to lead the discussion," Storm said.

"I will."

Sky smiled at him, which gave him a boost to counteract Storm's skepticism.

"I've fought for Helen in teams. I know strategy and the weaknesses of many of her creatures." If he couldn't fight with them like he wanted to—because if he went to Iceland, he would be forced to fight against them—he could at least help in this way and betray Hel to the furthest extent by exposing all her creatures' weaknesses.

When Storm nodded with appreciation, he added, "For instance, the hellhounds will fear Bryce's lasso. They'll avoid him and preferentially attack the rest of you. They can heal, but slowly and only in their wolf form. Lethal strikes are still just that. Fire Giants and Frost Giants have thick skulls, so they're top-heavy. If Bryce uses his lasso to yank them down at the ankles, he or someone else can finish them. They aren't easily pierced with bullets, so better to shoot for the jugular."

Bryce lifted his eyebrows. "You are a wealth of information. Good thing Sky had us keep you on."

Nico hoped that would turn out to be true.

CHAPTER

TWENTY

"You're not keeping your balance," Storm said flatly.

Sky grit her teeth. "It's hard to keep my balance when you're beating me to a pulp." Gone was any semblance of her chipper self.

For days, she'd been engrossed in manual labor. She'd been gouged with barbed wire, run until her lungs threatened to burst, suffered and healed more blisters than she could count, and every day Storm brought her out for sparring practice, intent on inflicting pain.

"Do you think the Dark Elves and Frost Giants won't try to beat you to a pulp?" her sister asked.

"I'm saying it's hard to concentrate and fight when I'm exhausted from healing myself every single day."

"You're going to be beaten down, bloody, and exhausted on the battlefield, and you have to get up and fight anyway. I have to prepare you for that."

"Bully," Sky muttered.

Storm lunged at her again, swinging. Sky attempted the maneuvers Storm had taught her, but once again found herself flat on her ass.

Shaking her head, Storm towered over Sky. "You have more grace than this. I've seen you on the dance floor."

Sky did like to dance. The last time Storm had seen her dance was probably at Raine's wedding. That had been a fun time. Storm brooded off to the side, but Sky had danced for hours with a half dozen partners who couldn't keep up with her.

She accepted Storm's hand and pulled herself up, grunting. "Sure. I've got style and grace when there's a music *beat*, not when I'm getting *beat-en*."

Storm pursed her lips. "Okay, we can play it that way."

"What way?"

Sky dusted the dirt off her leggings while Storm brought out her phone, tapped a few buttons, and started playing "Woman" by Doja Cat, tapping her foot to the beat.

"We'll start with this one as we go through all the fight moves I've been reviewing with you. This time, pretend we're dancing, choreographed to a song."

Setting her stance, Sky eyed her skeptically. "Okay."

To the song's beat, they moved arms and legs. They made the motions slower than they had been, certainly slower than an actual fight. As they moved, Sky gained a sense of the tempo and the rhythm of fighting. Maybe she could get the hang of this.

The next song Storm picked, "Break My Heart" by Dua Lipa, had a faster rhythm. Picking up their pace, they moved through the same rehearsed motions, but this time Sky kept her balance and didn't land on her backside.

Thirty minutes and eight songs later, with each escalating in speed, Sky was gasping for air, clutching a stitch in her side, and sporting a wide smile. Storm had still managed her fair share of blows against Sky, but she had deflected and redirected a record number.

"I did it!" She wrapped her arms around Storm's neck and

hugged, startling her sister. "You're right, it's like dancing. Only more painful." As she backed away, she rubbed her throbbing arms, sore from blocking the hard blows.

"Nicely done," Storm said with much less enthusiasm than Sky felt the occasion deserved. "Next, we'll fight with batons."

Sky's zealousness deflated as she wondered how much more painful those lessons would be.

LATER THAT DAY, Sky donned the outfit she and Will had picked up from Brok. Her 'battle armor' was a white cotton lace dress with three-quarter length sleeves. The hem came down to her ankles, and the skirt portion flowed loose to allow for free movement. She couldn't feel that the infused nanoparticle barrier added any weight or stiffness over normal cotton. Brok had thrown in a pair of white leather boots, explaining how she needed better footwear on the battlefield than her usual open-toed sandals. After pulling on her vambraces, she walked outside to the smaller corral, ready for her lesson with Nico.

As per his usual, he wore jeans and a t-shirt, and as per her usual, she tried not to stare.

"Let's talk a moment," Nico said, his lovely accent and deep voice washing over her.

Her heart fluttered at his words. She wanted to talk. She craved the fun of their interaction from the first few days in the hospital, but he'd distanced himself since coming to the ranch. Because of his apprehension, she vacillated with uncertainty about how to reconnect. She'd made him uncomfortable when she'd been forward in her shop, although her intentions were to be playful.

When she replayed events in her mind, she wondered if he'd seen her actions as too forceful. The man had been controlled by a manipulative she-demon with incredible powers. Hours after Sky had forced Wallace to shoot himself, she tried to seduce Nico. Perhaps he saw her as another controlling woman. She hadn't considered that when she'd backed him into the counter.

Perhaps that had been a mistake, but she hadn't sorted out when or how to rectify it. She debated dropping subtle hints with body language and see if he wanted to be the one to make the next move. Now that he wanted to talk, perhaps this was their opportunity.

"When you use the bow, what do you feel?" he asked.

Oh, right. He wants to talk strategy.

This was one of his strengths, and she needed to learn from him, not romanticize a relationship when he'd said he didn't want one.

She rolled her shoulders. "There's a physical connection where I can actually feel the handle in my left hand as it appears. I can grip it solidly. Same thing with the arrow, feeling the shaft and fletching between my fingertips and the stretch of the string. I also feel the low hum of it. The magic within it."

He nodded. "It sounds as though you connect with this mind and body. Which makes me wonder if there is an element of mind control involved."

He said the words *mind control* a bit clipped, making her wonder if he thought of Helen's power.

Is this the heart of his reluctance to connect with me?

Was he afraid she would use her powers on him the way Helen had if she could? She thought of the hospital and how he'd tensed when she'd used her powers on the physician. She thought again of Wallace's attack and Nico's pale face after she'd influenced Wallace to shoot himself in the foot.

She would have to show Nico she wasn't the type of person to manipulate people outside a few rare exceptions.

She extended her arm and drew back an arrow. "Yes, I do feel a magical connection, like I have summoned this magic in part with my mind and will, pulling it from the vambrace."

"I suspected. I think if we put those vambraces on someone without telekinetic abilities, they wouldn't work. With that in mind

—pun intended—I want you to hit a target with your mind rather than your vision.”

“Are you going to blindfold me, Master Obi-wan?”

Nico cocked his head to one side with a frown.

She dropped her arms to gape at him. “Oh my gosh, you don’t know *Star Wars* references? We have to fix this. When the war is over, a movie marathon is next. *Star Wars* and Marvel movies.”

His throat bobbed in a swallow, as if uncomfortable at the thought of concentrated time with her.

“I like you,” she blurted.

He didn’t make eye contact when he said, “We can’t.” Before she could argue, he added, “Feelings for me might make you hesitate if I’m ever turned against you by Helen. You can’t afford to hesitate.”

Sky wanted to argue with him, but he was in obvious distress on the subject. She wouldn’t continue to make him feel uncomfortable. She could let the topic go... for now.

Raising her arms, she readied another arrow. “What am I hitting?”

“That tree. A hundred yards out.”

She took aim as Nico took a few steps back.

“See if you can connect with the arrow with your mental magic.”

She nodded, focusing and tuning out the disappointment sweeping through her at the physical and emotional distance Nico put between them.

As she drew the string back, light flickered, momentarily blinding her. She let the arrow loose even as she blinked. Looking over at Nico, she noticed a mirror in his hand. He turned to look at the tree.

“You intentionally distracted me,” she said.

“There will be many distractions in battle. I want to know if you can make the shot regardless. And you can.”

She followed his gaze to see the arrow dissolving from the trunk of the tree.

"Again," he said. "Again, until your fingers are raw and your mind aches from the effort."

HELEN SOAKED IN A HOT BATH. From behind the closed bathroom door, she could hear the scampering of her servants. They were cleaning her bedroom of the body she'd left behind.

With the war nearing, she needed a boost of power. Killing the Vanir allowed her to absorb his power. The ritual was time-consuming and messy but cathartic. She needed cathartic to balance the stress of the impending battle.

Most days, she was surrounded by utter incompetence. It oozed from the pores of the creatures she enlisted and dripped from their tongues in the form of lies and half-truths to cover up their mistakes.

No matter. The war would come, and she would win by sheer numbers, even though her attempts to thwart the Valkyries before the battle had failed. She had thought killing prophets would stop the spread of hopefulness that the Valkyrie would defeat her in a battle of might. But Helen couldn't silence them all.

She'd also envisioned how preemptively targeting Valkyries would solve the problem, but she'd had no way of identifying them among the other eight billion people in the world. She knew they were out there, though, because one by one they had infiltrated her dreams. Their quest for power had pulled Helen in, but when she'd tried to intercede, she'd failed to kill even one of them. She had hoped the Frost Giant assassin and the Hellfire she'd launched would have dealt with them—and foolishly believed for a time one or the other had succeeded. But when she learned Bolverkr had died, the safest course was to assume he'd died a failure. And he had.

Not to worry. She had an army.

Three by three.

Three—or six—Shadow Guardians couldn't defeat hundreds of her creatures.

TWENTY-ONE

Nico took an electric sander to the barn walls as Bryce measured and cut fresh planks to replace the rotting, splintered, or brittle boards. Nico enjoyed the work, enjoyed immersing himself in manual labor and sweating out his worry and annoying self-pity. He could smooth the wood into a fine finish and imagine life being equally simple. What if all you needed was a little sanding to expose that healthy glow beneath the worn and weather-beaten layers? What if life could be as simple as repairing barns all day?

When Helen was defeated, would Nico have the luxury of imagining a future? He'd earned a degree at university, but he'd never visualized himself beyond that battle.

A battle he should never attend.

He recalled Brok's words, *"Sure, kid, whatever you say. Come back and see me when you figure out your destiny."*

Nico's role was to help the Shadow Guardians win the war through strategy and the intel he provided by being one of her personal hellhounds. He didn't need a weapon or suit of armor, both of which could make him a more formidable adversary when Helen called him back to her side.

He had to avoid that battle.

Besides the dwarf's words, Nico had to contend with Sky's looks of disappointment. They ran together each morning and ate dinner side by side. The rest of the time, they mostly trained and worked apart. When together, she was always edging closer to him, quick to touch or smile. And he repeatedly didn't return the affection. If he nurtured the feelings between them, the pain would be all the keener when they were torn apart.

At noon, Usha announced a lunch break by arriving with sandwiches and lemonade.

Nico and Bryce thanked her before rinsing dirt and wood dust off using a hose in the barn. They sat on hay bales to eat as she slipped back out the door.

"You're a hard worker, Nico. I admire that," Bryce commented.

Nico nodded. "I've always enjoyed manual labor. Takes the mind off..." his voice trailed. "Everything."

"You haven't settled in. You're polite enough but guarded. Like the new horse in the corral."

There was a new horse? Nico looked around the barn, chewing and swallowing a bite of ham and cheese on rye. They'd only recently brought Thunder, Dolly, and Faith to the ranch. Olivia, who'd dropped in to stay for a few weeks, had taken a trail ride with Storm and Bryce the other day.

Bryce chuckled. "It's a figure of speech."

"If Usha is correct, we're going to be on that battlefield together in a few weeks. So I suppose I am guarded."

"You don't believe the prophecies?"

Nico worried the man referred to the very prophecies coursing through the mind of his own daughter. Yet Bryce's tone was inquiring with no hint of defensiveness.

"I believe you five are meant to storm that Icelandic field. I don't know why I'm here."

"Ah, imposter syndrome."

"I beg your pardon?"

"Imposter syndrome is when you have all the qualifications to do what it is you're doing or what others think you should do, but you still doubt yourself. You feel unworthy. It's common. Doctors are taught about it because we feel it. All the time."

"Yes, unworthy. I'm not supposed to be here." Nico washed down another bite of the sandwich with lemonade.

Bryce gave an amused smile. "Hell, man, none of us are supposed to be here. I'm supposed to be practicing surgery in Texas while my daughter attends school, getting an education so she can be the scientist she dreams of becoming. Instead, my eight-year-old is a prophet, I've got a tattoo on my back to produce a spontaneous shield, I'm wearing a magic lasso, and I'm carrying around an engagement ring in my pocket as I wait for the opportunity to ask a Valkyrie to marry me. None of this makes a lick of sense, but we're all here for the ride, so you might as well make the most of it."

"Storm told you what I am?" When Bryce nodded, Nico continued, "Then you know why it's complicated—why my presence here is a danger to everyone."

"I'm sure that whatever hardships you've had to endure being who and what you are has made you fearful of what you might do, but I don't think Usha would put you under the same roof as the chosen Valkyries if you didn't belong here—if you were going to harm any of us."

"Storm knows better than to trust me," Nico grumbled.

"I love her, but God knows that woman's trust is hard to earn."

"You're going to propose?" Nico asked, snatching at the opportunity to change the subject.

Bryce grinned. "That's the plan. Although I'm thinking it takes more courage to flash a diamond ring bending on one knee than it does to kill a Frost Giant."

Nico chuckled. "She loves you and adores Olivia. She'll say yes."

"Thanks. I appreciate the vote of confidence."

Nico finished his food and hopped off his bale. As he worked, he mulled over Bryce's words.

Imposter syndrome.

Absurd.

And yet, of the six of them—seven counting Usha—only he and Storm felt Nico didn't belong.

Sky raced through the obstacle course on Thunder's back. Using only her thoughts to guide him, her hands were free to use the bow and arrow. In quick succession, she pulled from the quiver, drew back, and fired. She hit every target. She was better with her magical bow than she'd ever been with the tangible versions she'd shot in her youth. The mind-body-bow connection seemed to give her accuracy.

She could feel the old horse's enjoyment of the activity—how it made him feel young again even if he wasn't as fast as he'd been in his youth.

Next, Bryce created moving illusions for her—Frost Giants and Dark Elves attacking. She felled them with arrows as well.

Pleased with herself, she drew Thunder up beside Raine and smiled.

Raine patted the animal's neck. "Ten moving targets and seven stationary bulls-eyes. I'd say you haven't lost your touch. We can do another round through the obstacle course with the sword, then the gun."

"Let me breathe a minute. Want to ride a bit? Faith would like some attention."

"Sure."

Sky mentally summoned Faith, who trotted over to them, and Raine hoisted herself onto the horse's bare back.

"It was great of Will to bring Thunder, Dolly, and Faith here," Sky said.

Before moving here, Dolly and Faith had been on Bryce's property, and Storm had been paying for someone to feed and care for them.

Raine nodded. "Olivia was ecstatic to see her horses again. Storm and Bryce rode yesterday afternoon again with her."

Sky rolled her shoulders.

"Stiff?" Raine asked.

"Six weeks of running, fighting, and fixing. I hope I'm ready by Freyfaxi."

"You will be. You're doing great."

They passed by Nico at the barn. Bryce was joining him and together they were stacking bales of hay.

"That was one longing look," Raine said.

Sky turned to face forward. "Yeah, I'm pretty obvious, huh? Lusting after a guy who's been avoiding me."

"Thing is—" Raine adjusted her seat on the horse "—I've seen him cast some equally lingering stares in your direction when you're not looking."

"Really?" She had thought she'd seen mixed wariness and interest in Nico's eyes. Whenever she had a few moments between training and chores, she tried to summon the courage to talk to him. Then, she would remember the way he'd looked when she'd caged him in her shop—like a cornered colt ready to bolt—and give him space.

"Really."

"Okay. Next chance I get, I will root out his feelings for me. No more dancing around each other. What are you grinning about?"

"It's strange and a little refreshing to see you struggle to try to figure out if a man is interested in you. You've always just known by glimpsing his thoughts," Raine said.

"Refreshing? You mean infuriating."

"I think you like the challenge a bit."

Sky shifted her weight on Thunder's back. "A bit. Still hard to know if he truly doesn't want a relationship or doesn't think he should want one because of everything else surrounding us—danger and destiny."

"I'm betting my money on his hesitation is directed at the situation and not at a lack of interest in you."

"Then I'll push a little harder, and we'll see what happens."

CHAPTER
TWENTY-TWO

Nico ran across the expansive Montana range, all four paws pounding the dirt and wheatgrass. Catching the scent of a hare, he adjusted his stride to chase it, gaze locking onto the fleeing creature. He didn't eat animals in his wolf form, though he loved the hunt.

Another scent brought him to an abrupt halt. Raising his nose in the faint breeze, he inhaled, nostrils flaring. A flash of white crested a hill, running toward him. A bolt of worry struck Nico.

When the moon-colored wolf was within a hundred feet, he slowed to a trot then a walk. At twenty feet, he shifted into his human form.

Andrej was a blond-haired, blue-eyed European like his brother but a few inches shorter and stouter. He wore black slacks and a black button-down shirt—stark contrasts to his fair complexion.

"You're alive." His accent was thicker than Nico's as he spoke in a bitter tone.

Nico shifted into his human form. He wore only the pair of shorts he'd been sleeping in before his run. "I'm alive." He wasn't sure why his brother would assume he was dead, but perhaps that had worked in his favor for remaining in hiding. Until now, apparently.

"You haven't been replying to my text messages."

"I'm on sabbatical," Nico replied dryly.

"Bullshit."

Nico smirked. No matter how old they were, he could always garner a certain amusing satisfaction from aggravating his sibling.

"You didn't respond to Helen's summons, either. How is that possible?"

Nico jolted. "She summoned me?"

"She tried, but she couldn't feel you. She thinks you're dead."

"You're here to confirm that?" Nico's body thrummed with tension, ready for a fight if Andrej had been sent here with orders to maim or kill. Both brothers fully expected Helen intended to one day pit them against each other.

"Of course not. What's one more dead wolf to her? I snuck away and tracked you down. Your flight was Montana, then Texas. I couldn't pick up your scent in the city, so I backtracked here. You aren't the only one who can track. Now, how are you evading her? What magic is this?"

"I don't know," Nico admitted, though he'd speculated to himself that the Valkyrie served as some type of barrier between him and Helen because he hadn't been summoned since being in their presence.

"Fine. Don't tell me. You and your secrets," Andrej seethed.

If I knew the cause, would I tell Andrej?

His younger brother was so entrenched in the ways of the underworld that Nico wasn't sure Andrej would agree to be extricated from Helen's talons if the option existed. And if Andrej did agree, would his true motive be only to discover how freedom was achieved so Helen could break the spell? The white wolf may have been his brother in blood, but his loyalty resided with his commanding goddess of darkness.

Nico rolled his shoulders. "You know my heart holds no loyalty to

Helen. I've never kept that a secret. Everything I've ever done for her was under compulsion to do so." And everything he'd voluntarily done worked to counteract the evil she'd forced upon him.

"Better to wear just the two faces—man and wolf—rather than all the ones you use interchangeably. You've woven a web of lies."

"I freely admit to being a scheming underdog, but I've never lied about which side I'm rooting for to win." Nico relaxed slightly, convinced Andrej had no intention of fighting him tonight. "Tricky thing about Hel's ability to make us do her bidding—instructions must be precise and there are always loopholes."

"Loopholes," Andrej scoffed. "You're a killer, not a lawyer."

"I am a killer, but only when I'm forced to be."

Andrej shook his head in familiar disgust. "Always thinking you're better than the rest of us."

Nico wouldn't entertain this conversation again. He'd already told his brother how wrong such a statement was on many other occasions. He couldn't cure his brother of his own insecurities.

"So, you're not coming home?" Andrej demanded.

Home?

Helen's side wasn't home. It was hell.

Nico crossed his arms. "Am I voluntarily returning to Helen so she can send me on my next assignment to kill an innocent? No."

Andrej hefted a sigh, looking over the landscape. "What are you doing out here?"

"Sabbatical." He wouldn't tell his brother he was training with the three legendary Valkyrie sisters lest Helen extract the information unwillingly from him.

"When will you come back?" For a moment, Andrej sounded lost and alone, like the younger brother he was. He didn't make eye contact as he waited for Nico's answer.

Nico's heart ached for him, but he'd learned a long time ago that staying by his brother's side didn't translate into an ability to protect Andrej. Helen easily set them to different tasks and could just as easily make them attack each other, if for nothing more than her own entertainment.

"When I can't refuse Helen," Nico replied.

Andrej turned away, shifting back into wolf form.

Nico quickly added, "You can let her think I'm dead, Andrej. She doesn't need to know."

The white wolf bolted away from him.

Nico stood on the plain, taking in the smells of subalpine fir, bee balm, wild chives, and a distant storm brewing. Watching the wolf leave, Nico wondered if Andrej would or already had tracked him as far as Usha's ranch. If so, whatever knowledge he gained could be disastrous for the group.

Nico rubbed his neck.

Helen tried to summon me and failed. How is this possible?

Was there something in Sky's magic? He might sleep under her wards on the house, but they trained in the open fields. If the wards were responsible, he should have been able to feel Helen's pull on him when he was mulling about the ranch.

Was the ranch itself impenetrable to Helen's sorcery? He would have to ask Usha about that, but the more he considered the timing, the more he realized he had sensed nothing from Helen since a few days into his assignment as Sky's guardian. This predated the ranch and predated when he'd slept under Sky's wards.

Perhaps his other theory was correct—some powers of the Valkyrie formed a barrier between him and Helen. He tried to grasp on to this thread of hope, but doubt plagued him. An ocean stood between him and the goddess. When they were on the battlefield with her powers in full force, she would order him to kill his new family, and he would be forced to do so.

THE NEXT MORNING, Nico found Usha rocking on the porch, sipping coffee.

"My brother paid me a visit last night," he told her.

He waited for her rebuke. If he'd been reporting equally alarming news to Helen, she would've demanded to know what carelessness on Nico's part had led to danger following him.

Instead, Usha continued to rock calmly in her chair. "He's worried about you."

Nico deflated in the chair beside her. "Only worried about how much trouble he'll get into if I don't return to Helen." He stroked a hand along his jaw. "I wonder when this fantasy I'm living will end. When I'll be sent away, as I should have from the beginning."

"Everyone here sees your value. It's a shame that you do not."

"I bring value, but at monumental risk to your Shadow Guardians. If my brother tracked me here, Helen might as well."

"If Helen didn't so staunchly underestimate you, she might have put more effort into tracking you down rather than sending only Andrej."

Nico shook his head with a smirk. "She didn't even send him. He found me of his own accord."

"Do you think your brother will betray you?"

"I don't know. I'd like to believe some remnants of the boy I grew up with still exists within the predator he has become. He hasn't told Helen where I am. And I haven't told him why I'm here or who I'm helping."

"What does he stand to gain if he tells Helen your whereabouts?"

Nico shrugged. "He's already part of Helen's inner circle, unless my disappearance has damaged that tenuous connection. If she's lost faith in him because of me, then bringing me back would be a way to restore his status. Apart from that, I see no real benefit. She's been known to kill siblings who conspired against her. Andrej's safest option would be to let her think I'm dead. In this way, he's no longer associated with one of her stray dogs."

"We have talked, you and I, in our brief visits together. You've pitied your brother but never suggested he was ambitious in his servitude to the goddess of darkness and death." The creak of her rocking chair filled the few beats of silence between them.

"No," Nico said. "I wouldn't describe Andrej as ambitious. He does his duty out of fear and a loyalty fabricated by Helen's cruel actions. But even as we sit here and I postulate what fragments of good within him might still protect me, I can't deny the urge to warn everyone at the ranch. Parts of him loath me. My brother knows I am here, and this could present a problem for us."

"Then we'll trust your instincts and let them know at dinner. The group can decide if any action needs to be taken."

TWENTY-THREE

Olivia gave Sky a mischievous grin as they sat at the dining room table. "I told my suitcase there'll be no vacation this year. Now I'm dealing with emotional baggage."

Sky laughed. "Nice. Keep the jokes coming. I love them. Are you enjoying the ranch?"

"Yes. There are so many hills. It's so beautiful. I helped dad with the fence today. Then I brushed all the horses."

"I'm sure they loved the attention."

Nico and Will entered the dining room carrying dinner. Sky thought perhaps one of the sexiest things she might ever see was this blond-haired man in jeans fresh from cooking a wonderful smelling meal. She was especially famished after her long day of training and chores.

"Sarmale," Nico announced. "Cabbage rolls. They're stuffed with ground pork, bacon, rice, onions, tomato juice, and seasoning."

"I can smell the garlic." Anticipation lit Sky's voice as her mouth watered.

"Garlic keeps the vampires away." He winked at Olivia. "Old Romanian joke."

The girl giggled.

"Should be good." Will and Raine arrived, pouring red wine glasses. "You spent hours in the kitchen."

"Cooking is soothing," Nico said, dishing out heaps onto plates.

"That smells amazing," Bryce said. He kissed Storm's cheek as they parted to take their seats.

Conversation ensued about everyone's day as they filled their plates and ate forkfuls of Nico's entrée. Sky relaxed into the normalcy of it all, fantasizing about having her own large family around an enormous table one day. When she had children, she wanted to host every holiday.

Of course, she had to have a real fiancé before starting a family. And before that, she needed a boyfriend. So far in a house full of people with a chore and training list longer than War and Peace, she hadn't caught Nico alone yet. She could sneak into his room at night, but she wouldn't be quite that forward. Plus, most nights she was exhausted and putting her head on her pillow was her only objective.

"I've already spoken to Usha about this," Nico began, voice ringing above all the others as they quieted. "My brother Andrej visited me in the hills last night several miles from here. He tracked me to Montana. Helen doesn't know he found me, and he doesn't know the company I keep. Regardless, you should know there is danger in the little he knows and could lead to the discovery of more."

"Do we relocate?" Sky asked.

Bryce frowned. "With only a few weeks to go, where do we move a group this size and continue our training without drawing attention?" When he ran a hand over Olivia's hair, Sky felt his tendrils of worry about his daughter's safety.

"The wards are here," Raine added.

"We can set up an electronic perimeter alarm system. It's something we probably should have already done anyway," Will said.

"Won't stop a smart bomb," Storm said, glancing at Olivia as the girl ate.

Will clasped Bryce on the back. "That's what we have the magician for. And we have Storm's Spidey sense combined with Sky's ability to detect intruders."

"So, we stay?" Sky asked hopefully, not feeling any strong pull from the group to move.

"We stay," Storm confirmed.

Nico scanned the group, looking amazed, as if he'd feared his confession would lead to his eviction. Sky sent him a soft smile. For a moment, their gazes locked, and she felt that breath-taking connection they'd had their first few days together.

He started to extend a hand to her when Olivia pushed out her chair and stood, hand raising toward the ceiling.

Her eyes glazed.

"Love breaks binding bonds.
The harvest reaps blood and death.
Six shall fall marks light to call."

Olivia's eyes cleared, and she sat back down. "What's for dessert?" She looked around the table as everyone stared at her.

Bryce looked pale as he patted her hand.

"I'll get the colored pencils," Storm said.

"I'll get the ice cream." Sky hopped to her feet.

STORM ATTACKED, knives drawn. Nico dodged her swipes, amazed by her speed. He'd known she was deadly but had never actually fought her. He was grateful her "knives" were blunt wooden replicas and that he'd had as many years of fighting experience as her, even if he was a few years younger.

Several days after the cabbage dinner and Olivia's premonition, the five of them gathered for sparring. The others watched the fight. Nico had already beaten them one-on-one in escalating difficulty. These sparring sessions with the guardians enabled him to critique on weaknesses.

Bryce was quick with his lasso but needed to incorporate more illusions and his magical shield. The shield was as much offensive as defensive.

Will was fast with his gun, but Nico was faster, especially in confusing him between man and wolf form. In Will's defense, hellhounds and Midgard serpents would be the quickest creatures on the battlefield, so the FBI agent would be faster than ninety percent of the demons they faced.

Nico ducked from another swipe of Storm's knives. From his crouching position, he leaped up, changing into wolf form as he flipped over her head and snagged a muzzle full of her dark, braided hair. He kept his jaw clenched as he landed behind her, jerking her head back and landing her hard on her back. The breath whooshed out of her.

"Son of a bitch," she stammered.

Nico turned back into human form. "I'm not, actually. My parents didn't have the ability to change to wolf form." He extended a hand to help her up.

She took it, and he pulled her to her feet.

Sky clapped, making Nico feel a zing of pride.

When Storm glared at her, Sky scoffed. "Whatever. You can heal. And you've been pulverizing me for weeks, so it's only fair I get to see you knocked on your ass a few times."

Nico began his assessment, telling Storm, "You're fast and agile, which you'll have to be for close hand to hand combat with knives. Always go for the arteries and tendons. For the undead, take out the eyes and the Achilles. If they can't see you and can't walk, they're of little threat. If you can incapacitate them with your knives, move on to the next target and let Will or Raine take off their heads with their blades."

"He's beaten all of us one-on-one," Raine noted.

"I've been a predator my whole life. I've the advantage of experience."

"Four against one?" Bryce asked, a mischievous glint in his eye as he twirled his rope.

The wolf in Nico felt a surge of animalistic glee at the anticipation of a challenging fight.

"How is that fair?" Sky demanded.

"War isn't about fair," Will said.

Raine added, "It's obvious that Nico has superior skill. We need to try a scenario where we team up against a better adversary."

Even as they talked, Will, Raine, Storm, and Bryce circled Nico, who let the zinging anticipation of an exchange of might wash over him. Will held a wooden sword, Raine a wooden spear. Storm still had her wooden knives, as Bryce spun Gleipnir.

Storm lunged first, a move Nico expected because he'd dropped her on her butt only a moment ago and she would want revenge. He spun away from her as Raine jabbed forward with her blunt spear. Nico trapped it between his chest and arm.

As he pivoted, he lashed out a leg toward Will to strike his hilt as Will swiped down with his blade. The kick counteracted Will's blow and sent him stumbling back two steps.

Raine swiveled with Nico's movements in order to keep a grasp on her weapon. She freed it from Nico while he blocked another attack from Storm, but at the expense of blocking Bryce's plans to hurl the lasso. He pulled back the golden lariat before it accidentally struck her.

Will recovered quickly and advanced, sword slicing through the air. Nico crouched then sprang up, shifting to wolf form, and plowed into Storm's chest. Pushing off her, he twisted in midair to avoid a swipe from Raine and sailed through Will as he activated his Bifröst magic and became transparent for a moment.

Gold flashed before Nico's eyes as a Gleipnir cinched over his muzzle and brought him to the ground hard. A grunt whooshed out of him.

The predator in him hated to lose, but the rational man was relieved to know the Shadow Guardians worked well as a team, adapting and adjusting in battle, and could kill him if needed.

"Stop," Sky whimpered.

Will brought his sword to Nico's throat as Raine brought her spear toward his chest. Storm crowded close, ready to attack if Nico moved.

"Stop!" Sky's command came with psychic force, bringing everyone to their knees.

Nico shifted to human form, laying on the ground panting as Sky rushed to his side. "Sky, you can't—"

She looked around at the others who gaped at her with some mixture of fear and wariness in their expression. She'd hurt her family, brought them to their knees.

Tears swam in her eyes. "Oh, Frigg. I'm sorry. I'm so sorry."

"Shit." Will pushed to his feet, panting. "I'm glad she's on our side."

"I'm sorry," she repeated.

"It's okay," Raine said, voice breathless and strained. "This session was about seeing what we're capable of. You saw our powers. Now we've seen yours."

Sky chewed her lip, looking at the faces of the family she'd hurt.

Did she see their apprehension? Sense their fear? Nico wondered.

He did. He couldn't read minds, but he could see their intellects churning with the realization of the liability she might be if she interfered with the team taking down one of Helen's creatures.

Because that was exactly what Nico was.

Helen walked down the steps of her jet in her private hangar. She'd been on a whirlwind three-day trip checking on the status of her troops and ensuring all was in order. If only all her army could be housed in one location. That would've been easier on her. But hundreds of inhuman creatures would draw the attention of both human authority figures and Shadow Guardians. She had to be cautious.

Besides, some of them didn't get along in close quarters. Jotun and Fire Giants always butted heads, competing for superiority as if comparing the size of their dicks. And no one liked the stench and filth of the undead. Therefore, circumstances forced her to keep them hidden, keep them separate, and travel to their individual camps.

Andrej waited for her by the door of her limo.

Such a good dog.

If only she could ease the tension of travel by pleasuring herself with him. One day after the battle, she would. No one would question her sovereignty or authority then. Once she drained the Valkyrie of their power and took the magic for herself, she would command obedience from everyone, and all her desires could be fulfilled.

Her mood lightened, thinking of that rewarding day.

"Your queen has returned," she announced, reaching Andrej and placing a hand to his cheek.

She stopped abruptly. Rather than climb into the limo, she turned toward the hellhound in human form. His gaze was cast down—not unusual, but he had bristled under her touch, his jaw ticking.

She snatched his chin in her hand, forcing his eyes to meet hers. "You dare show me the slightest insubordination?" With some satisfaction, she noted his fear-infused expression as the icicles in her voice were on the verge of plunging into him.

"No, my queen."

"Then what is this mood of yours?"

"Nothing, my queen."

"Liar!" she snarled, moving her hand to his throat. She curled her fingers into soft flesh.

Andrej remained utterly frozen. He'd seen her rip the throat out of those who dared defy her. He would know better than to flee or fight.

"This is still about your brother?" she demanded, forcing the mental link between her and the Fenrir descendant in her grasp.

"Yes." He choked out the word.

"He lives?"

Andrej directed his gaze aside.

She curled her nails deeper around his throat where she could more easily rip it out, but without compressing his voice box entirely.

"Yes," he said.

She released him, taken aback.

Nico Wølfe lives even though he never answered my summons?

"Where is he?" She glanced at the red marks she'd left on Andrej's throat.

"The US."

"Be more specific."

"Montana."

"You know the precise location?" She wanted to rake her nails down his perfect face for making her drag the information out of him.

"Yes."

"You knew he defected, and I'm only now hearing of this? When I must force it out of you?"

"You previously indicated he was of little importance."

Pivoting, she lashed out a hand, striking him center chest. The blow sent him careening backward, across the smooth surface of the hangar.

Her temper boiled inside her. "Impertinence. You know precisely where he is?"

In obvious pain, he slowly straightened. "Yes, a ranch in Montana."

"Alone?"

"With a woman."

"Who?"

"I haven't met her. Only watched them from a distance."

"A lover?"

"I don't know the exact nature of their relationship."

In several long strides, she advanced on Andrej, had him backing into a wall.

"But you suspect." She seethed.

"Yes, I suspect they are together."

She fisted the lapels of his jacket, lifted him off the ground, and slammed him into the wall. She pinned him there as her gaze bore into him.

"I want Nico dead. Do you understand me? No one defies me. No one. Take a Fire Giant. The biggest. Kill Nico and the woman he's with."

Because the outrage still burned within her, she hurled Andrej across the room. He slid across the smooth floor before violently colliding with the wheels of the jet.

Helen turned, straightened her shirt and blouse, then walked calmly to the limousine. She didn't have time to waste on one wolf, but she wouldn't have him make a mockery of her either. Nor could she allow Nico's freedom from her spread ideas of disobedience among the other Fenrir descendants.

TWENTY-FOUR

That night, Sky approached Nico as he did pull-ups in the barn. She had finished her training and chores and managed a little energy left for her scheme. She wore a sleeveless blue shirt with a flaring slate skirt and sandals.

Nico was shirtless, glistening with sweat, and looking good enough to eat. This view topped the sight of him after cooking dinner. She'd been drooling over him since the first day they'd met, and although she couldn't read his mind, she'd caught a few licentious glances her way. Her discussions with Raine and Bryce had helped reinforce Nico's likely interest in her.

Time to woman-up.

They'd had attraction and chemistry from the start, but she'd allowed their relationship to linger in limbo far too long. She'd never been one to wait for the perfect moment. She liked to seize the opportunity herself, but Nico was different. He had wanted her to back off and she had.

Today, however, seeing him pinned to the ground by the Shadow Guardians brought flashes of the battle to mind. Life was too short and too fragile for unspoken and physically unexpressed emotions.

Tonight, she would speak and express everything building inside her since meeting Nico.

Because she couldn't outright hear his thoughts and feelings for her, she wouldn't know if she was pushing too hard or not hard enough. This was unfamiliar territory for her.

Exciting territory.

And because he would clearly never make the first move, the task clearly fell to her. When he dropped to the ground, she stood very close to him.

"Uh, hey." He glanced around the empty barn.

Hoping they were alone or looking for a way out? She wasn't sure.

"You've got this place looking amazing." She put her hands on her hips as she surveyed the interior, admiring the fresh paint, organization, and cleanliness. Summoning her resolve, she moved closer. "I like you, Nico. I'd like to kiss you."

Although he backed away to retreat, the heated look in his eyes conveyed a different message. She grinned as she continued to advance toward him, backing him into a structural beam.

"Kiss me," she whispered. She placed a hand on his chest and arched toward him so he wouldn't have to go far to meet her lips.

"Sky." His voice came out breathless as his hands wrapped around her bare arms, calloused palms scraping lightly against her skin.

They were so close that she could feel the rise and fall of his chest. She couldn't tell if he would pull her closer or push her away, as he seemed to battle with his desires. Her pride took a hit at his reluctance to kiss her immediately, but she didn't back down. Something held him back, and she suspected it was his curse and the trauma of having been ruled by Helen, not a lack of desire for her.

"Kiss me," Sky repeated.

As he pulled her against him, he unleashed a rumble, something like a surrendering growl. Finally, his lips touched hers, shredding the last of his hesitation.

His arms held her steady as tongues explored. The kiss became the focal point of her entire world, all of which silenced around her. His mouth was warm, soft, tantalizing, with an edge of raw hunger. A prelude to what would come next.

More.

She had to have more.

Kissing him deeper, she tried to convey her feelings and desires for him.

"What the hell are you doing?" Storm's voice cut through the silence like Heimdall's blade through flesh.

Sky spun, ready to unleash a few choice words at her sister's intrusion, when she realized Storm was glaring at Nico.

"I'm sorry," he told Storm. He looked stricken and ashamed, like she'd caught him stealing her knives.

Sky stepped back as if physically slapped. Surprise and hurt flared almost immediately to anger.

The hell with that.

He'd better not be sorry for kissing her. Not with a kiss so magical it seemed to suspend space and time.

"Excuse me," Sky snapped at the two of them, heat rising into her cheeks.

Storm stalked closer, pointing a finger at Nico. "I warned you."

"I know," he said.

The combination of Storm ignoring her and Nico's recalcitrant behavior had Sky wanting to tear into both of them.

"Hey," she barked, shoving a hand into Storm's shoulder to remind her she was standing right there. "I kissed him. So back off."

Storm turned a pair of blazing purple eyes on her. "Don't you understand what he is? You can't have a relationship with him."

Nico looked away, dejected.

Well, he's no help.

"I can have a relationship with whomever I damn well choose," Sky said.

"He's Fenrir bloodline. They are Hel's hounds, which means he answers to the goddess of darkness herself. When we fight the battle, he'll be on the losing side."

"I know that." Sky's stomach twisted as she clenched her teeth. She knew, though hearing it out loud was like a punch to the gut.

Nico still said nothing. Nothing about what the kiss meant to him and nothing in defense of how he needed to be here, had a purpose here.

Irritated, Sky spun toward him. "Can you excuse us, please?"

When he left the barn, slinking away like a scorned animal, she whirled on her sister, asking the question she'd wanted to know since Nico's first confession at being a spy. "Explain how someone you don't trust is in charge of protecting me?"

Storm took a deep breath. "Nico's been loyal to the Council for years. He gives us information on Helen's activities. He works for her but hates his forced subjugation enough to risk his life and her wrath in betraying her. I trust him to the extent of activities we assign him. I specifically told him to leave you alone. Emotionally."

Sky put her hands on her hips. "That's not an order you can give."

Storm shook her head. "Don't waste your feelings caring about him. He will rip your throat out on the battlefield because he must."

Sky backed into a wooden support beam, taking the news like another blow and gulping for air. She knew the reality of her sister's words, understood them, but the presentation was so vivid. Why did Storm always have to be so blunt?

"For the record, you are the one who insisted he stay and come with us to Montana." Storm pursed her lips as if in disbelief. "I saw the attraction, but you're a freaking clairvoyant. I thought I didn't have to worry about you falling for him since you could read him and would know what he's capable of."

"I can't read him. At. All." Sky wrapped arms around her knotting stomach. "It has been wonderful."

Storm rubbed her temple. "I didn't realize that. Wait." She paced. "If you can't read him, can you affect his mind?"

"No."

"Do you realize how vulnerable that makes you? You can't stop him telepathically if he comes after you. And you're not doing him any favors by encouraging him to have feelings for you. He will know what he's doing and hate himself and blame himself for not stopping. Odin help us. If Helen gets inside his head on that battlefield, she may learn just how valuable you are to him. You can become even more a target than you already are. A relationship can only hurt both of you."

Sky's chest squeezed. As little as breathing became a struggle. She didn't want to cause Nico pain, but her feelings were what they were.

"I love him."

"Dammit," Storm said on an exhale.

"Thanks for your support," she grumbled.

"Don't do this to yourself."

"I know how I feel. And you know what?" Tears flowed now, hot and unstoppable. Sky pushed a hand into her stomach, but that didn't stop the tidal wave of emotions. "If his fate is to fight for evil against his own will, then who in this world needs more love? I bet he's been an outcast his whole life with this curse hanging over him. Guess what? I know how that feels."

"Sky—"

She stepped back from the sympathy Storm radiated and wiped at her eyes. "No. It sucks to know exactly what people think of you and have no control. This is my choice. I'm going to show him love and compassion and forgiveness for things he was forced to do or will be forced to do in the future. My choice."

She marched out of the barn, cheeks burning and heart squeezing so hard she thought it might implode.

A hand grasped her forearm. "Okay, Sky," Storm said, "I just wanted to protect you. I'm sorry. I didn't mean to be so controlling. If you need to see these feelings through, see them through." Her sister pulled her into a hug.

"I need to be with him," Sky said, reining her sobs back under control. She pulled away and sniffed. "It's actually been refreshing to try to interpret him based on body language and nuances without automatically knowing what he's thinking—what's inside." She wondered now if Fenrir's bloodline or Helen's control of him blocked her, but that was a discovery to make some other time.

"Okay, well. Go get him, Sunshine. Go find out what's inside." Storm wiped away a tear on Sky's cheek and winked at her despite the worry in her eyes.

Nico left the barn and showered, still dizzy from the intoxicating kiss and reeling from Sky's dismissal of him. He should probably pack his bags and leave. He'd overstayed his welcome, and with the battle so close it was probably best he leave them to finish preparations without him.

He'd finished wrapping himself in a towel when Sky burst through the bathroom door with an expectant look on her face. Her red hair framed a pair of flushed cheeks and brilliant blue eyes. Blue eyes circled with red. She'd been crying. He felt like a complete jerk.

"I'm sorry," Nico said.

This is the end, he thought.

The inevitable moment when he would lose everything of value to him. Happiness with the Shadow Guardians and Sky had been a brief respite from the cruelty of a life he had no control over. Storm had probably convinced her that sending him packing was the right thing to do. She wasn't wrong.

Bile rose in his throat as he braced for Sky's wrath. Even though she couldn't read his thoughts, he wondered if she could bring him to his knees with a psychic blow. Of course she could. Even without using her power, one dejected look from her and he would fall to the floor and beg forgiveness.

"I hope you're apologizing for your meekness and not for that kiss," she snapped with an edge of playfulness.

"What?"

Her expression softened. "Put down this unbelievable burden you've been carrying around. You are one of us. One of the six. Even Storm knows this." Sky walked up to him, wrapping her arms around him. "I don't want to lose you."

He shook his head and shrank back from her, resisting the urge to hug her back, knowing it would only hurt more when he had to let go. "You're not understanding. You never had me. Our entire relationship is a sham, and not just because we aren't really engaged."

Part of him wanted the anger he deserved. Her eyes held far too much forgiveness he hadn't earned.

"What I feel is real," her voice was all soft compassion, despite his harsh words.

He couldn't bear it. "It isn't," he growled out the words.

She smiled with a caring expression that said she didn't have to read his mind because she knew him well enough to see his turmoil. "There's pain behind your frustration, Nico. You can push me away if that's what's easier for you to do, knowing you'll be forced to betray me and my family. You didn't have to help us, but you did. You didn't have to protect me and train me, but you did. I didn't have to fall in love with you, but I did."

"You... you can't," he stammered, head spinning at her words.

What had he done? He would only cause her more pain if she loved him. And if Helen ever found out...

"Was your assignment to seduce me?" she asked.

"No!" he barked.

"Then what I feel for you is because I know the real you. Your compassion. Your humor. Your work ethic. Your cooking skills. Heavenly cooking skills." She laid a hand on his bare chest. "I know what's in here."

His breath hitched. "That's not a good idea."

"Why? Because you'll be called to serve Helen soon? All the more reason to prove my love. I want you to know it's real, and it's there for you even when we're standing on opposite sides of the battlefield."

He gripped her hands firmly to prevent their migration lower. Her touch and her compassion were too much. "Sky." He managed in a warning tone even as he was already aroused by her.

"No means no," she said. "If you don't want to make love to me, I'll stop touching you. If you have any feelings for me, for us, then you'll help me make tonight incredible. But I won't wake up to regret tomorrow, and I couldn't bear it if you did."

"What you're asking—" He exhaled but didn't push away this time.

"I love you." The words rushed out of her. "I don't need to hear it back, and if a terrible curse means our time ends in Iceland, then I'm going to greedily take everything until then. Unless it isn't what you want. If you say no, I'll back off."

Her unyielding gaze, shining with longing and passion, emphasized the truth she spoke.

"Yes. I want you." He crushed his mouth to hers, tasting her soft, hungry lips. His hands roamed under her shirt over the warm, delicate skin of her back.

When he buried his face in her hair to kiss her neck, she smelled of strawberries and honeysuckle like the first time he'd met her. Like summer. He felt intoxicated. Bewitched.

When she broke the kiss to nibble his ear, he moaned and pushed against her. To his delight, she matched his desires with her own hungry kisses. She was shedding her clothing even as he carried her into her bedroom with her legs wrapped around his waist.

She gasped when he dropped her on the bed, but then was quick to discard the rest of her clothing.

As he slid his towel off, he drank in the sight of her pale skin and long red hair by the moonlight. "You are so beautiful."

With a hungry gaze, she stared back at him, biting her lip.

He bent over to cup her breasts and kiss her again. Her hands gripped his shoulders as she groaned in his mouth with heated urgency.

He took the emotional plunge—heart and soul. He gave all of himself over to this amazing woman, although he suspected he already had during his days of watching over her from a distance. Running his hands over her smooth skin, he loved the way her breath hitched under his touch.

If fate doomed him to fight for Helen, he would surrender to his feelings for Sky now. He could pour love into her—a lifetime's worth —that he couldn't give her later. Perhaps on the battlefield, when he was called to cross to Helen's side, his heart would be filled with such love for Sky that it would simply burst in his chest. He could die instantly and never have to fight against the woman he loved or the new family he'd found in her sisters and brothers.

He stroked and licked and caressed until Sky was a writhing ball of sensual groans. Until she climaxed under the touch of his fingers and tongue.

"Nico."

At his name, spoken with desire and need, something primal pulsed through him. The wolf rose to the surface. He flipped her onto her stomach and drove into her, taking even as he lost himself to her and her throaty words of encouragement.

Every stroke fulfilled a ferocious desire he'd had since the moment he'd met her. He held her close with every thrust until the world burst in light and decadent ecstasy.

TWENTY-FIVE

Sky floated in a nebulous sea of exquisite pleasure as her eyes focused on her surroundings and the soft bed beneath her. Twice, the man had brought her to an earth-shaking orgasm and over the brink. She'd never experienced such bliss.

"Forgive me," Nico choked.

Turning over, she focused on his face as she lay in his arms. "For what?" He'd only given her the best sex of her life.

He ran a hand over the neck muscle extending toward her shoulder blade.

The tender skin was marked where he'd bitten down as he held in her place for his orgasm. She'd barely registered the pain in the heat of the moment, and her own second sublime release had shortly followed.

"It's fine. It'll heal," she said.

She realized he couldn't even bring himself to look at her. With a hand lifting his chin, she faced his gaze to hers. "That was amazing."

Later, she could ponder how amazing meant she would be that much more devastated when he was torn away from her to serve his master. Right now, she needed to wipe away his look of regret and uncertainty.

"Did you hear me screaming '*yes*'? Because I'm pretty sure the entire house did."

"I've never lost control like that. I was rough."

"Passionate," she corrected. "And at no point did I feel threatened by you."

"I shouldn't have bitten you."

"Do you hear me complaining? Next time, I'll bite you, and then we'll be even." She gave him a wry smile as she wriggled her naked body against his. When she felt his arousal stir, she knew her reassurance was sinking in. "Besides, it's not like your bite will turn me into a werewolf, right?"

"No," he said with a chuckle. The tension in his beautiful face eased.

"So, we're good. Great, in fact." She pressed a kiss to his lips.

He kissed her slowly before drawing back. His hands slid lower, caressing as they moved along her bare skin.

"This time," he whispered. "I'll go slower and give you the attention you deserve."

She lay back on the bed, offering herself up with a smile. "Variety is the spice of life."

Nico stirred as sunlight streamed through the bedroom window. Sky lay against him, bare skin to bare skin. Her hair spread along her back in a tangled web of sunrise colors. Sharing a bed with this woman one night, it would never be enough. He'd given her everything he had, emptied himself, mind and body, into her.

She ran a hand along his torso, stopping at scars as if taking inventory. "I've been wondering how you joined me in my dream walk?"

"I have a sensitive sense of smell. The marijuana you smoked must have affected me almost as much as you. I joined your dream until you vanished to Iceland or the imaginary vision you described. I'd heard the stories of Helen's interference in Raine and Storm's dream walk. I was terrified I would lose you."

His phone chimed. He reached over and glanced at it in case it was Will or Bryce or one of the women telling him it was time he and Sky tended their chores.

Instead, it was Andrej texting, *She hunts for you.*

Nico tensed but set the phone back down.

"I hate thinking of everything Helen put you through." Sky hadn't seen the message but seemed to sense his sudden discomfort.

His mouth curved with a slight smile. "I gave her hell on every assignment, undermining her whenever I could." His smile faded at the memory of how he'd acquired some of those scars the Valkyrie touched. "Sky, I have killed people. People who didn't deserve to die."

"You're blaming yourself when you're the victim here. You can't change what she forced you to do. You can only change what you will do next."

"You should also know my brother will probably be on that battlefield fighting for Helen. Fighting with unprecedented wrath because of his feelings of being betrayed by me. And all the hate he carries for himself."

"Hate for what Helen forces him to do?"

"For what he has done." He brushed aside a strand of hair on her face, already regretting what he was about to tell her but feeling compelled to share part of his sordid past. "We knew at a young age we would be forced to serve Helen one day. She gathered a pack of us, as children, took us into the woods, and forced us to bow to her in the snow—a demonstration of how weak we are in the face of her force. She made all of us turn into our wolf form. Some of us for the first time. After that, we returned to our families, but our parents never treated us the same. They distanced themselves, and Andrej and I became closer."

Sky shifted her weight so she could look up at him while he told the story. The story of his broken life.

"We weren't called back to Helen until several years later. I was already planting subversive thoughts in Andrej's mind. Ways we could avoid Helen or outsmart her. We were a team back then, in grade school. But one night we arrived home after rugby practice to find Helen holding our parents prisoner. She said it was time to witness how fully we would do her bidding." Every muscle in his body tensed as he relived the nightmare. He'd told no one the story, never thought he would. But he wanted Sky to know all of him.

She threaded her fingers into his.

"Helen forced Andrej to change into his wolf form and kill our parents. He killed his own parents at her command." He took a shaky breath. "I lost my parents and my brother that day. With his will fully shattered, he gave himself over to her control, even when she wasn't directly ordering him. He's hated me ever since. I don't know if it's because she forced him and not me, while *I* was the one plotting to betray her. I don't know if it was because I failed him. I gave him false hope for all those years that we would find a way out from under her."

Sky's soothing fingertips stroked up and down his arm. She said nothing, but the comfort of her presence lifted a weight off him. Every time he shared a part of himself, he braced for judgment and rejection from Sky, but he only ever received understanding and now, somehow, love.

"Andrej left to work for Helen, and I used our inheritance to finish my education. Mostly to honor my parents, who had always wanted us to have a degree. After university, Helen called on me more and more, which made a steady job impossible. Soon, I was fully in her employment and seeing more of Andrej. His anger toward me has never relented."

"You've been through so much hardship, Nico. I wish I could wash away the pain for you. You're not alone anymore. You don't have to bear it alone." She stretched up and pressed a kiss to his lips.

Soft and sweet—a taste of what a life with her would be like. A life he couldn't have.

He placed a light kiss just below her ear. "You have been. Time spent with you eases all the pain. Running helps as well. Would you be terribly offended if I went for a run?"

She smiled. "Only if you're not terribly offended if I don't join you."

He chuckled, knowing she hated those daily cardiovascular workouts. "Of course not." He slid out of bed, pulling on a pair of boxers and an undershirt.

"Are you planning to run in your wolf form?"

"Yes."

"Does it hurt to change?"

"No. Early on, the transformation was slow and painful. Each time became faster, until it was instantaneous and painless."

"Can I watch you change?" she asked, voice coaxingly sweet, as if she was asking to watch him make breakfast shirtless. "The transformation is so fast. I noticed that when you were fighting Storm. I expected contortions and bones reshaping. Clothes tearing. Howling."

He cocked his head to one side. "You've watched too many werewolf movies."

"Yeah, yeah." She laughed, scooting to the end of the bed.

He transformed. Man one instant, large white wolf the next.

A wide smile lit her lovely face. She reached toward him and sank fingers into his fur. "And your clothes just become part of you?"

He nodded. Clothes and anything he was holding. He could switch from man to wolf holding a knife, and when he transformed back to man, he'd still be holding the blade.

Nico relished her touch. He'd never shown a woman his wolf form. Now, a beautiful, naked woman was stroking him.

She cupped his face, staring adoringly in his eyes. "Go run, Nico. I love you."

He changed back into human form, pocketed his phone, and kissed her goodbye.

ONCE OUT OF THE HOUSE, Nico sprinted, claws tearing into the dry ground and whipping over his face. Above, the moon drooped in a backdrop of pale blue morning sky above the rising sun, mocking him. What was he but a pale, practically translucent thing hovering in Sky's life, looking out of place in her bright magnificence?

All because he was owned, body and soul, by the most ruthless woman on earth.

Helen.

Pushing harder, his lungs and legs burned.

He had love, though. Some comfort could be found knowing he was capable of love, even though Helen would rip that away from him soon.

The vibration of his phone ringing had him turning back into human form. Withdrawing it from the pocket of his shorts, he answered Andrej's call.

"Hello?"

"So, you live."

Nico jolted at the bitter sound of a woman's voice. "Helen."

"How does it feel to betray your queen?"

"Righteous," he said harshly.

"I command you to return to me."

He felt no power in her words. No compulsion to obey.

"I command you to go to hell."

"Insolent—"

Heart thudding in his chest, he disconnected the call and powered down the phone. If she had Andrej's phone and this number he'd given only to his brother, Nico couldn't take the chance she might trace him using his mobile.

If she has Andrej's phone, what's happened to him?

Nico's stomach soured.

She hunts for you, Andrej's warning had read.

Transforming back to wolf, he ran again toward home. Toward family.

He tried to recall the last time Helen had commanded him. The last time she'd demanded a report from him.

Before Sky.

He skidded to a stop, mind churning.

Since the car accident, he hadn't heard from Helen. Not once. Not even a whisper. He was past due to report to her, and yet she hadn't lashed out at him. All this time, he'd thought perhaps it was the power of the sisters, some magic veil against Helen. That, or she'd assumed he was dead, as his brother had mentioned.

With all her power and resources, she hadn't reconnected with Nico. Hadn't found him, physically or telepathically.

He thought of the prophecy.

Love breaks binding bonds. Olivia's phrase had struck him as odd because he thought of love as something to build bonds. What if love broke *evil* bonds? What if it severed the hold Helen had over him?

If love had broken his bonds, could he stand by Sky's side on the battlefield?

Panting, he lifted his muzzle to the sky and unleashed a long, therapeutic howl. He began loping, a slow enough pace he wouldn't be exhausted or winded when he reached the house.

Nico considered what he knew about the other wolves. Orphans. Loners. Those who'd had loving families had lost them tragically.

Isolated.

If they hadn't been, Helen had made them so. They couldn't be allowed to have families because the love in such a unit would break the bond of wolf and she-demon.

Nico had a future with Sky after all.

CHAPTER
TWENTY-SIX

Sky dressed for the day in yoga pants and a t-shirt. She brushed the impossible tangles out of her hair, smiling at the memory of the lovemaking that had put them there.

She threw open the curtain and stared out at the expansive prairie and pale blue sky. The world felt new and bright. Hardships lay in wait ahead, but she wouldn't think about the future today. Only the present.

She bounded down the stairs and joined Usha in making breakfast. Raine and Storm were already seated at the bar counter, coffee mugs in hand.

"Is that going to be a nightly offense? If so, I'll need to invest in noise canceling headphones." Storm sipped her coffee.

"Whatever," Sky scoffed. "Like you and Bryce have been quiet every night."

Storm narrowed her eyes at Sky.

"You look really happy," Raine noted.

"Uh, yeah. That was only the most amazing night of my life." She sighed. "You know, when he trans—"

"I do not need details," Storm interjected.

"I want details," Raine said.

Usha tended to the eggs without looking up, as if wishing she couldn't hear their conversation.

Sky laughed. "I wasn't going to give details about sex. I was going to—" she stopped, following her sister's gaze to the back door where Nico stood.

He wore shorts, a t-shirt, and a broad smile. Something was different, like a weight had been lifted. He took several long strides, wrapped her in his arms, and spun her in a circle.

"Well, hello to you, too!" She laughed.

"I'm free." He set her back down and framed her face in his hands, staring into her eyes. "I'm free of Helen." He planted a kiss on her cheek before spinning around to face Usha.

He held Sky's hand as he said, "Olivia's prophecy says love breaks bonds. It's broken my bond with Helen, hasn't it?" He glanced back at Storm and Raine. "I haven't been summoned since I met Sky. Not even an inkling of Helen's connection. Now, I defied her openly when she called my phone. I'd thought before now it was perhaps some magic of the Valkyrie, but it's broken. Truly broken." He turned back to Usha as if looking for confirmation.

"What you propose makes sense," the elderly woman said, scraping scrambled eggs onto plates. "No man or animal can serve two masters. If love is your master, darkness cannot be."

"Three by three," Storm interjected. "Six of us are together on that battlefield. I'm sorry I doubted you."

Her relieved voice had Sky's senses delving deeper, feeling the conversation surface in Storm's mind she'd had with Nico about ending his life when he became a threat to her family. Sky shuddered away from the cold memory that wasn't hers.

"It feels right," Sky said. "It feels like we're complete."

Raine walked over and hugged Nico. "Welcome to the family."

Bryce and Will entered through the back door, stomping boots and pulling off gloves. By appearances, they had been out feeding and watering the horses.

"What are we celebrating?" Bryce asked.

"Nico is joining us." Sky couldn't stop the giddy smile stretching across her face.

Bryce arched an eyebrow in puzzlement. "Hasn't he already?"

"Officially out from under Helen's influence," Raine said.

"Officially on our side," Storm added.

"We need a real celebration," Sky declared, spinning jubilantly in a circle.

The men shook hands with Nico.

"How'd that happen?" Will asked.

Nico smiled at Sky. "I have a new family."

"Does this mean the two of you actually are engaged now?" Bryce asked with a wink.

Nico's throat bobbed in a swallow.

Sky chuckled to break the sudden awkwardness. "He never actually asked me the first time," she joked.

To her surprise, Nico dropped to one knee, grinning like a fool.

She laughed as heat rose into her cheeks. "Stop. You're ridiculous." When his expression turned intense, she put a hand to her chest. "Oh, Frigg. You're serious?" Her heart fluttered, climbing into her throat.

"Sky Thoren, you are master of my heart. I would marry you in an instant if you'd have me." He added in a loud whisper, "If you give me a little more time, I can make this more romantic. Or I can back off altogether."

Tears filled and spilled from her eyes. "I can't think of a more memorable engagement than all of us together. Yes, I will marry you."

SKY AND NICO borrowed Usha's truck to pick up supplies in town. Sky wanted a spread of meats, cheeses, and wine for the celebration tonight.

Nico tuned the radio. "What music do you like?"

Keeping one hand on the wheel in mock shock, she clutched the other to her heart. "Ah. At last. Something you don't know about me."

"I know you play country music in your store, but I didn't want to presume."

"I like country, but, yes, it's in my store all day more for the customers. Because I hear it all day in the store, I don't listen to it any other time. I like a variety. Jazz for relaxing. Classic rock for cleaning the house. Alternative rock for parties. Classical piano for working in the garden."

"How's this?" he asked.

"Walking the Wire" by Imagine Dragons played.

"Perfect."

They rode in comfortable lack of conversation, enjoying the music with Sky loving the normalcy of a couple driving to the store for shopping together. She tried to recall if she'd ever gone shopping with one of her boyfriends. Nope. Maybe this wasn't normal, but it felt good.

"You seem happy," Nico said.

"I'm enjoying a truck ride with my fiancé, Storm's not beating me to a pulp in training, and I'm not cleaning bathrooms."

She parked the truck in the lot of an Albertsons, and they walked into the store together. Once inside, he pushed the cart and she filled it. They discussed wines, a topic on which he seemed well-versed, having sampled a variety from around the world during his travels. She tried to gauge how he felt about shopping with her.

"What?" he asked.

"What?"

"You're staring."

"I'm shopping with a gorgeous man who is also my fiancé. Am I not allowed to stare?" At his head cocked to one side, she added, "Okay." She fidgeted with a plastic perishables bag. "This isn't mundane for you?"

"What do you mean?"

She lowered her voice. "You're a shapeshifting wolf. A fighter. Grocery shopping is…"

"Relaxing," he finished for her.

"Not beneath you?"

He chuckled. "No. Believe me when I say I welcome any activity resembling everyday life. Bonus points if I get to be with you." He wrapped an arm around her. "I'm a warrior by necessity and force, not preference." Releasing her, he placed a Cabernet in the cart beside a block of Gouda. "Anyway. Shouldn't I be asking the Valkyrie who can commune with the gods if grocery shopping is beneath her?"

"Ha. I'm just lil' ol' me."

"Little you taking on Helen herself."

Sky's cheeks flushed.

They made their way through self-checkout in assembly-line style. Yup, she could get used to shopping and living with the man.

After they loaded groceries in the truck, she slid into the driver's seat.

"There is a jewelry shop just down the road," Nico said. "We could peruse their ring selection."

"I—"

Dark thoughts clouded into Sky's brain.

Money. Money. Money.

She usually tuned out background thoughts from the general population, most of which had to do with running errands, fixations on using the bathroom, or work or relationship stress.

Fight. Watch them bleed.

"What's wrong?" Nico asked.

The way he always seemed in tune with her feelings amazed her. She reached over and held his hand for reassurance as she scanned the parking lot for the source of the violent perseverating thoughts.

There, her focus narrowed.

A man carrying a fifty-pound bag of dog food over one shoulder and a grocery bag in the other hand walked toward his pickup truck. As he climbed into his vehicle, Sky started her engine.

"That man. Green truck. I think maybe he's trafficking. I'm sensing cages and a thirst for violence. Let's follow him."

"Okay."

She put the truck in gear and followed the man's vehicle out of the parking lot. "Just okay? No words of caution? No frustration at the detour?"

"The purpose of the Shadow Guardians is to protect people. If you think someone's in danger, then we should investigate."

"But you aren't cautioning me about the danger we could encounter."

"I've seen what you can do with a bow and arrow, which you are currently wearing." He glanced down at the leather wrapping around her wrists.

"Okay. Let's do this."

He raised a finger in the air. "But when we get home, you'll be the one to explain to Storm why her mint chocolate chip ice cream is melted, not me."

Sky chuckled. "No problem. I'll take the heat on that one."

With Ed Sheeran singing about bad habits on the radio, Sky tailed the man to a gravel driveway where she was forced to drive past so she wouldn't alert him to her surveillance.

Nico cut the music and rolled down his window to breathe deeply as they cruised. "Find a place to park, and we'll double back on foot." He glanced down at the sandals she wore.

"My feet will be fine. What did you smell? You're scowling."

"Animals. Concentrated fur and feces."

"Cows? Horses?" They were in Montana, after all.

"Predators. But I'm too far away for much else."

She pulled off the side of the road in the lot of a small, abandoned gas station and glanced down at her own shoes. "How far is too far with your super snout?"

"Less than half a mile."

"Okay. That's doable." Blisters would heal.

They walked to the long drive where the man had maneuvered his truck. Nico lifted his nose to the air and sniffed deeply. He scrutinized the lanky trees and tall grass, making Sky wonder if he was looking for cameras, motion detectors, or just noting that someone didn't want this place seen from the road.

Nico frowned, as if contemplating a difficult decision. "I don't suppose if I asked you—pretty please with a strawberry on top—you would wait in the car?"

She smiled sweetly up at him. "That would be contrary to all the compliments you've been giving me about how amazing I'm doing with my training."

"I could shift to wolf form and make that run pretty quickly. Then return and report what I find."

She scowled at him, not wanting to separate.

"If it makes you feel any better—" he looked down at her sandals and back up to her eyes "—I'm not questioning your fighting abilities, just speed."

She put her hands on her hips. "I'm not sure that makes me feel better."

"I have another idea." He rubbed a hand over his jaw. "I've never tried this before, but you've seen that my clothing stays with me in wolf form, as do weapons. I'm told shapeshifters can also choose to take humans and animals into them."

She looked him up and down. "Into you? Where do I go exactly?"

"I can't explain the physics of it. And like I said, I've never tried with a person. My brother did it once when he was saving a mate. They were outnumbered by a hubble gang in an alley. Andrej wrapped his arms around his friend, changed to wolf form, and fled both of them out of danger."

"It won't be like that movie *The Fly* I saw with my parents once?" At Nico's blank look, she added, "Jeff Goldblum in the teleportation device?" She sighed. "Anyway, it's an old eighties movie where a fly gets into his device. They mix DNA, and he turns into a gigantic fly. It's as disgusting as you might imagine it would be."

Nico blinked at her. "You won't turn into a gigantic fly."

She smacked him on the arm but couldn't help smiling. "That wasn't what I meant."

He chuckled. "I've not heard of any situations where magic or DNA was transferred in the process. But if you're uncomfortable with the idea, we'll simply walk to wherever the scents take me."

She rolled her eyes at his obvious impatience with the situation.

"Fine. We'll try it your way, especially because there's melting ice cream at stake."

He wrapped his arms around her and shifted. One instant she was staring at his blond hair and the next instant she was eye level with the tall grass she'd been standing in.

Wow, this is amazing.

I can hear you. Nico's deep voice reverberated around her weightless, incorporeal self.

I can hear you, too!

You're good then? he asked.

Show me what you got, furball.

He took off at a sprint, and the sensation was almost indescribable. When she rode horses, the wind in her hair and the feel of the animal's torso beneath her made her feel powerful. With Nico, she was like particles along for the ride but could still feel the speed and wind.

You're fast! That's a fence. Whoa, whoa! Fence!

He never slowed as he majestically vaulted over the barbwire.

Wow. Just wow.

When they came to a rectangular structure of sheet metal, Nico slowed and crouched down in the tall grass. A hundred yards from the structure was a two-story home with white panels in need of painting. Lifting his snout to the air, he sniffed several times.

What do you smell?

Dogs.

Okay. I can see how that could be a kennel. So that affects my human trafficking theory. But he could be stopping here, at his home, feed the dogs before he goes out to do his dirty deeds.

Dirty deeds? Nico asked.

You know what I mean.

Nico cocked his head to one side, ears perked.

What is it? She was pretty sure she sounded like she was whispering although there was clearly no need to because their communication was telepathic.

Whimpering. Like suffering.

We need to get inside that shed right now.

TWENTY-SEVEN

Nico approached the structure. Closer to the corrugated metal walls, the smell of concentrated urine and feces grew stronger, making his nose twitch. And another smell. Blood, not the faint fragrance of an animal in heat or the over-powering coppery waft of fresh blood, but the pungent odor of dried blood. Old wounds.

When they reached the door on one end, it was slightly ajar with a padlock hanging loose. From inside, the whines of animals mixed with shuffling noises, perhaps their owner. After glancing around the exterior once for any signs of danger, Nico shifted back to human form.

Sky wobbled on her feet for a moment as she blinked. "Whoa. Head rush."

He placed a finger over his lips before pointing it toward the crack in the door. Her eyes widened as she pursed her lips, heeding his look of caution.

When he glanced at her vambraces, she immediately recognized his signal and raised her left arm. The majestic golden bow appeared. Taking a step back from the door, she pulled an arrow from her quiver and nocked it.

Odin, help me, this woman is dazzling and calm under pressure. Nico was falling more in love with her every day.

When she nodded her readiness, he grabbed the door, swung it open, and pivoted. The stench hit him first, overpowering, to say the least. The sight of caged and injured animals sickened him. His vision turned red with fury as he focused on the man at the far end, scooping dog food into bowls.

When a low growl escaped Nico's throat, all the animals silenced and turned to look at him. Some scampered to the corner of their cages while others stood at attention.

"Money and fighting," Sky began in a quiet, seething voice. "Not human trafficking, but dog trafficking. Dog fighting. Sweet Jesus." She raised her voice. "What kind of sick asshole are you?"

The man spun around in surprise, dropping a bowl of dog food he was holding. Some of the kibble rolled under the chain-link fence of the nearest pen, and the caged animal scarfed the small pieces.

Nico's chest rose and fell in heart-pounding rage. His throat constricted as he resisted the urge to change back to wolf form and rip this man's throat out.

The man scowled. "This is private property. I can shoot you."

"Only if you think you can draw a gun faster than my arrow lands in your chest."

Sky's remarkably calm voice tugged Nico off the precipice of losing control. He blinked to focus on the surrounding room. All the animals watched the exchange, alert and sensing danger. Nico looked at the different breeds—husky, pit bull, boxer, and even a wolf.

Sky rolled one shoulder. "Now, you're going to stay right there while we alert our FBI friends to your criminal activity."

The sound of boots crunching on the grass outside the structure had Nico spinning around.

"Hey, Arnie—"

Before the newly arriving man had a chance to register the intruders, Nico took offensive action. He grabbed the man by his flannel shirt—unbuttoned and draped over a t-shirt—and yanked it down around his arms, trapping them to his side, while simultaneously whipping his neck forward and head-butting the man.

The man stumbled back, but Nico kept his hold and dragged him into the kennel, slamming him against one of the chain-link doors. He squirmed, but Nico held him firm.

Arnie, obviously thinking he would use the distraction in his favor, had reached around his backside, presumably for a gun. Having completely trusted Nico to deal with the other man, Sky's gaze had never left Arnie. When he'd made his move, she had fired an arrow into the latch of the pen closest to the dog owner. The latch dropped open, and the animal inside instantly darted out, focusing his attention on his owner and snarling viciously.

Sky readied another arrow. "You pull out that gun, and I'll have him latch his teeth onto your balls faster than you can spell Mississippi."

The animal looked ready to spring at a moment's notice. Eyes wide with fear, Arnie looked down at the angry animal.

Nico gaped at Sky. "Fight-trained dogs fear their trainers and wouldn't attack. Is this you?"

"Yes. They're terrified, but I asked them for their help."

He gritted his teeth through a wave of nausea. "Don't. Please don't influence them. You don't know what it's like to have your actions dictated to you. Don't turn them into human aggressors when they're not."

Her face went pale. "Okay. I'm sorry. I didn't think—"

The dog turned and went back to his pen.

She swallowed. "I summoned Will. He's on his way."

An hour later, Sky stored away the groceries as Storm poured ice cream out of the carton and into a glass.

"Those poor animals were scared and hurting. You should've seen the look on Nico's face. I thought he was going to lose his shit, and then how were we going to explain that to authorities? I guess if he took a bite out of crime in his wolf form, we could've gotten away with saying the men were attacked by their own dogs. Except, apparently, they're trained to be terrified of their owners and wouldn't attack."

Like Helen, Sky thought.

That whole incident must have been one big triggering event for Nico, but he'd kept control. She'd felt awful when she realized he must have seen her control of the dog to face Arnie as a parallel to Helen giving hellhounds orders.

She had summoned Raine and Will telepathically while she and Nico held the men hostage. When he arrived, Will put the men in the cages as Sky and Nico fed, watered, and reassured the animals. Will then sent a call to the FBI, claiming an anonymous tip had come to him. Nico took Sky back to the truck in wolf form so they could leave the scene, and Will and Raine traveled via the Bifröst before authorities arrived on the property.

When Sky and Nico arrived back at Usha's, she unloaded the groceries as Nico was pulled to help Bryce feed the horses.

Storm took a sip of her milkshake. "Sounds like you and Nico made quite the team."

Sky stashed the last of the cheeses in the drawer and closed the refrigerator. "We were in sync the whole time. I can't read his mind, but we knew and trusted each other. I bet Raine and Will get that same sort of rush when they're working together—knowing someone has your back." She ran fingers along one arm. "I have goosebumps just thinking about it."

Holding her beverage, Storm leaned on the counter. "I'm happy for you. So happy for what you found and how you free each other."

Sky sniffed, reached for the ice cream carton, and turned, storing it in the freezer. "Okay. Stop or you'll make me cry. And we have a party to set up for, so no tears."

Sky was also afraid that if she continued to let emotions flow around Storm, she was at risk of letting slip Bryce's plans to propose tonight. She absolutely didn't want to ruin that surprise.

TWENTY-EIGHT

They had decorated the interior of the barn with strands of golden lights and hung a disco ball from the center of the ceiling. Storm had set up speakers and arranged a playlist. A table off to one side held half-eaten meats and cheeses on charcuterie boards and open wine bottles.

Sky, wearing a daisy sundress, swayed in Nico's arms to the music, completely relaxed after food and wine. Life was bliss.

All around, she could feel the warmth of everyone's love. Raine and Will danced as he whispered sweet nothings in her ear. She wore a burgundy dress she'd borrowed from Sky, and Will wore jeans and a white button shirt. Bryce spun Storm in a circle before bringing her back into his arms. He wore jeans, boots, and a mint green button-down shirt. She wore a bright smile, a pink flowing blouse over black leggings, and a sparkling diamond ring Bryce had given her earlier that evening. Even Usha, who sat in the cushioned recliner Nico had carried out for her, smiled and tapped her foot to the beat.

Bryce and Storm were missing Olivia, but once they'd heard Nico's brother had been slinking about, they'd had Will take her back to Maddie.

So much happiness.

Is this a glimpse into how amazing our life might be when the battle ends? So long as it ends in our favor.

The six of them were united now.

"I'm so sorry about earlier today," she told Nico. "I wasn't commanding the dog, just asking for help the same way I ask Thunder permission to ride, but I can see how my mental intrusion could violate the mind of an abused animal. I can see how that would be too much like what Helen does to her hounds."

He held her closer. "I was already distraught over seeing the pen and the animals. Your presence kept me calmer than I might have been, but when I thought you were controlling the dogs, I became angry. There *is* a difference between asking and ordering, but I appreciate you stopping the instant I asked you to."

She pulled back to look into his eyes. "If I ever do anything to make you uncomfortable, you only need to ask and I'll make adjustments."

"Thank you." Nico leaned closer, his deep voice in her ear. "I'll buy you a ring."

"Okay." She hadn't put much thought into the matter.

"Tomorrow. I'll go into town. There's a jewelry store."

She suspected he'd looked online sometime today and found one.

"There's no rush, Nico. I have you. Really have you."

"Always. But the engagement is sudden, and—"

"You're telling me." She snorted. "I woke up from surgery and had a fiancé."

Her teasing drew a smile from his otherwise earnest face.

"True," he said. "I've sprung betrothal on you twice now. But I want you to know how seriously I take a relationship with you, even though we haven't been together very long. I love you."

"Without the ability to read your thoughts, I'm getting better at interpreting your body language. Your actions convey your devotion, not a ring. Besides, we have time to know each other when the world is free of threats. At least the supernatural kind. What will you do with your freedom?"

"I worked for a time as an investor. I still have a few clients."

Arms around his neck, she ran fingers along his hairline. "That sounds like something you can do in Texas. Or remotely."

"I certainly hope so. I'm engaged to a pretty little thing who owns a holistic shop there. I intend to settle down with her. If she'll indulge me, I'd also like to entertain her with international travel a few times a year—London, Paris, Florence." He pressed a warm cheek to hers. "I've traveled to many beautiful places, and I could never enjoy them with anyone. I'd like to change that."

"Oh, I'd love to travel. I haven't vacationed abroad. I've always wanted a passport. I've lived vicariously through Storm's travel blog, dreaming of world expeditions."

"Expeditions, eh? We'll make that dream come true." He kissed the top of her head.

When the party wound down, the six of them stored perishables before heading to bed. Nico lingered with Sky a few minutes longer in the quiet kitchen.

"Tonight was wonderful," she said.

"Who says it's over?" he asked, voice husky.

Her gaze instantly smoldered toward him. His heart swelled at the thought of how this woman wanted him—now and forever. He didn't deserve her love and adoration, but he would enjoy it. He had a lifetime free of servitude to right the wrongs of his past. Starting with Sky. Starting with now.

She grabbed his hand and tugged him toward the stairs. When they were almost there, he pulled her back toward him and scooped her into his arms.

A gasp and a giggle escaped her before she clamped a hand over her mouth. He didn't bother to remind her that the two other couples in this household were madly in love, and no one would sleep right away after the romance building on the dance floor. Sky needn't worry about waking anyone with their nocturnal activities.

Climbing the steps, he buried his face in her neck and hair. Her strawberry scent intoxicated him.

When they reached her room, he slipped inside and set her down. By the time he'd closed the door and turned back around, she'd already shimmied out of her dress.

"You are so beautiful."

He backed her toward the bed, and she crawled onto it. On his hands and knees, he towered over her, drinking in the sight of her beautiful blue eyes and long hair covering the pillow before taking a long, languid kiss.

He left her panting as he undressed.

She cleared her throat. "So are you."

Climbing back over her, he explored her soft skin with his tongue as she ran tantalizing fingers over his muscles.

Slow, he told himself.

Long and slow. He slipped inside her and nearly lost control when she gasped and dug nails into his back.

Slowly, because even though he wanted a lifetime of this, had committed to it, his hopes and dreams could be short-lived if Helen won.

He took Sky slow and deep in long strokes as he watched every fluttering lash over her mesmerizing eyes while devouring each moan of delight with his mouth.

The friction built, rose, and peaked until nirvana crested over them in shaking, shuddering waves.

With bodies still entwined and merged, he sank on top of Sky, catching his breath as she clung to him.

Perfect. This woman was sheer bliss.

Grasping her hips, he rolled to position her on top.

"Nico!" His name was a surprised gasp.

Pressing his palms to her breast, he undulated his hips. "Again," he said in a low growl.

Her lips parted in surprise, but she was already moving over him, glittering eyes lost in euphoria.

NICO RAN under a densely starlit sky, diamonds sparkling at him like the diamond ring he would buy for Sky. Never in his life had he considered he would experience the freedom to love and marry.

The party had been a much-needed reprieve for their entire group. He was one of the six. He could accept that now. Before any more gatherings, they would have to win the battle against the goddess of the underworld. He felt invigorated, knowing his destiny was to fight *with* Valkyries. His dreams had been his future after all, but in a good way. The best way.

A familiar scent struck him, bringing him to a sudden halt. The gleaming white wolf stood on a mountain ridge, looking down at him. Nico's hair stood on end at Andrej's intrusion.

He waited, stark still, as Andrej made his way down the hillside. When he shifted to human form, Nico relaxed slightly. Perhaps his brother hadn't been sent to fight him. Nico always suspected Helen would one day pit them against each other. Except Andrej hated him so much, perhaps he didn't need any encouragement from his queen.

Nico transformed. "Brother."

"Still on sabbatical?" Andrej sneered.

"Helen still trying to command me?"

"Why can't she? What is this magic you discovered?"

"A special kind of magic. It's called love. Love broke Helen's power over me. She can't force me to do her bidding ever again."

"I can smell this woman on you. Who is she that you would risk your life and mine to be with?"

"She's everything to me."

"Love from a Valkyrie?" Andrej's expression darkened.

"You can choose love as well."

Andrej scoffed. "You know the demon I am. There's no love in this world for me."

"You're my brother. I love you."

Andrej flinched at his words then looked away.

"Wait." A jolt of alarm hit Nico. His brother had called Sky a Valkyrie, which meant he knew Nico was staying with the chosen trinity. If he knew, Helen probably knew. "Helen has found us?"

"You can't hide from her. No one can. She ordered me to kill you. And anyone with you."

Nico's blood ran cold. Icicles of fear bore into his skin like frozen claws.

"She didn't say how. She didn't say I couldn't warn you first. I didn't tell her you're with three women—"

"You've been spying on me."

"—three sisters—who I suspected are *the* three sisters." His tone was one of resignation and defeat, not gloating. "If I had, she might have sent more to kill all of you. It seems I've learned something from your deceptive ways, Nico. Go to your family." Andrej spoke the word family as if they were Nico's kin, not the man before him.

Angst rose to the surface, but Nico fought the urge to run home for a moment longer. "Join us."

Andrej's dark eyes turned hollow, lifeless. "I'm lost. Always have been. I'll see you on the battlefield."

Nico wanted to argue, but his pack was in danger. He had to leave his brother looking destitute and defeated.

A gift, his brother had given him, in his half-truths to Helen and this warning.

Spinning, Nico took off at a sprint and changed to wolf form mid stride. Claws raked the dirt as his chest heaved, his pace never slowing.

The smell of smoke in the wind struck his nostrils before the house came into view. The hair on his neck stood on end as his gut clenched.

He picked up his pace, legs pumping and adrenaline coursing

through him. Smoke, gnarled and toxic, curled into the night sky from under the roof of Usha's house.

Nico spotted the culprit. At the front of the house near the porch stood an eight-foot-tall monstrosity. He wore denim overalls with no shirt. Burnt orange-colored skin glowed red under the moonlight. The structure of his bald head was grossly abnormal, with cheekbones sharp enough to cut and a bony crown encircling his forehead.

Fire Giant.

Nico had never seen one so big and so inhuman in appearance. Helen had taken her genetic experiments to a frightening extreme. Her misfit couldn't enter the home because of Sky's wards, but that didn't mean he couldn't burn it to the ground and everyone inside it.

TWENTY-NINE

Sky woke with a start. The room was dark and the bed was empty. Nico was probably exercising his wolf. She would never feel slighted by his need for freedom. Outside exploration was a therapeutic release for him.

Running a hand along the sheets, she smiled at the memory of their recent lovemaking after the party. She wished they had more time together before the battle, but she would make the most of every moment. She would enrich Nico's time with her through the happiness he deserved.

Fear jolted through her with a sudden sensation they were all in danger. She sensed it through her sister Storm who had a keener ability to detect impending attacks. Throwing off her covers, Sky sent a psychic pulse to everyone in the house, waking them into action. Immediately, she heard the sounds of feet hitting the floor, murmurs, and shuffling.

Sky scooped up her wristbands and uru protective clothing from the corner of the room and raced for the door. As soon as she yanked it open, she smelled smoke. In addition, she sensed danger lurking beyond the house fire.

"Everybody out of the house!" Bryce hollered as he came down the hall.

We're under attack, Sky told everyone telepathically.

She tugged on her wristbands as she raced toward the front door, wondering where Nico was. She had no way of warning him.

"Me first." Storm approached from behind her and reached for the knob.

Because she was dressed in her defensive outfit, Storm was more prepared for battle. Knives out, she exited the front door. Sky followed, clothing bundled under one arm as she nocked a magical arrow.

A massive, reddish fist plowed toward Storm. As she dove out of its path and over the porch steps, Sky released an arrow. The hulking creature, bald head scraping the porch beams, turned as she fired. The arrowhead hit and embedded in his hip as his fist missed Storm and collided with the door frame. Wood cracked and splinters flew.

Sky reached for another arrow as the monster lashed out a hand, wrapping long, meaty fingers around her throat. His touch felt hot, searing.

Storm swiped a knife at him as she bounded back onto the porch, slicing a gash in his thigh. She was about to bring another blade into his side when he struck out with his free hand, knocking her into the air. She landed in a heap on the ground.

Sky's neck flared in searing pain. She was probably seconds from losing consciousness, either from lack of blood flow, lack of oxygen, or both.

Then from out of the night, Nico, teeth gnashing in a ball of fur and fury, clamped his mouth on the forearm attached to the hand strangling her.

The Fire Giant roared.

Air rushed into Sky's lungs when he released her. He tried to swipe at Nico, but the wolf was too fast. He jerked his head away, tearing flesh from the arm with him.

Still on the porch planks, Sky snatched another arrow from the invisible quiver and drove the pointed head into the creature's calf. As he screamed in pain, he kicked his leg out.

She rolled away but not fast enough. He caught her in the flank, sending her airborne. Pain flared through her side as she braced for the impending collision with the hard ground.

Instead, she slammed into Storm, who had dropped the knife in her hand she'd been preparing to throw in order to catch Sky. Her bundled clothing scattered along the dirt.

Storm let out a grunt as they hit the ground. "You're welcome," she heaved out.

Clutching her side, Sky struggled to get off her sister. The giant stalked toward them. Storm pushed to her feet, obviously slowed by pain, and collected her knives as the creature bore down on them. Sky was in no condition to escape his destructive path.

With a shudder, a crater opened between the sisters, and the giant came to an abrupt stop to avoid falling inside it. Sky glanced at the porch where Bryce was focused on holding his illusion of the crevice. In one hand, he spun his golden lariat, before hurling it. The rope looped around the creature's neck. When Bryce yanked, it cinched tight, and the Fire Giant jerked his hands back to grab at the lasso.

Storm took advantage of the creature's distraction, springing into action and leading with her knives. She thrust two up under his ribs as Nico leaped and caught the giant's neck in his powerful jaws just above Bryce's rope. Raine dashed forward, driving her spear through his chest.

With a ground-shaking impact, the demon collapsed to his knees. Behind him, flames engulfed Usha's ranch house.

Nico, Storm, and Raine scrambled back as the creature fell on his face and spontaneously combusted, filling the air with the putrid smell of sulfur.

The illusion of the hole in the ground faded.

Nico ran to Sky. When he reached her side, he transformed back into his human form, wearing only his jeans. "Are you okay?"

She nodded. "Nothing that won't heal. Are you hurt? Did you get burned?"

"In my wolf form, I'm impervious to fire. Guess it comes with being a hound of hell and servant to goddess of the underworld."

His words about his former master were spoken with a levity on the topic she'd never heard before. His soul was lighter with his new freedom.

Will materialized with Usha in his arms.

"Usha!" Raine called, rushing toward Will.

He laid Usha gently on the ground, her body looking pale and limp. "I found her on the back porch." He moved aside as he coughed.

Outside my wards.

Sky crawled on her hands and knees to the small woman, ignoring the pain of battered muscles and bones. She reached Usha's side at the same time as Bryce.

He felt for a pulse as Sky placed a hand over her heart, feeling for the woman's presence. She had a rim of burned skin around her neck. The fire giant had strangled her.

Bryce shook his head. "No pulse."

"Should we do CPR?" Raine asked, a desperate edge to her voice.

Bryce looked at her sympathetically but also hesitantly. Sky gleaned his thoughts—he didn't want to shatter Raine's hope but also didn't want to batter the body of a frail old woman with the trauma of chest compressions with little hope they could revive her to her former self. Sky understood. The damage was done—a brain deprived of oxygen for several minutes—even if they managed to get a heartbeat back.

"Her soul is gone," Sky said with finality.

"Oh, no." Raine dropped to her knees, turned to Will, and sobbed.

When Sky rocked back, Nico enveloped her in his arms. In the fire's backdrop, Storm stepped into Bryce's arms and buried her face in his neck. Behind them, the fire raged.

Everyone's anguish was palpable, but anger also swirled among them. Beneath that ran a river of guilt—Raine and Storm thinking they should have done something sooner or not have brought everyone to the ranch in the first place. When Sky looked at Nico, his doleful expression made her wonder if he blamed himself because he'd feared such an attack ever since his brother had found him.

Sky made a mental note to host a post-traumatic, decompressive group session. Chamomile tea and conversation would help them process the stress and loss of tonight. For now, the immediate threat was gone, and everyone needed to grieve.

CHAPTER

THIRTY

Despite the events at Usha's ranch, the sun had the audacity to shine. With the weight of grief in the air, Sky felt like unseen, bulbous drops of tear-laden rain were falling on Usha's casket. They stood outside a small, old church where a preacher spoke solemn words, but Sky only heard the murmur of everyone's sorrow.

None of the Shadow Guardians wore strictly funeral-black. Each wore their specialized nanoparticle clothing from Brok.

Gathered together, the threat of another offensive from Helen loomed over them. Memories of previous attacks swirled through everyone's minds. Helen had attacked each of the sisters individually in their dream walks. She'd launched a smart bomb at Bryce's daughter's birthday party. She'd sent a Dark Elf after Sky. Now this Fire Giant had delivered a disastrous blow.

Sky let the waves of despair from her family members wash over and around her.

As the preacher talked, the six of them remained motionless. Behind them sat a wave of mourners in black clothing, many of whom Will had transported here and would take home later. Sky knew only a few of the Shadow Guardians who'd arrived and none of the Council of Mjölnir elders. She tried to wall up her senses against the onslaught of melancholy thoughts from the larger group.

When the preacher's words of comfort ended, Sky sent a silent message to Bryce. As the casket lowered, she stepped forward, summoning her golden bow. Murmurs of surprise rippled through the crowd as she nocked an arrow, pointed toward the sky. After she unleashed it, it soared until it burst into a dozen fireworks, then a dozen more. Bryce kept the light show salute until Usha was safely in the ground.

AFTER THE SERVICE, everyone moved indoors for refreshments. As Sky sipped on a soda, a woman approached the six Shadow Guardians. She was dressed in black robes, her face drawn tight. She had dark skin, a broad nose with a small diamond in one nostril, and rich dark chocolate brown hair chopped short on one side and shaved close on the other. Her wide set of almond-shaped eyes had fragile appearing gold iris.

The group tensed—all but Will and Storm, who held up a reassuring hand. "This is Anka. She's Usha's granddaughter." Storm turned toward her. "I'm glad you could make it."

Anka nodded to everyone. The weight of her sadness added to the already oppressive atmosphere threatening to overtake Sky. Nico, seeming to sense her wavering strength, wrapped one arm around her waist, a much-needed gesture of love and support.

Anka addressed the group. "My grandmother spoke highly of the Valkyrie. All of you. Her death is our loss, but not hers. She has peace. And she will watch all of you take the battlefield in victory. She believes in you."

"We believed in her," Raine said.

"A lot of us owe who we are today to Usha," Will added.

"Can you each take a moment to share your relationship with her to the group? To honor her memory?" Anka gestured toward a large, framed photo of the woman on an easel standing on a raised platform.

"Of course," Raine said, walking up to address the crowd. She'd known Usha the longest of all of them and had trained under her since Usha first recruited her.

Will clinked a spoon against his glass to quiet the mourners.

Raine began. "I'm here to say a few words on Usha's behalf. She was my mentor, teaching me about the shadow world and helping me to become a Valkyrie. She guided me down the path, preparing me for what's to come."

When Raine stopped, voice cracking, Will joined her and spoke. "Usha opened my eyes to the power of Heimdall within me. Because of her, I pushed myself into the magic I had neglected and feared for years."

Magic, Sky gleaned, which had helped him save Raine, initially from Helen and subsequently on several other missions. He wouldn't have reached his full potential without Usha's insight.

Will added, "Because of her, I met this wonderful woman, my wife."

Storm and Bryce took Raine and Will's place by the photo.

"I respected her." Storm swallowed, taking a moment to compose herself and thinking of how she'd considered Usha a village elder of sorts. She'd sought her counsel more than once since meeting her a few years ago, despite the teasing she gave Raine about the organization being a cult. Storm had even respected the woman enough to accept Nico's assignment as Sky's protector, even though Storm disliked hellhounds. "She taught us teamwork. She taught us to value ourselves and others."

Bryce dwelled on how he'd revered the small woman in the short time he'd known her. "She was a dear woman with a quiet strength and never an unkind word." He thought of how she'd always been sweet to Olivia and had given him the kind of reassurance a single father needed, especially with a daughter who had frightening premonitions.

Nico and Sky took the platform. She looked out over the mourners, and for a moment, let the grief hit her before raising her walls. Sadness lingered among the group but so did love.

Some thought of Usha and others reminisced about loved ones lost. She saw Jake and Avery whom she'd met several years ago when Avery, a raven shapeshifter, had been searching for uru and Jake was the Shadow Guardian who'd protected her. Since then, they had continued to supply Brok with the valuable Asgardian ore.

Rosalyn and Apollo were among the group. She was the horse shapeshifter Shadow Guardian who had rescued Apollo, a healer, from Helen's lab in Germany. Since then, they had been working under the Eastern European Council of Mjölnir faction, trying to undermine Helen. In fact, their mission tomorrow weighed heavily on their mind. They'd learned the location of one portal Helen created to transport a group of creatures to Iceland. They were taking a dozen Shadow Guardians and some C4—demolition being one of Rosalyn's specialties—to shut it down.

Sky felt the magnitude of work everyone had been doing across the globe for years to undermine Helen. This had been a decades long game of chess—moving pawns and knights—until the final clash to take down the queen. But it was even more complicated than a single game. There were other foes to be fought on other continents throughout time, and there would be more after Helen. For now, she was the greatest threat Midgard had seen.

Nico's words broke Sky's concentration on the audience. "Usha never discriminated against me for what I am. She took a chance on me. She always made me feel like a teammate even when I'd still thought of myself as an outsider."

Sky squeezed his hand. "I only knew her the few months of our training, but she molded us into a team. When we take that battlefield, she will be with us in spirit."

AFTER WILL TOOK the other guests to their homes, the six of them met in the church. Sky sat in a pew behind Nico. She was utterly exhausted after feeling so many people's grief and thoughts off and on throughout the day at Usha's funeral.

Anka had stayed. She milled around the room, gathering floral decorations in front of her grandmother's photo.

"We need to separate," Bryce said, pacing the front room. He wore his lasso in a loose loop, ready for action, rather than as a belt. "We're too much of a target. We all know when the battle takes place, and since Helen has no intention of fighting fair, she's likely to strike again if we're all together."

"Safety in numbers," Raine countered, though her voice held no real conviction. She sat heavily on a pew opposite Sky.

"I think she's right," Sky interjected, leaning against a support beam that stretched to the ceiling. "It's only a few days, and we shouldn't separate."

"We should avoid populated areas, because I don't think Helen would care about civilian casualties." Storm gripped Bryce's hand when he came to stand by her.

"Will and I have his cabin," Raine said.

Will nodded, standing behind Raine with soothing hands resting on her shoulders. "Three rooms. We'll all fit. Minus the horses, who will need to be boarded somewhere."

"This is my fault," Nico said. "The attack is my fault."

Will shook his head. "We knew assembling like this was a necessary risk."

Nico shook his head. "My brother found our location. I should have moved us sooner. I thought with the wards and us together, we'd be safe. I'm sorry. She sent him after me, and that means Usha's death is on my hands."

"We all agreed to stay at the ranch," Bryce said.

"Usha's death is Helen's doing," Storm said. "No one else. We were as prepared as we could be with weapons at our bedsides and Sky's wards. Usha was outside the safety zone when the attack happened. You are one of the six. She knows you're a threat to her. She would have hunted you down, regardless of where we were."

Sky looked up at Nico, who stood beside her and extended a hand to him. "Nico and I need to go back to Brok. Now that Nico is officially part of the team—part of the six—he needs armor and weapons. Brok told us we'd be back."

Nico nodded, taking her hand and bringing it to his lips to kiss the knuckles.

"We need one more thing." Storm turned to Anka. "Is the orb still with Denny?"

"Yes, Denny has it."

"That was a good idea," Nico said, wrapping his body tighter around her in bed.

"Hmm. Yes."

"I think everyone benefited from your tea, incense, and reflections on Usha."

"Oh, you meant earlier with the group. Did it help you?" She slid her naked body back slightly to look at him.

"Yes."

"Good. I think spacing out in front of the TV helped, too."

After their private group therapy session, the six had gathered in Will's living room and watched a movie on his enormous flat screen. Now, everyone had retired to their bedrooms.

"That was my first time watching *Wonder Woman*."

"Really? How is that possible?"

"I mostly avoided any entertainment with the possibility of romance or defeating the villain. Why watch something so entirely different from anything I could ever have?"

"Until now."

"Until you."

They lay in silence for a moment as Sky stroked a languid finger along his biceps. He would never take for granted the miracle of her in his life.

"What do you know about Helen's motivations?" Sky asked. "I get that we all think she's evil, and she's clearly done things to justify that title, but was she just born that way or did something or someone influence her?"

"You mean like Aries influencing World War I in the movie?"

"Maybe an evil mentor. The anti-Usha."

"I don't know that anyone is aware of the full story. The rumors are that she killed her own parents at a young age. She maxed out their credit cards, took all their cash, and liquidated everything before disappearing into the shadow world. I pieced together that she made contacts with whomever sided with her beliefs that mere humans, like her parents, were unworthy to continue to live. She built her army at a young age, perhaps as a teenager, having heard of the prophecies. You can't tell by looking at her, but she's closer to sixty now. She's kept a younger appearance by sucking the life from her victims."

"She's had forty years to build her army?"

"Yes."

"When I met her in the dream walk, I could feel an inkling of her thoughts—all hate and anger. The thoughts were there, though partially muted, like she had semblances of mental walls erected. With you, I sense nothing. You're both creatures of Helheim, so how can I perceive some of her but none of you?"

Nico shifted his weight to drape one of Sky's legs over his hip. "She's a child of Loki, who was Asgardian and Jotun—both of which you can sense. Her command over hellhounds originates from her pet, Fenrir, but we are very different creatures from her."

"I see your logic." She wriggled closer. "I hope we can win this."

"We can win."

"There's no place I'd rather be on the precipice before battle than here in your arms."

"I'm so incredibly fortunate to have you." He buried his face in her neck.

THIRTY-ONE

Will transported Nico and Sky to Denny's house. Nico held Sky's hand, feeling the warm strength of her beside him. As rainbow lights danced around them, the smell of salt and nuts filled the air.

"Gah!" A broad-shouldered Black man startled, tossing up a bowl of mixed nuts he was carrying. "Seriously, Will, right into my living room?" The man looked around dismally at the scattered pistachios, cashews, and walnuts.

Will's lips turned up in an amused grin. "I thought Anka called and gave you a heads up."

"Hi, Denny." Sky tiptoed around the nuts strewn along the floor and gave Denny a hug. "This is Nico, my fiancé." She beamed when she said the word.

Nico smiled, delighted at the jubilant and effervescent way she introduced him. This was the first time she'd introduced him as her fiancé, and it sounded effortless and perfect.

Nico stretched over and shook hands with the man. Sky had explained to him how Denny was Storm's therapist and helped bring

Storm into the fold of the Shadow Guardians. "Pleasure to meet you."

"Likewise." He shot an annoyed glower at Will. "Though knocking at the front door would've been more appropriate. More... *normal.*"

"Do you want your neighbors to see a few people teleport onto your porch via rainbow?" Will asked.

Denny made a half-choked sound. "No." He walked over to a closet and pulled out a vacuum cleaner.

"I'll take care of the mess. You three have a chat." Will took the household tool as Denny led them to the back porch, away from the noise.

The humid Texas air struck Nico instantly when they stepped outside. The August heat clashing with his fur was going to be hell once he permanently lived in the state. Perhaps he could convince Sky to vacation elsewhere when the place was broiling under a summer sun.

"How are things going, Sky?" Denny asked. "You look lovely, by the way. Love and engagement suit you."

Nico instantly liked Denny. He took time to ask about her when probably the rest of the Shadow Guardians would skip the formalities and get down to business. There was a war coming and few people in their line of work took the time for such a consideration.

"Thanks. It's been—what's the saying—the best of times and the worst of times."

"I'm sorry for your loss. When Anka told me, I wanted to join you all at the funeral. She asked me not to go because she wasn't sure if it would be dangerous. All six of you gathered in one place."

"So, you and Anka?" Sky's blue eyes twinkled mischievously.

He cocked his head to one side. "I have a feeling you gleaned that rather than Storm having informed you."

"You kind of psychically shouted it when you said her name. The love jumped out like a sparkler coming to life."

He smiled, all white teeth and squinting eyes. "She's amazing.

We had quite the adventure of securing the orb. I think it shaved about ten years off my life, but she's adding them back."

"What's so special about this orb?" Nico asked.

"Let me fetch it for you." When Denny slid the back door open, the sound of his roaring vacuum cleaner could be heard. He walked inside, closed the door, and disappeared.

He returned a moment later with a plain black box. He opened it to reveal a golden orb. Norse letters and symbols were inscribed in the metal. Denny pulled it out and rolled it around in his hand. "It's capable of augmenting the powers of the person wielding it, so keeping it out of Helen's reach is prudent. I watched Anka's tele-kinetic abilities escalate twenty-fold as she used it to crush a horde of zombies attacking us."

"Zombies?" Nico asked.

"Uh, yeah. I call them zombies. I guess you call them draugr—Helen's undead."

"Storm thinks it can help us win the war," Sky said as Denny dropped the object into her hand. She gasped.

"What is it?" Nico asked, noting her surprise with concern.

"I can feel its power."

"Is it safe?" He wasn't sure he trusted magical relics, especially not if it was something Helen had sought.

"Powerful, but neutral. I don't sense any evil in and of itself, but I can see how Helen could use it to her advantage if it enhances power."

"Storm sent you to retrieve the orb, so perhaps she thinks you'll be the one to use it," Nico said.

"I did give Helen that psychic punch when she attacked me. I wonder if the orb would help me do something like that on the battlefield. It would be a huge advantage."

Nico eyed it warily. "You should test it first."

"That's a good idea," Denny added. "You don't know how you might react when it augments your power. It could drain you, incapacitate you, or worse. Who knows? It definitely drained Anka. Took her a few days to recover."

"Okay, I'll try it out when we're back at Will's cabin. Next stop, Brok, for Nico's armor and weapon."

"Keep it in the box when not in use, though," Denny cautioned. "Anka thinks Helen has a way to track it when it's not hidden. Like some type of magical beacon."

W ILL, Sky, and Nico arrived at Brok's property, Sky holding the black box containing the orb. Concealed, she couldn't feel the whisper of power it emanated. She was eager to try it. Of the group, she was the slowest runner and most inexperienced fighter. Using a relic of power would elevate her contribution to the six of them.

"Thanks, Will."

"Sense anything?" he asked.

She scanned the surroundings without feeling danger. The dilapidated landscape had her thinking how Brok could rebuild his home when the war was over. Perhaps the Shadow Guardians could help. The dwarf had sacrificed his own safety to help them.

And, hey, if he needs a barbed wire fence around his yard, I now know how to install one.

"No danger," she said.

Will nodded at her. "Message me when you need a pickup." With that, he vanished in a blaze of shimmering colors.

"Once more into the breach?" Nico asked.

Sky smiled. "Brok is going to say he told you so."

"Of that, I have no doubt."

They picked their way through the tall grass to the rubble where the hidden set of stairs lay. Sky sent a friendly psychic message to Brok so he would know Nico and she had arrived. After descending the steps, they knocked.

When the door swung open, the dwarf looked up at them. "Ha!"

He barked. "Could've saved yourself a trip and taken what I'd offered the first time."

"Then we wouldn't have had the pleasure of seeing you again," Sky said sweetly.

Brok motioned them inside with a hand. "Gave me more time to think, anyway." He plucked two sais off one wall.

More short sword than dagger, the sais were trident—one long blade and two short—but all three tips tapered. They were all black, though with a slight shimmer as if made of glass. The material reminded Sky of the obsidian walls of the cave in which she'd met Helen.

"Incredible." Nico took one and rotated it in his hands. "Not a standard Norse design though, since sais originated in Asia."

"True," Brok conceded. "But these babies have fibers from Lævateinn."

Nico arched an admiring eyebrow.

"Who's Lævateinn?" Sky asked.

"Not a who, but a what," Nico explained. "Lævateinn is a Norse magic wand crafted by Loki and said to have resided in Hel."

"What better way to kill the goddess of death's granddaughter than by a weapon made from an artifact from Hel by Loki," Brok said in a tone of self-satisfaction.

"Poetic," Sky said, even as she regarded the weapon with wariness. They were beautiful, even in their deadly glint. The sleek black was understated and seemed to complement Nico's composed personality.

"Even more poetic," Brok added, "is the symbolism of three."

Sky nodded. "Two trident sais. *Three by three, Hel's wrath to free.* Amazing."

Nico admired it as Sky produced a wad of cash courtesy of Storm and paid Brok.

"Thank you," Nico said to Brok. "I suspect we are off to the tailor now."

"Nah." Brok waved a hand at him. "I sized you up last time you were here and got the threads made." He tossed Nico an all-black suit of armor from out of a drawer. "But you don't get to be picky."

Nico tugged at the stretchy material.

"Try it on in the back room to make sure it fits."

Nico disappeared.

"Just a few more days until the battle," Sky said. "Any words of wisdom?"

"Yeah, win. No pressure, but we're all kind of counting on you."

Sky blew out a breath. "Yeah, I got that."

He scratched his thick beard. "For what it's worth, I believe in all of you."

Sky bent down and hugged him. "That's worth a lot."

His pain and worry washed over her. He had an extended family he cared about, despite living like a recluse.

Nico emerged wearing the skin-tight bodysuit. "Surprisingly breathable."

"Hubba, hubba." Sky gaped at him, admiring the way the material hugged every formed muscle of his body.

Brok grunted. "You can save the mushy, gushy stuff for when you're not in my workshop."

She sensed the dwarf's satisfaction with his work. He'd wanted to make something more representative of a superhero outfit for the six, and so he finally had.

"Thank you for everything," she told Brok.

A shrill alarm filled the room just as a wave of blood thirst struck Sky.

Attack. Kill. Feast.

Brok's eyes went wide as Nico grabbed his new weapons from the table beside him. He slipped his phone into a pocket on the thigh of his new outfit.

"Perimeter breach." Brok's brow furrowed as he hoisted himself onto a countertop and yanked an axe off one wall.

THIRTY-TWO

An ear-piercing scraping came from the ceiling above seconds before it was ripped away. Debris and wood planks collapsed into the room as Sky scrambled to safety under one workbench. Swatting away the falling dust, she tried to see what was happening.

Nico dodged fallen planks as Brok stood on a countertop, gripping his axe. Through the gaping and widening chasm in the roof, Sky glimpsed a flash of menacing ten-inch-long claws and shimmering iridescent scales. The enormous creature had a long, snorting proboscis and sickly red eyes. Vicious curved teeth tore the hole larger as the claws raked the debris away. The creature had dingy, pale yellow scales like cigarette-stained teeth that reflected the sun.

Sky had heard about the dragon shapeshifter Raine and Will had killed a few years ago, but Sky had never seen one. She certainly never imagined how tiny she would feel in the presence of one—or how awful its breath would stink. Had it been feasting on spoiled meat and rotten eggs?

As the dragon drew its head back, its chest expanded, the way a rib cage might to suck in a deep breath before blowing out birthday candles. When it let loose an exhale, a spray of fire rained down toward them.

Brok, seeming to have anticipated the flames, pivoted away while hurling his axe at the dragon's head. Although the blade glanced off its thick bony crown, the blow's force knocked his head to the side and sent the flames to one corner of the workshop instead of directly inside where all three of them would have been flame broiled. Despite the streak of fire being tangential, the temperature in the room skyrocketed, reminding Sky of a Texas afternoon in August even though they were in New Jersey.

As the creature shook his head and closed his mouth, he lashed out a limb toward Brok, who'd been reaching for another weapon. The claws raked along his back, knocking him to the floor.

Nico, who had dodged the dragon's flame, leaped off a pile of smoldering wreckage and brought one Lævateinn sai down to puncture the dragon's outstretched forelimb. Blood sprayed as the animal shrieked. It jerked its snapping jaw around, but before it could chomp into Nico, he rolled, shifted into wolf form, and sprung up, sinking canine teeth into the dragon's shoulder.

The creature rotated, bucked, and reached with his injured hand, wrapping talons around the wolf and flinging him aside. Nico slammed into a crooked rafter before falling into the room near Brok's limp body.

The dragon drew his head back again, angry red eyes flashing with his lust for death. Before he could spew fire, Sky stepped out of the hiding spot, stood, and readied her bow. Heart pounding, she fashioned a golden arrow and let it fly. With a whistle of speed, it sang through the air before piercing the soft flesh of the dragon's neck.

His eyes went wide as he back-pedaled away. Wailing, he extended a pair of yellow wings and launched into the air.

"Will!" Sky sent a psychic cry, dropping her hands to extinguish her magic bow. She bent over Brok and Nico, feeling for pulses.

They were both still alive. She breathed a slight sigh of relief, but only slightly. They were both badly injured. Brok couldn't heal and Nico had said his recovery was slow in wolf form.

"We'll get you out of here," she promised, sinking a shaking hand into Nico's fur.

In the distance, the dragon's screech made her think he was circling back around for another attack.

"Sunna," Brok croaked.

Sky sensed he wasn't asking the Norse god of the sun for help but mourning the complete destruction of his powerful telescope tool that had enabled him to harness the sun and create his masterpieces. The dragon's weight had crushed it beyond repair.

Will appeared in a shimmering rainbow, clutching his temple. "Ease up, Sky. You're—" His gaze landed on the bodies on the floor. "Oh, shit. Are they—"

"They're alive but severely injured." She reined in her fear and anguish to ease off the migraine she was giving Will.

"Can you fix them?" he asked.

With salves and herbs? Probably not.

"Just get us out of here," she ordered, snatching up the black box beside her.

"Where?"

"Anywhere, before Helen's dragon comes back. How about Bryce?"

Tears streamed down her face as she tried to think of what to do. Her medicinal remedies only went so far, which didn't include life-threatening injuries. Brok was losing a lot of blood, and Nico probably had organ and bone injury from his collision. Maybe the physician could help.

The world burst into bright colors.

She should have acted sooner instead of cowering under the counter. She should be the one with the injuries because she could heal herself.

As they arrived on a warm, grassy lawn, Bryce rushed out of Will's cabin.

As he knelt, she read the physician's thoughts. He needed his equipment, but even at a trauma center, he doubted they could be repaired. Regardless, he began barking orders at Will with what supplies he needed as he applied pressure to Brok's wounds.

Sky glanced at the black box.

Augmented magic.

She had imagined using it for psychic powers or one of her sisters using it to fight faster and harder in the upcoming battle, but what if it could augment healing magic and spread her power from herself to others?

She flipped open the box's lid and gripped the orb as she opened herself to its possibilities. Magic, like liquid satin, flowed through her veins. Time slowed as her awareness sharpened. She could sense everything around her, from the blades of bent grass to the breeze through leaves, to the birds perched on branches. Smells bombarded her—nearby honeysuckle, Will's perspiration, and Brok's blood.

Glowing golden tendrils flowed out from where she held the orb, snaking toward Brok like a dozen reeds in a breeze. They writhed under his clothes, the magic threads found his wounds and sealed them.

The thrill of success made Sky lightheaded and giddy, not the usual exhaustion she felt when she healed herself. She turned her focus to Nico, gold healing magic illuminating his white fur.

Yes. Better. More.

She could do so much more.

Will emerged from his house carrying Bryce's medical bag. Extending this new magic to Will, she found the old back injury he'd suffered when he'd fought Jör. She hadn't known it still pained him on wintry days or after battles. He also had lingering inflammation from smoke inhalation trying to save Usha. She healed both completely and searched for what else she could fix and continue to bask in the glorious power.

She found more on all of the men—old injuries, sprains, scars.

Healed. Healed. Healed.

She was an evangelical pastor healing her flock, except she didn't have to move or preach, just focus.

Who else?

A deer in the woods with an injured ankle.

Healed.

A rabbit in a hole with an illness.

Healed.

A butterfly in—

"Sky?" Someone was shaking her.

But she had a world to heal. More. Just a bit more.

"Sky? Dammit, Will, Bryce, how do we snap her out of this trance? Sky! She's going to kill herself." The panic in Nico's voice brought her vision into focus. He was in his human form, hands clasped on her face. Pale blue eyes filled with fear. "*Raza de soare,* come back to me."

She let go of the orb and collapsed into him.

"WE WERE ATTACKED BY A DRAGON," Sky said, the orb resting in its box on her lap. She couldn't believe the words coming out of her own mouth.

A freaking dragon!

She sat beside Nico as the Shadow Guardians assembled in Will and Raine's living room. Nico kept one arm around her, rubbing along her arm intermittently in a show of support. Raine and Will sat on a catty-corner sofa while Storm paced near Bryce, who stared out one window. Brok sat by the fire swathed in a blanket and looking pale.

A large wooden chandelier of beautiful twisting craftsmanship hung from tall beams. A stone fireplace created a lovely focal point, though it wasn't currently lit, considering it was a warm summer afternoon.

"She has another dragon," Raine said with a shudder.

"I thought Nid was her only pet of that magnitude," Nico said. "And he's dead."

Sky gleaned images from her sister's mind of Raine and Will attacking Nid, slaying a dragon who'd been attacking other Shadow Guardians on a beach.

"How bad is the yellow one wounded?" Storm asked.

"Not mortally," Sky said grimly.

Will nodded. "I heard him circling above, turning to make another attack before we left Brok's place."

"The battle is soon. He might not be fully healed by then," Raine suggested.

"Since we didn't know she had another dragon, we can't also assume she doesn't have another Apollo," Nico said. "I've been out of her inner circle for several months, so both are possible."

"Apollo?" Sky asked, though she immediately gleaned the answer from Will and Raine. "A healer who's on our side," she said. "And he was in a public place when Nico and Brok were injured, so Will couldn't transport us to him."

Will nodded. "I was about to fetch him and bring him here when you started healing them. And me." He twisted his back as he spoke, amazed to be pain free, Sky sensed.

Storm crossed her arms. "We now have confirmation the orb can augment anyone's powers. And it takes strength from the user."

"So it seems," Sky said, still feeling lightheaded.

She had this orb for a reason; she was sure of it. But she didn't think the intent was for her to kill herself while healing everybody else. Clearly she couldn't tell during its use when she was on the brink of pushing too far. And if Nico or one of her sisters couldn't snap her out of the magical death trance because they were busy fighting on the battlefield, Sky would cease to exist.

Scrubbing hands over her face, Sky said, "I need to practice with it. Get better."

"We've only a few days."

"Yeah," she turned to Storm, "so, better not waste time. I'm not saying I'd use this right away in the fight. But if things aren't going in our favor on the battlefield and we're facing fourth quarter, fourth down, and fifty yards to go, we need a Hail Mary option."

Bryce frowned. "To play devil's advocate, we kept that thing hidden from Helen for a reason. If we bring it to Iceland and she gets her tentacles on it, it's game over."

Brok cleared his throat. "It might be game over if you don't have it."

THIRTY-THREE

"You saw the box?" Helen asked.

"Yes, my queen. The redheaded Valkyrie had it in her possession." Sid, Helen's shapeshifting dragon, looked worse for wear with a bruise near one eye and a bandage around his neck and left hand.

Helen stroked her chin as she considered this development. Months ago, she'd lost the magical orb when Andrej had been ambushed at a hangar in Texas. She suspected the Valkyrie had defeated her draugr and taken it. Now, she had confirmation from Sid that one of the Valkyrie possessed Odin's Orb.

Helen would have been more excited if Sid had gotten his dingy claws on the box, but this new development was promising. If the Valkyrie were carrying it around on an outing this close to the day of the battle, they were probably planning on bringing it to the battle-field. Once there, Helen could home in on which Valkyrie used it and take it from her.

She smiled. Helen need only wait for the orb to come to her.

WHILE WILL and Raine took Brok to stay with Ida and Wyatt, Sky and Nico meandered through Will's wooded hills. She'd recovered from yesterday's ordeal with the dragon, though still felt shaken. Between the Fire Giant and the shapeshifting dragon, she was gaining more temerity. Yet she didn't feel ready for a battle of epic proportions.

They stopped near a babbling brook, and she settled down in front of a small, withered shrub.

"You're healing shrubs today?" Nico asked, a teasing tone in his voice, though she heard the worry too.

He'd told her last night that he was worried the orb would take her life entirely if she tried to heal her family on the battlefield. That, or she'd be so distracted using it that an attacker would seize the moment to end her.

She opened the black box. "I thought I'd start with something small. Manageable."

Nico paced several feet away from her, obviously anxious about her intentions to master the orb. Perhaps master was too lofty a goal. At the very least, she wanted to set boundaries on the give and take between relic and magic user.

Sitting cross-legged and holding the orb in her right hand, Sky focused on the shrub. The magic within the orb whispered to her of power and possibilities.

One shrub. No funny business.

She let her senses crawl from the shriveled leaves to the browned branches to the brittle trunk and into the roots. No. This one was dead. Dead and gone.

There was no reviving it.

She reached out, feeling and connecting with the surrounding life. Nico was alive and vibrant near her. Interesting how her telepathic skills couldn't reach him, but sensing his health and life through the orb was possible. As was healing him with it.

The earth beneath her teemed with subterranean creatures—ants, worms, beetles, and chipmunks. She might think twice about sitting on the dirt floor again, knowing the thousands of things alive beneath her.

She focused on a rattlesnake just on the other side of the creek as it bit down into a mouse. She felt them both.

Predator and prey.

One full of life, soon to feast. The other facing the last few beats of its heart. Unless she turned the tide. Gripping the orb tighter, she infused life back into the mouse. This time, however, she didn't take from her life force; she took from the snake's. Within seconds, the mouse sprang forth, freeing itself from the dead rattler's mouth.

Sky opened her eyes and blinked. Nico was sitting on a rock, watching her with those pale blue eyes.

He looked back-and-forth from her to the bush. His mouth drew in a thin line. "No luck?"

"This particular bush was not salvageable."

"Oh. Do you want to find a different plant?"

"I already tested the orb. I healed a mouse. He'll be coming out of that hole soon."

"Where?"

"There." She pointed.

As if on cue, the small rodent shuffled out of the dirt between the branching roots of a tree, then scurried away.

Nico sniffed. "You don't seem any worse for wear. And you didn't lock yourself into a trance." His tone was cautiously optimistic.

"I didn't use my own life force this time."

"Come again? How does that work?"

"In those roots, under all that dirt, is also a dead rattlesnake. I could feel both of their lives, so I shifted the essence of one to the other."

Nico's eyes widened. He leaped across the ravine, transforming into his wolf form in midair and landing lithely by the tree roots. He dug in with claws, followed by his snout. As he drew back, the dead snake was firmly between his teeth.

She stood and gave him a tsk. "Seriously? I kiss that mouth."

The wolf dropped the snake, looking remorseful.

She started to laugh, but the visual confirmation of what she'd done sickened her. "I can kill one thing to save another." Could she take Helen's life this way? Was she strong enough to take on the goddess of the underworld?

Nico transformed back into human form, tall and fit, and picked up the snake to examine it. "It's better than using your own life. If you didn't have magical healing abilities, that last feat saving Brok and me would've killed you."

"I know." She held up the orb. "But this is still a crazy sick amount of power for anybody. I'm tempted to destroy it rather than risk Helen ever getting her hands on it. If it can augment my healing powers, enabling me to transfer life from one organism to another, what scary powers of hers can she magnify? I don't think I want to know the answer to that."

He crossed the stream, jumping in human form this time, and walked to her. "I'd venture to say she'd use it to augment her ability to drain others of power. As it stands now, she has a ritual she can perform to kill and leach power, but it's time consuming." He placed his hand over hers and curved her fingers around the orb. "Keep it, Sky. I have faith you will both protect it and know the best time to use it."

"I hope you're right." With a shudder and chill running down her spine, despite the warm summer sun, she slipped the golden device back into its case.

Tomorrow, they would know.

THIRTY-FOUR

Sky stared out over a battlefield of fire and ice. Active volcanoes loomed to her right, and snow-capped mountains rose to her left. Although the volcanoes weren't spewing lava as they had in her dreams, pockets of steam billowed out of the ground, spindling up to mix with the overcast sky. The battlefield was an uneven combination of rock and grass.

Helen's army waited in the distance. From afar, Sky could discern a mixture of bloodlines among the undead.

Hundreds of undead.

They were shriveled, sickly looking creatures with mottled slate skin and loose scraps of clothing. They had more of a decomposed look compared to Dark Elves, who were human in size and appearance, with waxy gray skin.

Several enormous Frost Giants stood in the group, their bluish hue looking like they were fresh off the glacier. They wore black pants and black, sleeveless vests, which Sky suspected were made of bullet-resistant material.

Midgard serpent bloodlines, with their burnt red tones, weaved impatiently among the soldiers of undead like crimson snakes through blackened, diseased foliage.

Large, imposing Fire Giants with taut muscles under orange skin crowded among the group. They were shirtless, and Sky suspected that was to inflict maximum damage with their burning contact.

Three dozen normal looking men and women stood among the obvious creatures. She suspected these were the shapeshifting descendants of Fenrir who would transform into wolves on Helen's command.

At the end of the battlefield, Hel's pale skin glistened out from under a black silk jumpsuit with a flowing obsidian cape. She sat atop a dragon. The same yellow-scaled, four-legged, winged creature who had attacked them at Brok's.

Beside Sky, Nico slipped his hand into hers. He wore his skin-tight, black, uru nanoparticle, protective outfit.

"That's a whole hell of a lot of ugly," Bryce said. He wore jeans and a t-shirt with his golden lasso at his waist.

"She's definitely been breeding them bigger and stronger than what is among the general population." Raine hefted the weight of her baton in hand. She wore her agent suit with hair slicked back in a ponytail.

Will stood beside her, gun holstered. He would pull out Hǫfuð from the Bifröst when the battle started.

Storm stood beside Bryce. She wore all black, spinning her knives with cool violet eyes fixed on her targets. The calm before the storm.

The six made their way down the hillside. When they reached the bottom, Helen's dragon unleashed a vicious roar. Her troops sprinted toward them, all fiery determination and snarling lips.

Even from a distance, Sky could feel their hate, their anger, and their pain. So much hate, not just for the Shadow Guardians but for the world in general. Existence had not been kind to these creatures. Helen had not been kind to them. The undead hadn't been left in peace. The new creatures she'd created over the last several decades had been born in pain and subjected to the agony of accelerated growth in an environment where they knew no love and no compassion.

A tear slipped down Sky's cheek. There was no salvation for them, and death would be a mercy.

The people she loved radiated power and forgiveness. They didn't hate the evil they were about to destroy but pitied it. Their resolve was stronger than the force of the wall of monsters rushing toward them at breakneck speed.

One hundred feet.

Fifty feet.

The undead were the slowest of the group, so in the lead were Midgard serpents, wolves beholden to Helen, Frost Giants, and Fire Giants.

Twenty-five feet.

When they were within fifteen feet, sprinting, Bryce pulsed out his force field. The golden semi-translucent shield burst to life before any of the creatures could react and slow. In mid-run and leap, they struck the solid wall of magic. The impact was like running full speed into concrete. Faces, limbs, and torsos cracked as bones splintered.

Behind the first wave, the rest of the creatures slowed. When Bryce dropped the shield, he also let down the illusion he'd been holding. Sky had remained on the ledge, unseen with an arrow nocked. She began unleashing them, one after another. Raine had been poised on the ice side of the battlefield and attacked while Storm took offensive action from the fire side. The creatures jolted at the sudden appearance of the Valkyries and scrambled to engage in the fight.

The only people who had actually been beneath Bryce's shield were the men. As soon as he dropped the magical barrier, Will opened fire with his gun as Nico transformed into a wolf and launched himself at the throat of a Frost Giant.

Sky's position had two advantages—three, according to Nico, who wanted her out of the thick of the battle. She could volley arrows into the crowd, but she could also see the movement of Helen's army higher up from the battlefield. With her abilities, she could communicate with anyone—except Nico—on her team, moving them into position like chess pieces.

All around Nico, the scent of death filled the air. With his teeth and his sais, he struck down the enemies surrounding them. Dark Elves weren't particularly hard to kill, but there were so damn many of them. For every one he killed, three more rushed him. He was outnumbered, but he wasn't alone.

He had his pack, his new brothers and sisters. Perhaps they didn't grow fur and fangs like he did, but they were family. He would fight with them to the bitter end.

He would try to avoid fighting other Fenrir. Some of them had fully embraced Helen's control and evil, but others were mere puppets on a string, unable to resist her influence—like Andrej, although even he was starting to defy her.

Where is my brother? Nico wondered.

He stayed close to Will and Bryce, who both had some pretty ingenious magic. Bryce's shield was absolutely impenetrable, and he could raise and lower it in a split-second, but his work of illusion was equally impressive. He created incorporeal replicas of himself, who the enemy wasted time and energy attacking. Will shimmered with rainbow colors in and out of his location, confusing his attackers.

Nico couldn't see Raine or Storm through the flocks of their enemy, but he heard the dying screams of the Valkyries' victims.

An arrow sank into a woman who was mid-transformation into a wolf as she launched herself at Nico. The creature collapsed to the ground in a puff of ash. Sky had just saved his life. Again. She was fast and accurate at launching those arrows.

But despite the guardians' superior abilities, they were vastly outnumbered. Nico wondered how they would ever plow through

Helen's pets to reach the she-demon. In the distance, she sat atop a massive dragon, content to watch her own creations suffer and die.

For her own gain.

Nico transformed back to his human form after killing an undead, when the fist of a Frost Giant plowed into his jaw, knocking him off his feet. A red wolf, teeth bared, leaped for Nico's throat.

A blur of white streaked into Nico's vision, knocking the red wolf off course. The two animals tumbled, growling with gnashing teeth and raking claws. The white wolf transformed into Andrej and wrapped his arm around the red wolf as he slit its throat.

Nico gaped in surprise. "Andrej, you're free?"

"I guess you were right about love," Andrej said between pants of breath. "I was fighting my way toward you and felt this rush of protectiveness. Suddenly, Helen's pressing commands to fight and kill the Guardians vanished. I'm free."

"Andrej, will you fight with us?" Nico placed a hand on his brother's shoulder, chest swelling with relief and pride.

His brother nodded. "I'll help you finish this."

SKY LAUNCHED ARROW AFTER ARROW, never missing a target, even if her shots weren't all deadly. She knew she was good and was relieved to see she could perform under pressure, but she wondered how much of her success was related to the sheer number of creatures on the battlefield. Maybe she wasn't missing because they filled every space and she couldn't miss.

No, she was definitely hitting the ones who presented the most immediate threat to her family.

Nico fought flawlessly. When he needed to run, leap, or dodge, he seamlessly shifted into his wolf form with claws and gnashing teeth, taking out Dark Elves. He shifted back to his human form intermittently to swipe his sais through the undead. Coming at them with so many different modalities, his opponents couldn't predict which way he would attack.

Nearby, Bryce was just as unpredictable. His shield varied between complete body armor and a simple deflective oval on his left arm. He would raise it and drop it intermittently while roping his enemies and creating opportunities for Will to strike them down by sword or bullet.

Although Will had no shield and no teeth, he was no less vicious. He had a gun in one hand—the one Brok had enchanted to never run out of bullets—and a sword in the other. Using his Bifröst ring, the FBI agent vacillated between a solid and semi-solid state, flickering in and out, so any creatures who encroached close enough to strike went right through him before he felled them.

Raine whirled and twirled with Gungnir. The uru spear ripped through flesh as easily as a sword. With grace and focus, she struck down the Dark Elves and undead swarming around her. A Frost Giant burst onto the scene, massive fists swinging like clubs, and Sky launched an arrow at his head. It struck his temple but didn't put him down. Fortunately, it at least slowed him long enough for Raine to pivot and thrust her spear into his neck, finishing him.

Storm whipped around her enemies, knives flashing. Up close and personal, she sliced and kicked, spinning through Hel's minions like a Tasmanian devil. Like the storm she was.

A Fire Giant swung what looked like a spiked bat and Storm rolled, but the weapon clipped her shoulder. She wobbled in a crouched position. Sky shot an arrow into the creature's chest. He roared and tried to yank it out, snapping it in half, but it vanished, leaving the wound in place.

Storm launched herself upward, sinking her knives between his ribs and into his heart. Sky shot another arrow into a hellhound as it ran toward Storm. He tumbled across the ground before skidding to a stop and bursting into ash at her feet.

Sky marveled at how well everyone was doing, but she also noted Helen surveying the battlefield from a distance. She wasn't attacking. Why wasn't she attacking?

She was gathering intelligence, Sky realized. Watching the way the Shadow Guardians fought in order to anticipate their moves.

She's also letting us wear ourselves out, exhaust ourselves. And we are.

No amount of cardiovascular preparedness could enable these men and women to fight nonstop.

Helen knew that.

She would wait for the opportune time when they were injured and exhausted.

And she wants the orb, Sky gleaned. Helen was waiting to see where it appeared on the battlefield so she could seize it.

Sky sent psychic messages to everyone, words of encouragement at how they were thinning Helen's ranks. She had them moved into position deeper and closer to Helen. She could almost feel the gloating satisfaction from the she-demon. The Shadow Guardians were completely surrounded by her deadly creatures. Her abominations.

CHAPTER

THIRTY-FIVE

On Thunder's back, Sky moved along the ridge, still taking shots into the chaos below. There were too many of them. Despite all of her sisters' efforts over the last few years to bring down Helen, and despite all the creatures they'd killed, the goddess of the underworld reincarnated had still created a nearly impenetrable force.

Bryce was the first to go down. He faced off with a Fire Giant, the biggest on the field, and lassoed its neck. The creature twisted a hand around the rope secured over his head and yanked. Momentum caused Bryce to surge forward at the same instant the Fire Giant raised his sword.

Sky launched an arrow, but by the time it struck the Fire Giant between the eyes, he'd already impaled Bryce. The cowboy stumbled backward, pulling out the sword before he dropped to the ground.

Storm screamed in rage, but she was halfway across the battlefield, surrounded by wolves. As she turned toward her fallen lover, four hellhounds pounced, and she went down beneath a mound of matted, bloody fur.

Raine was in no shape to help, as she was engulfed in a fresh wave of the undead. They clawed at her, red blooming through her white shirt, and she vanished beneath the darkness, Gungnir falling to the ground. Sky continued to unleash arrows as fast as she could, but Raine didn't rise out of the ashes.

Will seemed to have exhausted his Bifröst magic and either lost or holstered his gun in favor of Hǫfuð. Three Frost Giants surrounded him, wrestling him to the ground before one of them picked up Will's limp body, raised him above his head, and threw him onto a pile of rocks at the base of the mountain. He fell, unmoving.

At the same time as Will and Raine were being crushed, Nico and Andrej fought side-by-side against a swarm of ax-wielding Dark Elves. Nico transformed into his human form and sank his sais into an attacker. Andrej covered his back, sinking teeth into another just as a third plunged his ax into Andrej's back. Nico cried out his brother's name before killing three more Dark Elves in a blur of motion between wolf and human form before a club from a swinging Fire Giant struck his chest.

Helen unleashed a bone chilling cackle of victory.

Six shall fall, marks light to call.

Sky reached into the folds of her dress and grasped the orb to call the light. Closing her eyes, she focused on the beating hearts of the battlefield. Her family was still alive, but just barely. On an exhale, she concentrated on Helen's abominations. Ending their lives meant ending their suffering and also saving her family's lives. With her will, she activated the magic within the orb, transferring life-sustaining energy from Helen's creatures to Raine, Will, Storm, Bryce, Andrej, and Nico.

Like a tidal wave starting closest to Sky, the cascade of transference rolled its way toward Helen, manifesting as her creatures of darkness fell to the ground, turning into a combination of ash and sludge. Helen was unreachable across the divide, but Sky could still obliterate her army.

The last thing Sky heard before collapsing on the back of Thunder was Helen's outraged roar and the loud bellow of a dragon.

. . .

Nico surged to his feet, feeling a wave of power pulse through him and around him. Not only had the orb and Sky's magic healed his battle wounds, but it had given him renewed energy.

Around him, the bodies of Helen's fallen decomposed. Dark Elves morphed into bubbling piles of primordial ooze. Fire Giants had been reduced to ash and Frost Giants crystallized then melted. Helen's hounds lay on the ground, panting. Sky had spared their lives but left them weakened. Nico suspected she was granting them a chance at redemption, since they would be free of Helen's influence once the six defeated the goddess of darkness.

The other guardians were standing, brushing off dirt and grime and picking up their weapons. His *raza de soare* had done it. She had used the orb and their last resort. Bryce rolled his shoulders and looped his lasso. Storm collected the last of her scattered knives. Raine pulled Gungnir out of a dissolving Midgard serpent. Will shoved to his feet, gun in one hand and sword in the other. Andrej rested on his hands and knees, dazed and panting but fantastically alive.

To Nico's relief, Sky pushed herself up laboriously to sit up on the back of her horse. She looked pale and drained, even from a distance. Fortunately, they had killed half the creatures before she'd had to use the orb.

A shadow crossed overhead. When Nico looked up, his stomach plummeted. Helen rode through the air atop her sickly yellow dragon, streaking toward Sky. The demon was after the orb. With the power of the relic, Helen could create the apocalypse she so desperately wanted without needing the army they had just eradicated.

Helen unleashed her slender silver spear, and it cut through the air toward Sky like deadly, luminous lightning.

The sleek weapon was heading straight for Sky's chest.

Suddenly, Thunder reared, taking the spear to the center of his thorax. As the horse collapsed, Sky screamed—the sound of anguish and shattered hope—as she disappeared beneath him.

Odin help her. Please let her still be alive.

Nico wouldn't know until they finished with Helen.

Hot rage filled him, and he turned toward the goddess with revenge on his mind.

Bryce had already leaped into action with his lasso looped around one leg of the dragon. He and Will pulled with all their might and anchored the rope around a large rock to keep the creature tethered. The dragon bucked, flapping gargantuan wings to escape, but Gleipnir held true.

Raine lined up her spear, aiming for the dragon's heaving, exposed chest.

When Nico made eye contact with Storm, she was bending and picking up a shield left by a dead Fire Giant and nodding in his direction, then toward the dragon.

Nico jerked his head once in understanding and then sprinted toward her. He shifted to wolf form ten feet from her and leaped onto the shield at a full sprint. She angled it above her and, using the force of her thighs and arms, pushed up, giving Nico the extra thrust he needed to launch into the air directly at Helen.

He clamped down on her shoulder just as she was pulling back a thin bow and black arrow with an aim of hitting Bryce. Her blood tasted rancid in his mouth. With a shriek, Helen dropped her weapon.

At that instant, Raine's spear plunged into the dragon's chest. His wings went limp as he fell.

Helen had one hand raking toward Nico and the other trying to grasp for purchase on the falling dragon. As she floundered, Nico transformed back into his human form and sank the blade of one sai into her throat.

When he threw himself away from the crash landing, shifting into wolf form so he would be more protected from injury, Helen filled the sky with an ear-piercing scream of agony and rage as her body turned ashen and folded in on itself.

He hit the ground hard and rolled to avoid the dragon as he crashed to the rocky surface. With determined speed, Will pounced and cut off the creature's head with his sword.

Nico raced to Sky's side, laboring up the rocky hillside. When he reached her, he shifted back to human form, ignoring the stabbing pain in his side he was certain was a cracked rib.

Breathing.

Merciful Asgard, she's breathing.

CHAPTER

THIRTY-SIX

Sky had fallen.

Now she was floating, lighter than air. Had she died? That would be a shame. She had so much more she wanted to do with her life.

Rainbow lights flickered in her blurred vision. She wanted to move, see where she was and where she was going, but her limbs felt like limp noodles. When she could focus, she saw Nico haloed in red, orange, and blue light.

"My guardian angel," she said wistfully. He had survived and was looking well.

Looking down at her, he smiled with adoration. "I'm still not sure I deserve that accolade."

She jolted, realizing she didn't know the status of the battle. "Is everyone—?"

"Our family is fine."

Our family.

She liked the sound of that.

"Oh, Thunder. I couldn't save him." Her heart panged at the sudden memory. She'd been too weak when he'd fallen from the direct blow to the chest.

"He saved a lot of lives today, protecting our *Raza de soare*. Thunder will enjoy his next journey in animal Valhalla for his bravery and his sacrifice."

She remembered the horse's bold defiance when he reared up to block Helen's spear. He'd been proud and unafraid to face death to save her.

Soft blankets enveloped her.

"Rest now. Just rest."

"You'll be here?" she asked. "You'll stay with me?"

"Forever."

SKY WOKE to the sound of a door clicking open. She sat up in bed to see Nico strolling in, carrying a tray with an omelet, coffee, orange juice, and a side of strawberries.

She pushed to sit up. "Careful, a girl could get used to this."

"You've done nothing but sleep for the last day, so I thought you might be hungry."

"You thought right."

He set the tray down on the nightstand.

She reached for the strawberries, popping one cut half into her mouth. "I can't believe it's really over. You killed her. We're free."

"It was definitely a joint effort, but yeah, she's gone."

She sipped the juice. "So much hate and anger. Hundreds dead on that battlefield because of her. How many would have just tried to live normal lives if not for influence and manipulation?"

"The important thing is that it's over. And you should know Andrej tells me you have quite a few grateful wolves freed from servitude to Helen."

"Good. That's good to hear. And you? What will you do with your freedom?"

"Back to finance. I'm ready for peaceful living."

"I can get behind peaceful. You still think you want to marry a wellness shop owner? Now that the world is your oyster you can go anywhere and do anything."

"There is only you, Sky. I'll go all those places I want to go and see all those things I want to see, but with you by my side." He sat down on the bed beside her, leaned over, and kissed her. Tender and sweet.

She would've liked to turn the kiss into something more, but she was still weak from expending so much power the day before yesterday. They kept the kiss long and lingering, as comfortable and drawn out as a warm summer afternoon.

A shimmer of light illuminated her doorway, but Sky didn't stop her kiss.

Raine gave a tsk. "Get a room."

Nico leaned back, smiling, and Sky cocked her head to one side. "This *is* my room."

"Oh. So it is." Raine strolled inside with Storm following behind her.

Will and Bryce hung back, outside the room.

"You've got your color back. I guess it's partly due to rest and partly something else." Storm's gaze flickered to Nico briefly, but without any semblance of the distrust she once had.

Sky smiled. "He is a pretty amazing fiancé."

Storm kicked the wood corner of one supporting bed post. "Yeah, I guess you can keep him."

Sky blinked at her. "Thanks for your approval, but I was already planning to."

EPILOGUE

EIGHT MONTHS LATER

Sky thought her heart might burst from so much joy. Happiness came from within her and swirled around her as the guests sat in rows of white chairs.

They held the wedding at Bryce's ranch, where Bryce, Storm, and Olivia had returned to make a home. At the new barn off to the right, Dolly and Faith watched events with curiosity. Above them, wispy white clouds filled a blue sky. One, she could imagine, was the tail of Thunder streaking across the sky from his new pasture in heaven. The Texas temperatures in April were cool and not too humid.

Sky walked on the rose petals Olivia had scattered down the aisle, and her father walked beside her, one arm looped gently through her elbow, the other arm looped through Storm's. The three of them approached the gazebo where Bryce and Nico stood, waiting in starched tuxedos.

The groomsmen, Will, Denny, and Andrej, were all handsome in black. Raine, Anka, and Rosalyn stood beside them as bridesmaids dressed in flowing purple gowns. Olivia, in a white and purple dress, stood beside her father, beaming a smile at the brides. Among the guests were Ida and Maddie, both in tears, Avery, Jake, and Apollo. Other attendees were friends of Sky's, Bryce's, and their parents.

When they reached the gazebo, Wyatt passed the women's hands off to their grooms. Brok stood on a platform, ready to officiate the ceremony. He'd scrubbed off his workshop grime, donned a suit, and held an officiant book containing his notes. In the months after the battle, the Shadow Guardians had helped rebuild his workshop. During that time, Sky had learned he was an ordained minister. He gave the women a smile and a wink.

Sky turned toward Nico, who was grinning at her. "You look spectacular," he said.

"And the tuxedo suits you," she whispered back.

When Brok began speaking, Sky thought of the next chapter to come in everyone's life. Raine and Will had their ongoing FBI work—there would always be a need for law enforcement of both hubbles and Norse bloodlines. Bryce and Storm would continue to raise Olivia, and he planned to go back to being a surgeon. Storm wanted to take them traveling during summer and holiday breaks and planned to continue helping Raine and Will when needed.

Sky and Nico had plans to travel the world. He wanted to show her the beauty she'd never seen, the beauty he'd never been able to appreciate. For their honeymoon, they would start with Eastern Europe.

They had risked their lives to save the world. They ought to take the time to see everything it had to offer.

*****BRIEF NOTE FROM THE AUTHOR*****

I hope you enjoyed The Shadow Guardians Trilogy. Keep scrolling to learn more about my other series.

Raven's Flight, prequel novella
Raine Down, Book 1
Rosalyn's Run, novella
Storm Surge, Book 2
Anka's Orb, novella
Sky Fall, Book 3

CHARACTER LIST
- BOOK THREE

Leads

- Sky Thoren - Valkyrie
- Nico Wølfe - shapeshifter

Valkyrie Adversaries

- Helen ógn (Hel) - descendent of the ruler of Helheim

Shadow Guardians Supportive Team

- Usha Bakshi - US representative on the Council of Mjölnir
- Brok Waldorf - dwarf and weapon's maker
- Denny Smith - psychologist
- Anka - tattoo Artist
- Avery - raven shapeshifter
- Jake - Vanir and UK based Shadow Guardian

- Apollo - Vanir healer
- Rosalyn - shapeshifter and Shadow Guardian

Main Characters' Family Members

- Storm Thoren - assassin and Valkyrie
- Bryce Chambers - physician and Vanir illusionist
- Will Decker - Storm's brother-in-law, descendent of Heimdall
- Raine Thoren-Decker - Storm's sister, Valkyrie, Shadow Guardian
- Maddie Chambers - Bryce's mother
- Olivia Chambers - Bryce's daughter

NORSE NAMES

Mjölnir - Thor's hammer
Yggdrasil - Norse tree of knowledge
Gungnir - the Spear of Odin
Mistilteinn - sword of Hrómundr Gripsson
Gleipnir - the silk ribbon that held Fenrir, Helen's fiendish wolf.
Lævateinn - magic wand crafted by Loki and said to have resided in Hel

~~NINE REALMS~~

Niflheim (Old Norse: "Niðavellir") - realm of frost and mist. This was the darkest and coldest realms and contained the spring Hvergelmir protected by the dragon Nidhug (Old Norse: Níðhöggr). The spring was the source of Élivágar, the seven rivers.

Muspelheim (Old Norse: "Múspellsheimr") - land of fire. Fraught with lava, flames, and smoke. Surtr reined over this land where Fire Giants and fire demons lived.

Asgard (Old Norse: "Ásgarðr") - home of the gods and goddesses (Aesir) and ruled by Odin. He was married to Frigg and possibly also Freya (some scholars postulate they may be the same woman).

Midgard (Old Norse: "Miðgarðr") - Earth. Midgard and Asgard were connected by the Bifröst, or Rainbow Bridge.

Jotunheim (Old Norse: "Jötunheimr") - realm of wilderness, forests, and snowy mountains. This is home of the Frost Giants (Jotun) who were the sworn enemies of the Asgardians. Utgard, the king, lived in a fortress of ice and snow.

Vanaheim (Old Norse: "Vanaheimr") - home of Vanir gods. Vanir were masters of sorcery, magic, and prophecy.

Alfheim (Old Norse: "Álfheimr or Ljósálfheimr") - home of the Light Elves. These minor gods of nature and fertility were known for having inspired poetry, art, and music.

Svartalfheim (Old Norse: "Niðavellir or Svartálfaheimr") - home of the Dwarves. Known for their master craftsmanship, these dwarves lived under rocks, in caves, and underground.

Helheim - home of the dishonorable dead. This realm was grim, cold, and devoid of happiness. Hel (daughter of Loki by some legends and daughter of Odin by others) ruled Helheim with her wolf, Fenrir, by her side.

DEAR READER

I hope you enjoyed The Shadow Guardians Trilogy. I would love to have you join my mailing list. I promise I won't spam you. I only send an email when I have a new book released, giveaways, or special discounts. And I'll never sell your information. You can also unsubscribe at any time.

You can also follow me on any of these social media platforms. Check out my Etsy page for signed paperbacks.

Also, as an independent author, I rely heavily on readers to spread the word about books they've read. If you enjoyed this story, kindly let others know by posing a brief comment on social media or leave a review where you purchased it.

Thank you for reading,

www.cbsamet.com

OTHER BOOKS BY CB SAMET

Olympian Awakenings Trilogy

Urban fantasy Greek Mythology Adventure

Grab the prequel exclusively HERE.

Stone Hearts

Winds of Destiny

Flame and Shadow

The Rider Files

ROMANTIC SUSPENSE NOVELS

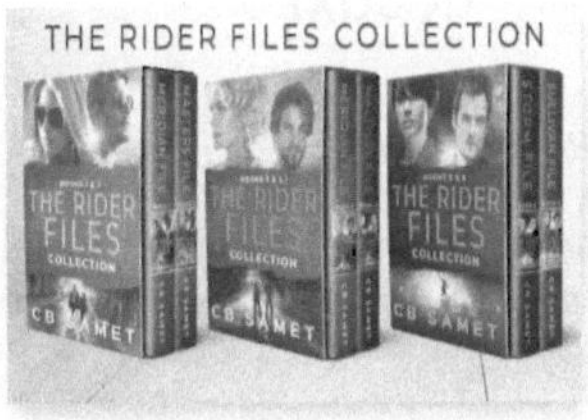

Join the Rider File protection team as they guard and defend their clients from deadly villains. Using their unique skillset and wits, they serve and protect

Meridian File / Masters File / Box Set 1

McMillan File / Maltisse File /Box Set 2

Storm File / Sullivan File / Box Set 3

Sharp File / Sizani File / Box Set 4

Rivera File / Rucker File / Box Set 5

Richmond File / Redwood File / Box Set 6

Atlas File / Angel File / Box Set 7

~~~

The Dr. Whyte Adventure Novels

Perfect for thriller lovers!

Black Gold

Whyte Knight

Gray Horizon

~~~

Sweet Romantic Suspense

"Well-written... tales of love and ghosts."

— KIRKUS REVIEW

IN BOXED SETS

Romancing the Spirit Series #1

Sadie's Spirit / Willow's Windfall

Cassie's Chase / Pheobe's Pharaoh

Vanessa's Valentine / Autumn's Angel

Romancing the Spirit Series #2

Carol's Christmas / Allison's Alibi

Gracelynn's Genie / Michelle's Miracle

Heather's Hero / Chloe's Cupid

Romancing the Spirit Series #3

Sabrina's Storm / Jenny's Justice

Stella's Star / Gigi's Gift

Pheonix's Phantom / Fiona's Freedom

~~~

Love action/adventure and strong female leads in a fantasy world? Book 1 won 2nd Place Evvy Award in fantasy.

Check out my other genre:

The Avant Champion Fantasy Series

The Avant Champion: Rising

Malakai: An Avant Champion Origin of Malos Story (prequel)

The Avant Champion: Honor

The Avant Champion: Ashes

Brothers' Bond: An Avant Champion Malakai Story

The Avant Champion: Conquest

Isabel: An Avant Champion novelette

The Avant Champion: Redeem